"The a...
that I ...

Jack's anguish was evident in his voice.

Liz stifled a gasp of dismay. Forgetting her self-imposed boundaries, she laid a compassionate hand on his arm.

"Six more months and the adoption would have been final," Jack said with a shake of his head. "Liz...I know you and I haven't always seen eye-to-eye, but I believe we're in agreement that Kassie should stay with me." He hesitated, then played a trump card he would have preferred to withhold. "I'm sure you realize your sister would have wanted it that way."

"Of course Kassie should stay with you," Liz answered. "I'll do whatever I can."

Jack took a deep breath, bracing himself for the inevitable storm of protest. "I need you to marry me."

Dear Reader,

We've got some great reading for you this month, but I'll bet you already knew that. Suzanne Carey is back with *Whose Baby?* The title already tells you that a custody battle is at the heart of this story, but it's Suzanne's name that guarantees all the emotional intensity you want to find between the covers.

Maggie Shayne's *The Littlest Cowboy* launches a new miniseries this month, THE TEXAS BRAND. These rough, tough, ranchin' Texans will win your heart, just as Sheriff Garrett Brand wins the hearts of lovely Chelsea Brennan and her tiny nephew. If you like mysterious and somewhat spooky goings-on, you'll love Marcia Evanick's *His Chosen Bride,* a marriage-of-convenience story with a paranormal twist. Clara Wimberly's hero in *You Must Remember This* is a mysterious stranger—mysterious even to himself, because his memory is gone and he has no idea who he is or what has brought him to Sarah James's door. One thing's for certain, though: it's love that keeps him there. In *Undercover Husband,* Leann Harris creates a heroine who thinks she's a widow, then finds out she might not be when a handsome—and somehow familiar—stranger walks through her door. Finally, I know you'll love *Prince Joe,* the hero of Suzanne Brockmann's new book, part of her TALL, DARK AND DANGEROUS miniseries. This is a royal impostor story, with a rough-around-the-edges hero who suddenly has to wear the crown.

Don't miss a single one of these exciting books, and come back next month for more of the best romance around—only in Silhouette Intimate Moments.

Yours,

Leslie Wainger

Leslie Wainger
Senior Editor and Editorial Coordinator

Please address questions and book requests to:
Silhouette Reader Service
U.S.: 3010 Walden Ave., P.O. Box 1325, Buffalo, NY 14269
Canadian: P.O. Box 609, Fort Erie, Ont. L2A 5X3

WHOSE BABY?

SUZANNE CAREY

INTIMATE MOMENTS®

Published by Silhouette Books
America's Publisher of Contemporary Romance

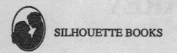

SILHOUETTE BOOKS

ISBN 0-373-07715-7

WHOSE BABY?

Printed in U.S.A.

SUZANNE CAREY

is a former reporter and magazine editor who prefers to write romance novels because they add to the sum total of love in the world.

Chapter 1

Whose baby would she be this time next year? *His?* Or some unknown couple's?

His expression austere, his handsome jaw clenched with his determination to keep her, attorney Jack Kelleher held Kassie Elizabeth, the fourteen-month-old Korean orphan he and his late wife, Sharon, had been in the process of adopting, as a priest from St. John's Church in nearby Leesburg read the committal service.

The baby's almond-shaped eyes were intent as she played with his tie tack, oblivious to the solemn rite of passage that was unfolding. Chubby in white tights beneath the hem of her Chesterfield spring coat, her little legs dangled trustingly against him.

As the priest droned on, a gust of wind swept the historic cemetery, which predated the Civil War, ruffling Jack's thick, dark hair. It was March, on the cusp of April, a brisk, faintly raw northern Virginia day characterized by sodden earth, intermittent sunlight and swollen tree buds.

The adoption wouldn't be final for six months. With Sharon gone and the adoption agency refusing to budge from its policy of placing the youngsters in its care with two-parent families, the outcome was anybody's guess.

As a widower, Jack no longer qualified, though he passed muster as a parent, and his six-figure income easily met the financial test. Ironic, wasn't it, given his growing reputation as a legal champion of fathers' rights, to find himself in that kind of predicament? The fact that he'd patched up his differences with Sharon on the express condition that they adopt a child together only exacerbated his strong sense of life's unjust, paradoxical nature.

What a mockery it is, pretending to mourn, when all I feel is disgust and a kind of emptiness, he reflected bitterly. *The relief that will come later, if and when Kassie's mine to keep, isn't even a blip on the horizon yet.*

Liz might be able to help if he could talk her into it. Outwardly continuing to focus on the priest's words and the spray of yellow gladioli that rested on his late wife's coffin lid, Jack let his thoughts stray to his slim, red-headed sister-in-law, who stood slightly to his left, the sleeve of her elegantly tailored black business suit all but brushing against his coat.

What would she say when he outlined his plan to her? Would she turn him down flat without pausing to consider it? Or insist she needed time to think? Ten to one she'd consider the favor he wanted too much of a sacrifice. Having her around for a while would be the opposite of sacrifice for him, he acknowledged. Letting her go after they accomplished what they set out to do would be the difficult part.

They went back a way together, he and Liz—further than he and Sharon had by nearly a month. They'd met as opposing attorneys in a sharply contested custody battle in which his client, the children's father, had emerged triumphant. As adversaries, he and Liz had struck sparks—both argumentatively and sexually. Charmed by her nimble brain, crisp courtroom manner and leggy grace, he'd yearned to get to know her better just as soon as it was ethically correct for him to suggest it.

When he'd asked her out for drinks following the judge's decision, she'd agreed. But, to his chagrin, she'd refused to date him. Their outlooks were "too different," in her opinion. She was a career-oriented, independent woman. She doubted he could abide the type, given the way he'd trashed her working-mother client.

By some quirk of fate, Sharon had chosen that precise moment to wander into the fern-bedecked bar and grill where they were seated, precluding a response from him. A bit stiffly, because her dander was up, Liz had introduced them. He'd been astonished to learn that they were twins, as they looked nothing like each other.

"Same womb, different egg. We're fraternal," Sharon had laughed, explaining their disparity in a nutshell.

When Liz had excused herself to make a business call a few minutes later, he and Sharon had continued to chat. On impulse, he'd asked her to have dinner with him instead—in a clumsy attempt to show Liz what she was missing, he'd realized afterward.

Blond, outgoing, an expert flatterer, Sharon had eased her sister's rejection of him. Ripe for the picking, he'd ended up in bed with her that night and dated her a few more times before getting involved in another time-consuming case. He'd been horrified when, a month af-

ter his final rendezvous with her, she'd announced that she
was expecting his baby.

His feeling that Liz didn't particularly care for him had
only grown during the course of his five-year marriage to
her sister. Thrown together on family birthdays and holidays, they'd continued to butt heads over the most in-
consequential of topics. Emotionally she'd kept her
distance. Still, when the chips were down, he thought she
respected him. As Kassie's adoptive aunt, she'd been un-
stinting in her affection.

Conscious of his physical proximity though she
couldn't begin to guess what was on his mind, Liz tried
not to glance in Jack's direction. *Does he find Sharon's
death as unbelievable as I do?* she wondered, aching over
her twin's tragic fate and certain he was experiencing
similar emotions.

One minute Sharon had been alive and well, on the way
to her college reunion. The next, her body parts had lain
scattered, like those of a hundred-and-twenty other passengers, in an Indiana cornfield. Try as she would, Liz
couldn't get that fact to register in her head. Being forced
to wait three weeks to hold the funeral until Federal Avi-
ation Administration investigators had completed their
work at the crash site and released the victims' remains
had only made her loss more difficult to assimilate.

Thank God Jack didn't accompany her, Liz thought,
suppressing a shudder. *Without him, Kassie would be
forever lost to us.* The fact that a place in her heart would
have withered if her dark-haired brother-in-law had been
killed, as well, was something she didn't want to think
about.

Though Sharon hadn't always lived by his rules, Jack
had proven to be a somewhat traditional parent. When
she'd brought up the topic of her college reunion, he'd

declined to accompany her, insisting that one of Kassie's parents needed to stay around, though the child had a live-in nurse. Or so Sharon had reported during her final phone conversation with Liz.

"It looks like I'll be flying to Chicago alone," she'd disclosed in a cheerful tone that hadn't invited sympathy. "Still, I'll have fun, don't you think? I've made a point of staying in touch with my college buddies and former roommate."

Now the world was empty of her, and Jack was facing what promised to be a protracted struggle to keep the baby. *If there's anything I can do to help, short of getting emotionally entangled with him, I'll do it,* Liz thought. *I love Kassie dearly. And it's beginning to look as if I'll never marry and have a child of my own. I want to keep her in the family as much as he does.*

It was just that she doubted her strict policy of noninvolvement with him would survive too much togetherness. The last thing she wanted to do was stumble into providing her grieving brother-in-law with sexual comfort. Yet she knew that was a distinct possibility if she and Jack spent a great deal of time together. Too easily her feelings for him and his probable neediness could push them in that direction.

Sexy, tough and too quick by half, "Black Jack" Kelleher, as he was known in Washington, D.C., legal circles, had laid siege to her heart from the moment they'd met. Skeptical of what she considered his Machiavellian tactics and male chauvinistic bent, she'd found herself responding to him on an elemental level.

To her regret, when she'd turned down his dinner invitation five years earlier, the opportunity hadn't come again. The bottom had dropped out of her stomach a month and a half later when Sharon had confided she and

Jack were expecting a child and had set an early wedding date.

A month after the ceremony, which had been limited to immediate family members, Sharon had lost the baby. To everyone's surprise, she hadn't been able to conceive again. Despite the shotgun nature of their marriage and a wide disparity in their tastes and interests, her union with Jack had proven to be a stable one, though once or twice Liz had surmised an oddly haunted look on his face.

It was only recently, after Kassie had arrived to brighten their lives, that Liz had begun to wonder if something had gone wrong between them. Jack had seemed so grim and disapproving of her sister—Sharon so blithely indifferent to him.

Whatever their problems—and they'd had their share of them, she suspected—she'd maintained a strict "don't ask" policy where their relationship was concerned. Unfortunately, though she'd done everything humanly possible to root it out, time had only caused her attraction to Jack to deepen. Even now, as she mourned the twin she'd always loved like a part of herself, she was acutely conscious of his after-shave, his compelling physical presence.

She knew her devout, conventional parents, Frank and Patsy Heflin, would be horrified if they suspected she had a thing for him. From their point of view, though Sharon was dead, any interest in Jack on her part would be construed as poaching.

For reasons of her own, she was forced to agree that he should remain off limits. From the none-too-subtle hints Sharon had dropped from time to time, she'd gathered that her sister's physical relationship with Jack had continued to run hot despite their differences. Feeding on crumbs where Sharon had banqueted had little appeal.

Rosemary would probably understand. From beneath lowered lashes, Liz studied Jack's stylish, sixty-four-year-old mother, who was standing on the far side of Eloise McWhurter, Kassie's nurse. As a by-product of Sharon's marriage to Jack, Liz and the widowed Rosemary Kelleher had become friends. They often shopped together, exchanging confidences over lunch or dinner at least once a month.

No doubt our friendship came about because we're so much alike, Liz thought. A political activist and former county commission chairman in neighboring Maryland, Rosemary was savvy, self-directed and independent with a capital *I*. In Liz's estimation, her strong-woman persona had always been something of a thorn in Jack's side, though he was clearly crazy about her.

Liz's train of thought scattered as the priest who was conducting Sharon's burial service fell silent and the sexton stepped forward with his assistant to lower Sharon's coffin into the grave. At Patsy's suggestion, they'd decided to scatter flowers in lieu of earth atop Sharon's casket in a final gesture of farewell. "My poor, dear girl would have have preferred them," Patsy had sobbed, dabbing at red-rimmed eyes with a lace-trimmed handkerchief.

As they'd left the church following Sharon's funeral Mass, Jack had asked Liz to be the first. "As her twin, you were closer to her than anyone," he'd suggested.

About to argue with him on principle, she'd realized it was neither the time nor the place. Accordingly, at a nod from the funeral director, she approached the edge of the rectangular earthen pit that contained her sister's coffin and let a white chrysanthemum slip from her grasp.

"Goodbye, Shar... be happy wherever you are," she told her twin silently. "If heaven's anything like life, you'll be voted the prettiest, most popular girl there, and get the guy everyone else wants.''

Turning away before the tears that were welling up inside her could spill, she had to brush past Jack, who was still holding Kassie in his arms. ''Can you stay on at the house for a few minutes this afternoon after everyone else has left?'' he asked in a low voice, his craggy-handsome features stark with what she believed was the overwhelming grief he felt. ''I need to talk to you.''

Briefly searching his face, she nodded without answering. What can he possibly want to discuss, today of all days? she wondered, her heart aching as she watched her father attempt to ease her mother's pain as they released two of Sharon's favorite Casablanca lilies and then simply held each other.

With Jack's help, Kassie managed to toss a pink rosebud onto the little heap of flowers below. ''Da-da-da,'' she said with shy solemnity, resting her cheek against his lapel.

The priest from St. John's Church read a final benediction, after everyone who wanted to toss a flower for remembrance had been given the opportunity to do so. They were free to leave. Even more focused on her brother-in-law than previously as a result of his puzzling request, Liz did her best not to let her feelings show as she joined in the all-around exchange of hugs that took place. She was careful to turn Jack's brusque embrace into an occasion for kissing Kassie and whispering a few love words to the child that brought a smile to her face.

Each commemorative ''holy card'' that had been handed out by the funeral director at the inception of the service had been accompanied by an invitation to visit Jack's place afterward for drinks and moral support. If the number of people who'd turned up at the cemetery was any indication of the crowd they could expect, his restored 1791 farmhouse would be bursting at the seams.

As arranged, Frank and Patsy would accompany Jack, Kassie and the baby's nurse in the funeral home's shiny black limousine.

I hate postmortems at a time like this, Liz thought as she got into the passenger seat of Rosemary's Cadillac. All I want to do at the moment is remember my sister and weep. Still, she supposed such get-togethers had a point. Without question, her mother would be comforted by all the sympathy and praise for Sharon that would be offered her.

The narrow country road that led south from the exquisitely preserved village of Waterford toward Jack's farm wound over rolling hills between patches of woods, greening pastures and country estates. Though most of the homes in the area were extremely expensive by anyone's standard, few could be called mansions in the strictest sense. However, many were part and parcel of the nation's history. Altered and expanded by a succession of owners, some predated the American Revolution by several decades.

"Hard to believe Sharon's gone, isn't it," Rosemary commented after a long silence as they turned in between Jack's ivy-covered gateposts. "Life can be unbelievably short sometimes."

Liz nodded, sensing that no answer was required.

"I watched you with Kassie at the graveside," Jack's mother added, giving her a sidelong look. "You really love that child, don't you?"

"I guess that's obvious."

"Maybe it's time you got married and had one of your own."

You're telling me, Liz thought. Another couple of years and it'll be too late. When push had come to shove, she'd never really loved any of the decent, successful men who'd wandered into her life and hung around long enough to propose marriage to her. Measured against Jack, despite his flaws, none of them had made the grade. Somehow, his strong, subtly mocking features had gotten in the way of her caring for them.

A couple of twists and turns down a narrow lane bordered by oaks and evergreens, and the house came into view. Built of mellow red brick in the early Federal style, it had a matching wing that had been constructed later and a fieldstone add-on kitchen to the rear. Its steep, slate-roofed attic was punctuated by dormers. Set with a combination of replacement glass and the original wavy, irregular panes, its west-facing windows graciously gave back the late-afternoon sunlight.

The property also had a stone barn and several outbuildings, including a heartwood pine log cabin which had been moved to the site and restored to become a housekeeper's residence. Beyond it, a pond that was home to a family of ducks glinted beneath a copse of willows.

Though it was somewhat impractical for a bachelor who worked in town, Jack had owned the house for the past eight years. He'd been living there when he, Liz and Sharon had met. Once they were wed, Sharon had tried to talk him into selling it and moving back to D.C., specifically to a luxury apartment in the much-vaunted Watergate complex.

His answer had been an unequivocal no each time she'd suggested it. While Liz knew her twin had craved daily access to big-league shopping, museums and theaters, fancy restaurants and an active social life—that she'd hated being "buried in the country up to her neck," as she'd put it—she'd never been able to find it in her heart to blame Jack for his refusal.

To her, the rambling but elegant house and its seventy-five acres or so of prime real estate comprised an idyllic spot to raise horses, dogs and children—all of which, to her surprise, had interested him. Just being there made her think of might-have-beens that were better left unarticulated.

The funeral home's limousine was just leaving as they approached. Meanwhile, a number of cars were already parked in the oval turnaround near the front steps. More were coming up the drive as they drove around to the side and halted beside the kitchen entrance.

"I thought we'd go in the back way...make sure everything's set up properly for the horde," Rosemary suggested.

"Fine with me," Liz said.

Getting out of the car, she braced herself for the part of hostess she'd have to play for the next several hours. The discipline of her courtroom experience would stand her in good stead, she supposed. Just the same, rehashing Sharon's death with sundry relatives, friends and quite a few people who were total strangers to her wasn't a pleasant prospect. In the process, she'd be forced to watch Sharon's unattached female friends fawning over Jack in his newly acquired role of widower, and confront her tangled feelings about her parents.

Slim, energetic, with Jack's discerning blue gaze, Rosemary reached over to pat her hand affectionately. "Losing Sharon was the hard part," she reminded. "This get-together will be history in a couple of hours. It won't be so bad if we keep busy and let insensitive comments roll off our shoulders."

Irish, Jack's silky, wheaten terrier, came forward to meet them, wagging his feathery tail and thrusting a cold, welcoming nose into Liz's hand as she got out of the car. Affectionately ruffling the dog's blond fur, she followed Rosemary up the steps to the pantry entrance.

Inside the huge, old-fashioned kitchen, which featured a massive brick fireplace, French provincial tile and an island range with a chopping-block counter and bar-stool seating, the assorted catering staff Jack had hired for the occasion was bustling about, adding last-minute touches to trays of canapés, assorted relishes and finger sandwiches. As they watched, additional batches of canapés emerged from Jack's twin ovens on oversize cookie sheets.

The sound of arriving mourners reached them from the foyer and the formal living room, where a discreet but well-stocked bar had been set up. A uniformed butler hurried in that direction with a tray of glasses and several buckets of ice on a service cart.

"So," Rosemary commented, surveying the scene with diamond-studded hands perched on slender hips. "It looks like everything's on track here. Want to run upstairs and grab a few minutes for yourself? If so, I'll cover for you."

Though the offer was a tempting one, Liz didn't dare take her up on it. For one thing, Patsy would object. "Thanks...that would be nice," she answered. "But the fact is, Jack needs us. Besides, I want to keep an eye on Kassie. We mustn't let her get too exhausted or worn-out over this."

Running her fingers through her hair in a futile effort to tame it, and smoothing the lines of her black designer suit with somewhat better success, Liz entered the living room. Like Rosemary, who was right behind her, she was immediately engulfed by friends and extended-family members.

Words of commiseration and would-be understanding washed over her. "Darlin', I'm so sorry," one woman said, crushing her in a perfume-laden embrace. "It must be awful, losing your twin!" "Whatever will Jack do without her, now that they've adopted a baby?" another asked. "Your mother was always so proud of her. She must be inconsolable."

Thank heaven there were a few people Liz didn't know, and who didn't know her, like that dark-haired, fairly good-looking man who stood nursing a glass of sherry by one of the dining room windows. Murmuring what she hoped were appropriate responses to everyone who spoke to her, Liz glanced about for her parents. Her father, a retired police commissioner who spent most of his time puttering and swearing in his garage workshop, was hoisting what was doubtless his second Scotch on the rocks with some of his former sergeants and lieutenants.

Blond like Sharon, though these days her hair color emanated from the beauty shop, Patsy had elected to hold court on a curving, French silk sofa her dead daughter had purchased during a recent redecorating binge. Tears slipped down her cheeks as she relived the memories captured in one of Sharon's scrapbooks with several female relatives.

"No mother could have asked for a sweeter, more loving daughter," she proclaimed in her husky smoker's drawl. "I thought I'd burst with pride when she was named homecoming queen at Bethesda-Chevy Chase during her senior year. This is the feature story that ran in the local paper..."

Bending forward to study the clipping, the woman closest to Patsy shook her head. "She certainly was beautiful."

Abruptly Patsy was weeping in earnest. "I don't know what I'm going to do without her, Irene," she choked.

From the moment they'd received the tragic news of Sharon's demise, neither of Liz's parents had allowed her to comfort them. If she tried to hug them, they seemed to shrink from her. It didn't seem to occur to them that she was devastated, too, and might need a hand to hold.

It was almost as if they wished she'd gone down in Sharon's place. Such thoughts were overly dramatic and self-punishing, of course, born of survivor's guilt and her own very real grief for her sister, and she didn't really believe them. Still, she'd faced the truth as a ten-year-old— Sharon had always been their parents' favorite. Compared with Sharon's popularity and her coup in snagging a rich, handsome husband, the many scholarships Liz had won, her juris doctorate with honors from George Washington University and her successful legal career had been treated as run-of-the-mill accomplishments.

The little girl in her kept trying to please them—particularly now that she longed to comfort them in their sorrow. Abandoning her hostess duties for a moment, she approached her mother from behind and laid a tentative hand on her shoulder. "Anything I can do, Mom?" she asked, her heart in her voice.

"Wha...at?" Patsy Heflin raised her head in surprise, then shrugged dismissively. "Oh, it's you, dear. No, not really. Just keep an eye on Kassie, if you would. And do your best to make sure everything runs smoothly, so poor, dear Jack needn't concern himself."

Across the large, sunny room, which was decorated with expensive French provincial antiques and glowing

Chinese carpets, "poor, dear Jack" was receiving con-
dolences from a long line of well-wishers and, it appeared, fending off the first indirect advances of eligible
female friends and acquaintances. As Liz turned and
drifted away from the group on the French silk sofa, their
eyes met and held—his blue and somehow demanding
beneath dark brows.

Will he ask me to help in his upcoming fight with the
adoption agency? she wondered. If so, I'll be happy to do
it, even if it means taking a leave of absence from the
firm. On a deeper level, the thought of being alone with
him—even for a few minutes—was doing devastating
things to her composure. Would some wobble in her
voice, some fleeting rash of goose bumps, betray her
feelings for him? With Sharon gone, it was a risk she was
reluctant to take.

For his part, Jack had observed the brief interaction
between Liz and her mother. When is Patsy going to grow
up and realize what a terrific daughter she has in Liz? he
wondered. She's worth half a dozen of her sister and then
some. A moment later, Eloise McWhurter, who'd been
feeding Kassie a late lunch in an alcove off the dining
room, brought the baby to him so he could make the
rounds with her briefly, before she was put down for her
nap.

When he looked again, Liz had disappeared into the
kitchen with Rosemary to deal with a minicrisis that had
erupted among the caterers. Somewhat the worse for wear
from too much Scotch and sympathy, Jack's in-laws took
to hanging on him and telling anyone who would listen
what a wonderful husband he'd been to their beloved
daughter. Effectively monopolized, he was aware Liz had
helped Eloise put Kassie to bed.

A few minutes later Liz, minus her suit jacket, stepped briefly back into the living room to tally the dwindling number of funeral guests. At last it was possible to snatch a moment to herself, freshen up and say goodbye to Sharon in her own way. Darting up the curving mahogany stairs that led to the second floor, Liz walked through her sister's ruffly, rose-sprigged bedroom into the adjoining bath. So expressive of her dead twin's taste, its gold faucets, monogrammed towels and movie-star lighting caused a little lump to form in her throat.

Funny, isn't it, the way Shar and Jack maintained separate bedrooms despite what she always described as a dynamite physical relationship? she mused as she powdered her nose and applied fresh lipstick. For me, simply having sex wouldn't have been enough. I'd have wanted to sleep with him—get close emotionally and spiritually.

Suppressing her curiosity about Jack's somewhat more utilitarian personal quarters, which were partially visible through a half-open door, Liz returned to her sister's bedroom. Lightly running her hand down one of the pineapple-carved bedposts that graced the antique, canopied four-poster, she plumped one of the many throw pillows and then wandered over to Sharon's dressing table.

Bottles of expensive perfume, several pieces of carelessly discarded costume jewelry and a mother-of-pearl brush, comb and mirror set lay where her sister had left them. The lump in Liz's throat became more pronounced when she realized several of her twin's long, blond hairs had caught in the brush's bristles.

Aware Sharon kept personal papers in one of the dressing table drawers, Liz stifled an urge to go through them as a way of making one last connection with her sister. They're Jack's property now, she thought. It's he who should have that privilege.

Gradually the sound of car doors slamming in the driveway below became more intermittent. Liz was standing at the window of her sister's bedroom, watching her parents' sedan disappear through the front gate and hoping a sober friend was driving them, when she turned, sensing Jack's presence.

She wasn't sure how long he'd been standing there, just inside the hall door, watching her with something in his eyes she couldn't fathom. She only knew that he threw her off balance.

"Has...everyone gone, then?" she asked, feeling as if she must say something.

How beautiful and competent looking she is in her pleated white silk blouse and narrow black skirt, with that glorious mass of hair curling about her shoulders like an oversized halo, he thought with a little twist of regret and longing. She's completely out of place amid Sharon's frills and furbelows. With everything that was male and love starved in him, he longed to reach out and touch her, simply to feel the texture of her clothing beneath his fingertips.

Somehow he managed to restrain himself. "Just about," he answered. "Rosemary's still puttering around in the kitchen, putting things to rights. Would you like to walk down by the pond, beneath the willows? Or shall we have our talk here, on your sister's love seat?"

Troubled by the thought of too much intimacy, Liz chose the former option. "The pond," she said decisively, "provided I can borrow a pair of Sharon's yard shoes. I have a feeling the banks are fairly muddy."

The pond, which lay wholly within the boundaries of Jack's farm, was actually a small lake. Pausing as they went out the kitchen door to let Rosemary know where they were going and give Liz a moment to put on her jacket and exchange her black kidskin pumps for a pair of rubber-soled loafers, Jack led the way down a gravel path to the water's edge.

He's certainly making a big deal of this, Liz thought, keenly aware of the way their steps fell into a complementary rhythm and the close-but-not-touching juxtaposition of his hand to hers. It's as if he plans to ask a favor so enormous that he needs to orchestrate a careful buildup. Whatever it was, she got the strong impression he didn't want Rosemary or any of his household employees to hear them discussing it.

Holding back a handful of trailing willow branches so Liz could pass beneath them, Jack dusted off the seat of a wrought-iron bench with his pocket handkerchief. Though she tried to avoid it, they brushed against each other as she took her place beside him. All her carefully smothered attraction to him blazed up, giving her the goose bumps she'd anticipated.

He was out of reach, despite Sharon's death, for reasons she'd already enumerated. Henceforth, she wouldn't have to see him as often. She'd get back on an even keel.

"So," she asked, unconsciously mimicking Rosemary's straightforwardness. "What was it you wanted to talk to me about?"

Jack's eyes blazed with blue intensity. "You know the adoption agency people have been making noises ever since the crash, about their policy of not placing children in single-parent households," he reminded her. "And that's what mine has become. Naturally, I've pointed out the advantages Kassie will have as my daughter and assured them how much I love her. But..."

Thanks to a case she'd been involved in several years earlier, Liz knew something about the agency involved. It was very conservative in its philosophy and unyielding in its policies.

"It's not enough for them, is it?" she speculated.

"No, it isn't," he agreed.

A small silence rested between them, fraught with unhappy possibilities.

"They're demanding I return her next week," Jack added, the anguish he felt painfully evident in his voice.

Liz stifled a gasp of dismay. Forgetting her self-imposed boundaries, and the dangers of physical contact with him, she laid a compassionate hand on his sleeve.

The gesture made him long to take her in his arms. "It seems they already have a substitute couple waiting to receive her," he went on. "They've threatened that if I don't hand her back to them immediately, they'll take the matter to court."

He was an expert at playing legal hardball—with a growing reputation as the man fathers would do well to retain in high-profile custody cases. Yet Liz knew how formidable even the best of odds could seem when an attorney's own emotions hung in the balance. To make matters worse, his efforts to keep Kassie would get prominent play in the *Washington News-Press*—maybe even the wire services and TV magazines. His prominence would guarantee it. So would the human interest angle of his status as a newly bereaved widower.

His privacy will be shredded, she thought. If he loses, Kassie will be taken from him. His legal reputation could suffer a bruising blow, as well.

"Six more months, and the adoption would have been final," Jack added with a bitter shake of his head. "Liz . . . I know you and I haven't always seen eye to eye in custody matters. Yet I have to believe we're in agreement that Kassie should stay with me.'' He hesitated, then played a trump card he'd have preferred to withhold. ''I'm sure you realize Sharon would have wanted it that way.''

It was one of the oldest tactics in the book and he needn't have resorted to it. When it came to Kassie, she was firmly in his camp. ''Of course I think she should stay with you,'' she answered. ''As far as I'm concerned, you're her father. And that's it. I'll be glad to testify on your behalf...join in the pleadings as colitigant if you think it would help.''

Jack's silence in response to her offer was deafening. With unmistakable urgency, his hands closed over hers, causing little stabs of awareness and longing to pierce her vulnerability. In the pellucid seconds that followed, she almost held her breath.

What additional boon, what untoward promise was he seeking?

There wasn't any way to ask for what he wanted without laying his cards on the table. The worst she could do was turn him down. Refuse to speak to him again. And poison his in-laws' minds against him. Jack decided to go for it.

''I need you to do more, Liz,'' he said, bracing himself for her inevitable storm of protest. ''I need you to marry me and knock the adoption agency's specious argument out from under them.''

Chapter 2

Liz was speechless. Was it possible she'd misunderstood? Or was he making a bad joke? Had losing Sharon unhinged him mentally? Whatever the case, she couldn't believe her unorthodox, but usually decent, brother-in-law had actually proposed marriage to her on the day of her sister's funeral.

It's just as I thought, Jack told himself with regret, attempting to read the multitude of emotions that were warring on her face. I'm the last man on earth she'd consider, even if our situation were completely different. All those daydreams I had about her, the might-have-beens I tormented myself with whenever the going with Sharon got rough, were so much smoke and mirrors—unadulterated fantasy-making in search of comfort.

"It would only be for six months or so, until the adoption was final," he replied, taking care to sound even-handed and reasonable in his request. "A marriage of convenience, to use the old-fashioned term. Kassie has

Eloise to care for her, and your work wouldn't have to suffer. It goes without saying that I wouldn't expect a husband's rights and privileges. When we parted company, you'd be eligible for an annulment.''

Incredibly, he was serious. And she was shaking. *If I thought for one second that he wanted me for myself, I'd jump at the chance no matter what people thought,* she realized, giving him a stricken look. *But of course he doesn't harbor any such feelings. He's determined to keep Kassie, that's all…by recruiting me as a substitute mother for her until the adoption agency has signed off on his petition. Being married to him under those circumstances would be like starving to death in a candy store, or expiring of thirst within a few feet of a water fountain.*

Fearful she'd trip over her tongue when she tried to answer him, Liz took a deep breath. ''Jack,'' she said, falling back on the discipline of her professional demeanor as she withdrew her hands and got to her feet, ''you're panicking because of Sharon's death and the trauma we've all weathered this afternoon. No such drastic measures will be necessary. If your petition to adopt Kassie ends up in court, you'll win. You usually do. I have enormous faith in you.''

She respected his legal acumen. That was something, he supposed. But it wasn't what he needed from her. He needed her to be his partner in outfoxing the adoption agency, if not the love he was aching for. He wasn't the sort of man to hand his child over to strangers without a fight, and he didn't plan to give up on her help simply because she'd turned down his first request.

He stood also. ''Winning's by no means assured in this case, and if you give it a moment's thought, you'll realize that, Liz,'' he said. ''We're operating in a relatively untried area of the law here. Never mind that I'm in the right and I can make a hell of a good argument for keeping Kassie. I don't want to take chances where she's concerned.''

Neither did Liz, if it came to that. With a steady air that belied her inner trembling, she didn't make it easy for him. "You've emerged triumphant in more than one precedent-setting lawsuit, Jack," she reminded. "And you can do it again. The fact that the outcome is so important to you only makes it more likely that you'll win. You'll fight like the very devil to keep her. And when you do, you're damn near invincible. I don't see why you think—"

"Larry Barnes is likely to be the judge on the case. You know what that means. He's a wild card, judicially. And he shares the agency's ultraconservative outlook. Though a natural child isn't taken from his or her surviving parent after a death . . . and, in my opinion, Kassie shouldn't be either . . . it's my guess that, other factors being equal, he'll find for them.''

Liz knew Judge Barnes, too, though she'd had cause to wish she didn't on more than one occasion. He was opinionated, quirky, a jurist who liked to legislate from the bench and hand down surprise verdicts. Much as she hated to admit it, Jack had a valid point. Still, there was always appeal. In any reasonable venue, she believed, he'd triumph.

"If you lost your case, and I'm by no means convinced that would happen, it wouldn't need to be the end of the road," she argued. "You have an excellent record on appeal, and—"

Interrupting with what she took for impatience on his part, Jack slammed the door on her line of reasoning. "Unfortunately," he said, "before I can file my brief with a higher court, Kassie will be returned to the agency and be placed with new prospective parents. She'll be frightened and confused...maybe even shut down emotionally. Just about the time she gets settled, *if* she's able to bridge that gap, my appeal will be heard. If I win then, I'll have lost, anyway, because uprooting her a second time could be extremely damaging.''

Abandoned by her birth mother, and with no acknowledged father in sight, the baby girl Jack and Sharon had named Kassandra Elizabeth had been found filthy and crying with hunger in a Seoul, Korea, sewer by some children, who took her to a nearby orphanage. Her luck had improved dramatically when an American adoption agency, Children From Across the Sea, had offered to assume responsibility for her and bring her to the United States.

In Liz's opinion, the precious tot she now considered her niece had suffered enough displacement and anomie for several lifetimes. Little Kassie deserved a chance to stay in the home where she'd experienced her first real sense of belonging—with the dark-haired American daddy she'd grown to love and trust.

She'd do whatever she could to bring that about. But she didn't think she could marry Jack—not even temporarily, as he was suggesting. It would be too risky, too devastating for her from an emotional standpoint. However religiously she tried to hide it, he'd discover how she felt about him. And feel sorry for her. Or take advantage of it. Either way, she'd be totally, abjectly humiliated.

She'd have to find some other means of helping him. Unfortunately, Jack seemed to feel he had just two choices: give up the baby daughter he loved so much or talk Liz into participating in his scheme. To her distress, she knew how persistent he was. If she didn't concede at least part of what he wanted—or seem to leave the door open to that possibility—he wouldn't give her a moment's respite.

To complicate things, his craggy countenance and brazen Irish charm were just out of reach. The bond of her attraction to him seemed to tighten until she found it difficult to draw breath.

She couldn't afford to waver. "Look," she said, sounding unbelievably calm and logical to her listening ears, "we've just buried Sharon this afternoon. We're both upset and grieving. Our judgment is bound to be somewhat skewed. We don't have to settle on a course of action yet. If you butt heads with the adoption agency in court and it looks as if you're about to lose, we can talk about it again."

Keenly aware of the barriers Liz had always erected to anything more than a superficial relationship with him, Jack figured it was the best he was going to get. She might be crazy about Kassie and mourn Sharon with a twin's uncritical affection. But when it came to him, she preferred to keep her distance.

He'd have to settle for what he could get. "Okay, if you mean it," he answered, managing subtly to expand on what she had promised him.

There was nothing further to discuss. Continuing to stand there, a breath apart in the filtered sunlight, they'd probably get into a row over baseball, or the weather. It had been known to happen. *If I'd agreed to go out with him five years ago instead of leaving the door open for my sister, we'd probably have continued to be at each other's throats,* Liz thought. *A long-term relationship between us would never have worked.* Still, she found it difficult not to imagine a contrary situation. If they'd become lovers, she guessed, she'd have put up with a great deal of guff from him.

"We'll stay in touch," she assured him, pushing down unwanted yearnings. "You have my work and home numbers. I hope you'll keep me up-to-date on what's happening."

Instead of phoning, he'd find some excuse to meet with her in person and press his case. "You can count on it, Liz," he said.

By unspoken accord they headed back to the house, her long legs effortlessly keeping pace with his, their hands almost brushing. As they approached the back entry, where Jack paused to pet Irish and unsnap the dog from his line so he could follow them into the house, they could hear Kassie wailing. What on earth had gotten into her? She'd been napping peacefully just a short time earlier.

Eloise had brought her downstairs. Both the nurse and Rosemary were trying to comfort her without success. Though she willingly let Jack take her, and her sobs subsided somewhat, big tears continued to slide down the baby's chubby cheeks.

It's as if she senses what happened today and needs to grieve like the rest of us, Liz thought. A more likely explanation suggested that Kassie was teething. Whatever was upsetting her little niece, Liz couldn't bear for the child to be unhappy. "Let me try," she said holding out her arms. "The last time I was here, this happened. I took her outdoors and . . . presto! . . . she was all smiles again."

On her last visit to the Kelleher farm, Liz's sister had been alive. Jack had been absent, absorbed in a complex case. While Liz had played with Kassie outdoors, Sharon had taken a personal call in her boudoir, then joined them on the lawn with an unusually pleased expression on her face. Liz remembered thinking that, aside from a satisfying career, her sister had everything a woman could possibly want.

Now she was gone, dead at the age of thirty-two.

"Sounds like a good idea," Jack said, ratifying Liz's suggestion.

Perhaps to escape the lingering atmosphere of the afternoon's get-together, which was reinforced by too many hothouse bouquets and a plethora of empty liquor bottles, not to mention the continued presence of the caterers Jack had hired, who were gathering up litter and generally putting the place to rights, he, Rosemary and Eloise decided to accompany them.

Kassie was soon laughing with almond-eyed impishness as she reached for butterflies and just-opened cherry blossoms. For the butterflies, escape from her chubby fists was easy. Gently, so as not to dampen the child's enthusiasm, Liz showed her how to sniff the blossoms and touch them gently, so they wouldn't be crushed.

On the verge of walking unaided, Kassie took a turn around the lawn with Liz steadying her. She was wreathed in smiles when her aunt handed her back to Eloise. What a great mother Liz would make if she weren't so tied to her career, Jack thought, watching with bittersweet pleasure as she kissed the baby's cheek. Despite her focus on the law, mothering seemed to come naturally to her. He realized that, if he dared to voice his sentiments aloud, she'd consider them the height of male chauvinism and lodge a protest.

Rosemary chose that moment to murmur that she was ready to start for home.

"That means I have to leave, too, since I rode with you," Liz said, welcoming a chance to escape so as not to be subjected to additional pressure from Jack.

"I could drive you home later, if you felt like hanging around for supper," he offered.

She quickly shook her head. "Thanks. But I couldn't eat a bite. Besides, I have some work to go over this evening. That reminds me...for the next couple of weeks, I'll be in Los Angeles. Call MacDonald Royer at my firm if you need to get in touch with me. He'll know where I'm staying."

That night, in the solitary comfort of her mellow brick Georgetown row house, and the following day, during a seemingly interminable flight to the West Coast, Liz did her best to go over the arguments she planned to advance on behalf of her firm's client. To her chagrin, she found it difficult to concentrate. She couldn't seem to get her handsome brother-in-law and his stunning marriage proposal out of her head.

Calling herself every kind of fool as her plane crossed high above the southern Rockies, she imagined herself and Jack actually carrying out his plan. Wed by a justice of the peace with as little fanfare as possible, they'd inform the court of Jack's change in status. They'd have to live under the same roof, of course. For the duration, his Waterford-area farm would become her address.

Social workers for the adoption agency would be all over them, trying to determine if their marriage was genuine. But they wouldn't be privy to whether she and Jack actually shared a bed.

That's what it might come down to, though, she acknowledged ruefully. Thrown together for months on end, we *might* end up becoming lovers. It could happen so easily. In a weak moment, Jack would turn to me for sex and, caught up in my feelings for him, I'd reciprocate. But he'd never love me. I'm too different from Sharon for him ever to feel that way.

The stubborn soul in her clung to the possibility. Burying her face against the skimpy airline pillow she'd propped next to the window beside her seat, Liz let herself drown in imagined vistas of Jack's mouth crushing hers, his strong but articulate fingers stripping off her Donna Karan business suit and silk blouse to reveal the pulsating woman who yearned to claim him.

If my fantasies ever became fact, she admitted to herself, my parents would disown us. And I'd get burned. The better part of valor would be to avoid getting involved with him in the first place. And to stop allowing her yen for him to close her eyes to other possibilities. Unlike her sister, she had a long life ahead of her, or so she expected. The best thing she could do for herself would be to turn her back on Jack's allure and find someone who could make her feel secure and reasonably happy.

As Liz researched the case she'd been sent west to handle and attempted to settle it out of court, she was too busy to read the papers or watch much television. When she didn't hear from Jack, she told herself that was because his custody battle with the adoption agency had been resolved in his favor. It meant an easy out for her. Life would go on as before. Though it hadn't happened in the five-plus years she'd known her brother-in-law, eventually someone else would come along with roguish eyes and a sexy grin and make her forget about him.

Meanwhile, back in Washington, Jack had refused to turn Kassie over to the adoption agency. Its director had filed suit. Because of Jack's preeminence in litigating high-profile fathers' rights cases, and the multiple human interest angles of his situation, such as his recent bereavement and Kassie's traumatic early history, the news media quickly had picked up the story. One of the major networks used it as a lead-in for a "trend" piece on the burgeoning struggle for fathers' rights.

"You might say it's a case of 'physician, heal thyself,'" the network newscaster commented. "Except that, in the case of Baby Kassandra, we're talking law, not medicine. The question is, can top-drawer attorney Jack Kelleher win custody for himself as he's done for so many fathers?"

Ten days after Liz's departure for California, Judge Barnes held an expedited hearing in the case. More nervous than he'd been since he tried his first case as a recent law school graduate, Jack wore a single-breasted, pin-striped suit to court and did his best not to appear too flamboyant. Though he sensed that Larry Barnes liked him, he knew full well the judge preferred to be the star of the proceedings himself.

He kept his arguments low-key but forceful and didn't shrink from infusing them with emotion. He'd been married when he and his wife had applied in good faith to become Kassie's parents. Through no fault of his, he was now a widower. If the adoption had become final before Sharon's death, the agency would have had no power to take Kassie away from him.

But that hypothetical situation wasn't the mainstay of his argument. "Almost certainly, a number of natural children under the age of eighteen lost a parent in the crash that killed my wife," he said. "Yet, to my knowledge, no one has come forward to press the claim that their remaining parents, who are understandably grieving, have somehow become unfit to raise them. Such a claim would be unthinkable and, if acted upon by the courts as CFAS proposes Your Honor act in this case, terribly destructive to everyone involved.

"I beg Your Honor to believe and consider that I love my daughter as much as if I'd given life to her...*more,* because she was so longed for, and she so desperately needed us. And that I'm the same good father to her I was before I was widowed. The agency's reports on Kassandra's placement to date...copies of which I have filed with my brief...note the 'strong bond of attachment between father and daughter.' If that bond is ripped asunder, I'll suffer, but that isn't the most important consideration here.

"The most important consideration is that *Kassandra will suffer, too.* As Your Honor may know, she was found abandoned as a newborn in a Seoul, Korea, sewer. She lived the critical first months of her young life in a crowded orphanage. Now she's lost the only mother she's ever known. I'm her sole remaining reference point in this world, the one tried-and-true source of human affection she has left. If she's wrenched from my care and handed over to strangers, the damage to her will be incalculable."

As expected, the agency's attorneys insisted that to abrogate its right to impose terms and conditions in a single case, such as the one before the court, would set a precedent that could make a shambles of adoption proceedings everywhere. Without commenting on the arguments for either side and asking very few questions, Judge Barnes announced they'd have his decision in two weeks.

On his way out of the courtroom, Jack ran into a fellow attorney and longtime friend, Rob Anderson, who'd recently lost an important case in Larry Barnes's court and had another on the docket. Aware Jack's case was coming up, Rob had slipped into the back of the courtroom.

"So...what do you think?" Jack questioned him apprehensively. "Did I make any headway with him?"

Rob shook his head. "I hate to say it, old buddy," he admitted with obvious reluctance, "but it's gotten so I can read old Larry's coughs and twitches. For what it's worth, I think he's going to find for the agency unless you can come up with a powerful argument to the contrary that hasn't already been presented. If you don't have one, you'd better make your peace with it."

Devastated at the prospect of losing Kassie and keenly aware of what a lengthy battle on appeal could do to her, Jack hoisted a Scotch on the rocks with Rob at a nearby bar and then drove home to Virginia. Turning the situation over in his mind, he could find only one bright spot on the horizon. And that was Liz. He firmly believed that, if he could talk her into helping him, his troubles pertaining to Kassie's adoption would be over.

Having spoken with her boss, Mac Royer, earlier in the week, he knew where she was staying. But he couldn't phone her the moment he walked in the door. Given the three-hour time difference between the Washington area and the West Coast, she was probably elbow-deep in negotiations. She wouldn't thank him for interrupting them.

Besides, Kassie was clamoring for his attention. It struck him that might not always be the case. Giving Eloise the evening off, he unwound by building plastic block towers with his daughter on the sunporch, then spooned specially prepared chicken, carrots and applesauce into her rosebud mouth as she bounced enthusiastically in her high chair. She'd reached the point of demanding to help feed herself and, banging her spoon on her high chair tray for emphasis, she managed to get food all over herself. That meant a bath, which Kassie adored. Kneeling beside the tub in his pin-striped trousers with rolled-up shirtsleeves as she flung suds around the room, Jack got soaked to the skin.

He was wearing an old blue bathrobe that matched his eyes by the time she snuggled in his lap for a story session before being put to bed. The book, Robert Louis Stevenson's *A Child's Garden of Verses,* illustrated by Gyo Fujikawa, had been his as a kid. He could remember Rosemary reading it to him. That evening, repeating the ritual with his daughter gave him a powerful sense of continuity that was undercut by worry. Kassie's mine, he thought fiercely. And I'm hers, every bit as much as if we were blood related. It would be criminal for Larry Barnes to set our bond aside as if it had no meaning.

It was going on eleven by the time that, still clad in his robe with his second Scotch of the day resting on the drum table beside his chair, Jack phoned Liz from his study. Exhausted but jubilant, she'd just walked in the door following a lengthy, last-ditch meeting in which she and the opposition had managed to negotiate an acceptable out-of-court settlement.

"Hello!" she exclaimed in an exuberant, high-energy tone, snatching up the receiver as she kicked off her shoes.

"Hi, Liz" came the answer. "How's it going?"

The faintly smoky, full-bodied voice that met her ears caused a little shiver to ripple down her spine. After a week and a half of silence, Jack was back in touch. With the kind of certainty that resides deep in the bone, she knew exactly what he wanted.

Soberly she sank into the most convenient easy chair. "Well, thanks," she answered. "We reached agreement this afternoon. Fill me in on what's been happening in Washington."

He gave her a succinct accounting, the organizing principle of his rapier-keen intellect strongly in evidence.

Unless she was willing to wed him for the duration, Kassie would be lost to them. No ifs, ands or buts.

Liz felt herself go weak. "How can you be sure?" she asked, stalling. "From what you've told me, you have just your hunch and that of Rob Anderson to go on. Judge Barnes might surprise you and give you the decision you want."

Jack pictured her stretched out on her hotel bed in her stocking feet with her narrow, exquisitely tailored suit skirt creeping up her shapely thighs. Her silk blouse would be untucked. Doubtless she was running long, graceful fingers through her luxuriant tangle of red hair as she spoke to him.

"There isn't going to be any surprise salvation," he answered. "Rob knows Larry Barnes like the back of his hand. And I trust my instincts. We've lost unless you're willing to help."

I *can't!* thought Liz, panic rising in her throat. I turn to jelly at the thought of living under the same roof with him. If I had to see him every day, share a breakfast table with him, I'd be a basket case.

Silence was his only answer. Hoping to forestall an outright refusal on her part, he asked when she was coming home.

"I hope to board a plane for Washington in the morning," she answered reluctantly.

At once he demanded her arrival time and flight number.

Thanks to her assignment, which had been taxing and open-ended, she'd fallen asleep each night almost the moment her head had hit the pillow. She hadn't had much time to worry about what would happen if Judge Barnes ruled against Jack. Or anything like a firm departure date in order to plan for return flight reservations. Informing him she didn't have a reservation yet was like trying to derail an express train with a bobby pin.

"I'm glad you're coming home tomorrow," he answered. "We need to talk. Tell you what...you can phone my secretary with the details from the airport, before boarding your plane. I'll pick you up... at National, right?... and take you out to dinner. We can talk then."

That night Liz tossed and turned until her body begged for sleep. She was hollow-eyed the following evening when she deplaned at Washington National at 7:17 p.m. eastern time. As promised, Jack was there to meet her, a black, folding umbrella tucked beneath one arm, his firmly hewn but ruggedly handsome features arranged in a profoundly serious expression.

To her embarrassment, he greeted her with a quick but forceful embrace. She could smell his after-shave, feel the sandpapery beginnings of his five o'clock shadow as his cheek grazed hers.

"Did you check any luggage?" he asked, taking a half step back to look at her.

Her fellow passengers probably took them for man and wife. Lovers would have kissed. Liz shook her head. "Just this garment bag. I've learned to travel light."

"Let me take it for you. My car's outside." Shouldering the bag, Jack took possession of her arm.

"You mean...it's parked at the curb? You didn't leave it in one of the lots?"

"Too much of a hassle," he answered dismissively. "I bribed one of the porters to keep an eye on it."

Outside, the rain had stopped. Its shiny black finish beaded with raindrops, Jack's Infiniti hadn't been towed or ticketed. Handing the porter who'd obliged him an extra ten dollars, he held the passenger door open for her, then crossed in front and got behind the wheel.

"Where would you like to eat?" he asked, starting the engine and pulling smoothly into the airport's heavy flow of traffic.

"I'm not all that hungry," Liz responded.

It was the first time they'd gone anywhere alone together, with the exception of the day five years earlier where they'd shared drinks after a case and she had introduced him to Sharon. Catching a faint suggestion of her perfume, he drew it consciously into his lungs. Unlike Sharon's customary choice in fragrances, it was haunting but subtle—as elusive as Liz was. He'd been celibate a long time, hunkered down in a bad marriage because he didn't much believe in divorce. Besides, Sharon had vowed to fight the one time he'd suggested it.

Now he was free, and the urge to be with the woman he wanted was almost overwhelming. He wanted to reach across the bubble of space that separated them and brush his knuckles against the front of her gray silk blouse where its wrap front hung open slightly, sagging from its hook-and-eye fastenings.

To imagine stroking her clothing and possibly the curve of her breast was too erotic even to think about at the moment. He'd get them in an accident if he continued to indulge himself. They were in the process of crossing the Key Bridge into the District of Columbia and fortunately he was too self-possessed to make a move on her without letting a lot of water pass under it first. He was supposed to be mourning for her sister. Baring his feelings would be the quickest way to earn her censure, he guessed, if not her outright condemnation.

"We'll make it Clyde's, then," he said smoothly. "I could use something substantial like a burger. Or maybe some crab cakes."

It was a weekday evening, slightly past the peak dinner hour. Still, Clyde's was crowded. A discreet tip to the headwaiter secured them a secluded table. Seated across from Jack beneath a thriving collection of Boston ferns, Liz perused the menu. She was hungry, after all. Or so she thought. Then again, maybe she simply needed something to do with a knife and fork so she wouldn't have to gaze at him attentively every single second.

She ordered a chef's salad while he settled for a guacamole burger with onions. He hoped the latter would keep him from getting too close. In his opinion, she looked tired, a little tense. The delicate freckled skin beneath her big hazel eyes was smudged with shadow.

He requested a bottle of wine, as well. "So," he murmured, his blue gaze burning into hers, albeit with low intensity. "Where do we start? On the phone, you seemed to say you didn't think it would be necessary for us to take any action until Judge Barnes hands down his decision. Yet I greatly fear that, for Kassie, it would be too late. The adoption agency's lawyers have asked that she be turned over immediately if a ruling is handed down in their favor and I decide to appeal."

All too well, Liz remembered the scenario he'd outlined for her beside the pond on his farm the day of her sister's funeral. She had to agree that to be wrested from Jack's arms and handed over to strangers would be horribly traumatic for the precious tot she loved so much, particularly given her early history. A yank back later, though it be to the daddy who'd raised her from the time she was six months old, might be more than Kassie could take.

"Tell me again how the hearing went," she requested. "When you called me in Los Angeles, I didn't take notes."

Aware how meticulous she could be regarding the details of a legal case, Jack complied, offering her the most complete and dispassionate rendering it was in his power to give. The food came, and their discussion lagged slightly as he devoured his burger, having eaten next to nothing since breakfast.

For her part, Liz picked absently at her salad. In light of the arguments he'd recapped, along with the limited but pointed questions the judge had interposed, she found herself coming to the same conclusion he and Rob Anderson had. Though it was possible Judge Barnes would find for him, it was far from certain. Meanwhile, she couldn't bear for him to lose Kassie. Or for her little niece to suffer. She didn't want something bad to happen because she'd refused to get involved.

It was beginning to look as if she'd have to do what Jack was begging her to consider. When they finished eating, Jack picked up their bottle of wine, which was half-empty, and offered to refill her glass. Possessed by a sudden urge to be home, Liz declined gently and issued an unexpected invitation.

"Why don't we take it back to my place, where we can kick off our shoes and hash out what to do?" she suggested.

They were going to be spending an awful lot of time together. Just how much remained to be seen. To Sharon's distress after their marriage, Jack had turned out to be a dyed-in-the-wool homebody.

I'll have to put in some extra hours at my law practice if I want to sidestep too much togetherness, she decided as he handed her into his sleek, luxurious car and drove her to her O Street NW address. *Otherwise I'll be butting heads with him and tormenting myself over his nearness on a daily basis.*

Thanks to the timer she set whenever she expected to be out for the evening or out of town, the interior of her small but gracious row house was bathed in lampglow. Unlocking the front door, Liz waved Jack toward the living room.

"Make yourself comfortable," she bade him, taking off her suit jacket and stepping out of her high-heeled pumps. "I'll get us some glasses and put on the stereo."

Though they'd been in-laws for half a decade, Jack hadn't set foot inside her place before. In a way, he considered that scandalous. She'd always come to them on birthdays and holidays—in part, he supposed, because that was what her parents had preferred. It wasn't any secret to him that Frank and Patsy enjoyed basking in the affluence his Virginia farm always seemed to evoke for them. He just couldn't understand why they refused to view Liz's career and her exquisite piece of Georgetown real estate as symbols of the hard-fought success they so obviously represented.

He couldn't help lingering in her black-and-white marble-tiled foyer for a moment. To his amazement, its neutral, shantung-covered walls were hung like the rooms of a portrait gallery, with countless silver-framed snapshots of her and Sharon as children, most of which he'd never seen.

True, Sharon had kept a scrapbook in which she'd mounted keepsakes of her personal triumphs, including photos of her first ballet recital, her reign as homecoming queen, a subsequent modeling assignment. Patsy had shown it to him on more than one occasion. But Sharon hadn't bothered to include any heartwarming candids of her and Liz minus their two front teeth, making mud pies or learning to skate on the C & O Canal with chapped cheeks and rubbery ankles.

Liz had cherished every glorious, awkward moment. As he scrutinized her collection, which he guessed she'd had blown up from the original negatives, he couldn't help but see how different the sisters had been at an early age. While Sharon had preened for the camera, clearly aware of her own "cuteness," Liz had grinned or frowned unaffectedly. As a youngster she hadn't been the least self-conscious or self-involved. She'd been immersed in the magic of childhood up to her elbows.

It's what I want for Kassie, he thought with a lump in his throat. *She* can make it happen. He had just one question. If he succeeded in getting her to marry him, how was he going to keep her once the adoption was final? Kidnapping wasn't legal, and he supposed he couldn't. He'd have to settle for what he could get.

Liz's style of decorating was different from Sharon's, too, he noted as he walked into the living room and sank into one of the cushy, off-white sofas that stood at right angles to her Federal era fireplace. It was nothing if not eclectic. She'd mixed flowering plants, Queen Anne furniture and glowing oriental rugs with Giacometti-type sculpture, an early Sam Gilliam canvas and a pair of David Hockney etchings.

He shut his eyes briefly with pleasure as the strains of Ralph Vaughn Williams's "Lark Ascending" stole softly into the room. A moment later, Liz joined him bearing a pair of balloon-shaped wineglasses and took a seat opposite him. Leaning forward, he poured and gave back her glass.

"To Kassie and to keeping her in the family," she said, voicing the toast he'd been about to propose.

"Amen to that," he answered on a husky note.

Clicking glasses, they each took a sip.

"The question is, how to accomplish it," he added, returning to the crux of their discussion.

It was Liz's chance to pose a question she wished she'd put to him the day of Sharon's funeral.

"I know you're convinced getting married again is your only option," she murmured. "And . . . who knows? You may be right. I just don't understand why you must have *me* as Kassie's stand-in mom. Surely you have other friends who . . ."

If he laid bare the full range of his reasons for choosing her, or seemed to be giving her sister's memory short shrift, she'd run for cover. He wouldn't have a prayer of convincing her.

"I can't imagine another woman as my wife . . . or any one else in Sharon's place, even temporarily," he insisted, quickly amending his original statement. "Nobody loves Kassie as much as you do. You're *family*. You have a stake in what happens to her."

His explanation made sense—maybe a little too much sense, from her point of view, but that couldn't be helped. She'd have to do what he was suggesting.

"I suppose we'll have to tie the knot, the way you argued on the day of Sharon's funeral," she answered, praying the cauldron of emotions she felt wouldn't boil over. "How do you propose we go about it? We'll have to explain to my folks and your mother first, or they're going to think some pretty rotten thoughts about us."

Jack couldn't believe his ears. Did she mean it? If so, they were home free! Though Larry Barnes might suspect their union was a phony, it wasn't within his purview to investigate. The adoption agency's insistence that he be a married man to retain Kassie's custody would be satisfied. Any carping that he had a different wife than the

one name on the original petition could be resolved by
some sort of compromise. A lengthier approval time...

These and other thoughts raced through his head,
burning up at most a couple of seconds. With a rush of
adrenaline, he tugged Liz to her feet.

"Liz, Liz, you're really going to do it?" he exclaimed,
hope colliding with relief and joy and another emotion
he'd vowed to keep under wraps for a long time yet.

"Yes," she answered, unable to keep her lower lip from
trembling.

"Ah, but I love you for it!"

His embrace was fierce yet profoundly cherishing. For
several seconds, Liz leaned into it, drawing his warmth
and the unspeakable wonder of letting him touch her that
way into the empty places where she'd always wanted him.

Chapter 3

Letting go of her, Jack gave Liz a lopsided grin. Did she have any notion how good she was to hold? Or what a temptation she'd be when they were living together? He'd spend most of his time wanting her.

"You were saying?" he asked, making light of the way he'd overpowered her.

She'd wanted to drown in the mingled aromas of his expensive after-shave and crisply laundered shirt. From beneath them, she'd caught a whiff of his unique, masculine skin scent. She hoped he wouldn't notice the longing and mild arousal that must be written on her face.

If their plan to keep Kassie was to work, she'd have to keep a tighter rein on her emotions. Absorb the delicious shock of touching him without letting him see what it cost. In other words, maintain her equilibrium. To be married to him, though in name only, and live at his Waterford-area farm until he was granted final custody of her little niece would be unbearable if he ever guessed at her feelings for him.

Somehow she managed to sound breezy and un-moved—the quintessential spinster lawyer who'd had dozens of boyfriends and never fallen for any of them. "Just that our parents—my mom, in particular—will think we've been carrying on an affair behind Sharon's back unless we tell them up-front what we're planning and give them a chance to talk us out of it," she said.

They resumed their places, facing each other in the room's soft light. "But we won't let them, will we?" Jack said. "Talk us out of it, I mean. I thought we'd tie the knot Friday, if that's okay. With the decision due any day, time is of the essence."

It would be breathtakingly quick. "No, of course not," she managed. "But you know Patsy. It's going to be dif-ficult."

Finishing the rest of their wine, they decided to host a family get-together at Jack's house on Monday, with the stated purpose of discussing Kassie's case. Jack would give his housekeeper the night off and cook for them. Only when everyone else had aired their thoughts would they put their plan forward and argue its merits.

They said good-night a short time later at Liz's front door, sealing their bargain with a lingering handshake, an all but nonexistent brush of Jack's lips against her cheek.

"I don't know how to thank you, Liz," her handsome brother-in-law said softly, with a little shake of his head. "You're the best sister-in-law a man could want. What you've agreed to do goes well beyond the call of duty...."

Firmly in command of herself again, Liz smiled up at him. "I'm the only sister-in-law you've got," she cor-rected him. "As for *duty,* it doesn't apply to Kassie.

Whatever I do to help you keep her comes straight from the heart.''

When Liz phoned her parents the following morning, they were dubious about her request. "I don't know what else your father and I can do to change the adoption agency's mind, or talk the judge into siding with Jack," Patsy complained, as usual doing most of the talking for both of them. "We wrote the letters he asked us to write, and I don't mind telling you they were very complimentary. I shouldn't worry if I were you, dear. Jack's one of the best lawyers in his field. He'll come up with something.''

Typically, Patsy had neglected to mention Liz's similar expertise, or suggest it might be useful. Well, Liz was used to being overlooked. "We've talked it over, Mom," she answered. "And we think the outcome's seriously in doubt. Couldn't you and Dad drive out for dinner? You aren't that busy. And it just might help.''

Informed Rosemary had been invited, her parents agreed to come. But Patsy was still skeptical. "I can't help feeling a little bit surprised at the way you and Jack have put your heads together over this," she remarked in her husky drawl after Liz's dad had hung up the phone in his workshop. "When Sharon was alive, the two of you barely spoke to each other.''

She's going to think I dreamed the whole thing up so I could lay claim to my sister's husband, Liz thought apprehensively. I wonder if we can convince her otherwise. "It's because of my love for Kassie and determination to do what Shar would have wanted that I've agreed to help him," she insisted.

The heady perfume of lilacs, which were in a riot of bloom just outside Jack's half-open windows, mingled with the wine-and-onion rich scent of *coq au vin* as Liz ran down his curving mahogany staircase to meet her parents at his front door. Dressed in cream-colored raw silk slacks and a matching short-sleeved sweater instead of her usual lawyerly attire, she'd just finished rocking Kassie to sleep—a much cherished task that filled one of the empty places in her heart.

"Hi, Mom...Dad...thanks for coming!" she said, breathlessly kissing their cheeks and noting with distaste the fairly strong aroma of Scotch on her father's breath. In her opinion, he'd been drinking too much since his retirement. "Jack and Rosemary are in the kitchen," she added. "Jack's cooking tonight. Both Eloise and Mrs. Rivers have the evening off. Instead of eating in the dining room, we...that is, Jack and I...thought everyone might be more comfortable seated around the island counter...."

She stopped, realizing from the look on her mother's face that she was talking excessively. She probably sounded nervous.

A bit condescendingly, her mother patted her shoulder. "That stands to reason, dear. With your lack of experience in the kitchen, I didn't think *you'd* be doing the honors."

The myth, of course, was that Sharon had been an expert cook, when in fact she'd hardly ever prepared a meal. Still, she'd been a whiz at planning them.

Swathed in a blue barbecue apron that accentuated the color of his eyes, with his shirtsleeves rolled up to reveal muscular forearms, Jack wished her parents a friendly but subdued hello. "Chicken French-style and a salad," he announced, shaking hands with Frank and giving Patsy the requisite hug. "I doubt if it's as good as Mrs. Rivers's version. But I did my best."

Having watched him assemble the ingredients as she fed Kassie, and having inhaled their mingled aroma as she played with the child and put her to bed, Liz was willing to bet his *coq au vin* was delectable. Settling her parents at the counter, she filled the water glasses while Jack finished tossing the salad.

It looked as if she'd be sitting next to him. The island counter, which abutted the range top on one end, was ringed by five bar stools. Three were already occupied. Taking her place and bowing her head as her father gave the blessing, she took care not to brush against the man who would be her husband by Friday if their parents didn't talk them out of it.

A testimonial to Jack's culinary skill, the *coq au vin* fairly melted in Liz's mouth though she was almost too edgy to eat it. To her chagrin, the meal went quickly, with Patsy picking at her portion while Frank shoveled his into his mouth with the same gusto he devoted to hamburgers. Only Rosemary seemed to savor hers to the fullest. Yet even she was quieter than usual, as if she guessed something extraordinary was in the offing. *I hope she doesn't think badly of us when all's said and done,* Liz thought. *Mom and Dad will probably be suspicious of my motives. But it's her opinion that matters to me the most.*

Clearing the table, Jack offered dessert, some profiteroles he'd picked up at a bakery in Leesburg. Except for Frank, there weren't any takers. "Okay," Jack said, pouring coffee for everyone and then resuming his seat while Liz passed the cream and sugar. "As you know, Liz and I invited you here in order to brainstorm about keeping Kassie. We agree, after considerable discussion, that there's a good chance the judge will find for the adoption agency. If that happens—''

"You'll appeal."

The interjection was Patsy's. Here we go, Liz thought, bracing herself.

Jack nodded soberly. "It seems pretty straightforward, doesn't it? And I'd have a decent chance of winning, in my opinion. Unfortunately, there's a major drawback..."

Using much the same language he'd chosen to communicate his fears to Liz on the day of Sharon's funeral, Jack outlined the pitfalls he foresaw for the baby they all loved. "The last thing I want is for the underpinnings of home and family to be knocked out from under her...not once but *twice*," he said urgently. "Given her abandonment at birth, I'm not sure she'd bounce back from it."

"You can't give her up to save her," Rosemary interposed. "She'd be devastated. And we all love her too much. Surely some way can be found..."

Jack glanced at his mother. "What do you suggest? The agency refuses to budge from its position of denying custody to single parents. Now that I'm a widower..."

As the discussion had gotten underway, Liz's father had remained on its periphery, sipping steadily at the dry bordeaux Jack had selected to accompany their meal. Now he jumped in with both feet.

"You could get married again," he suggested.

Everyone, including Liz and Jack, turned to him in astonishment. "Frank...for God's sake!" Patsy cried, going livid with anger and embarrassment. "How can you say such a thing, with Sharon buried less than a month? It must be the liquor talking. Apologize this instant!"

His ruddy face flushing a deeper shade of red, Liz's father did as he was told. "Sorry, honeybun," he mumbled. "I was only kidding. Honest. It just seemed like the most straightforward solution, y'know."

Never one to accept an apology without first thoroughly chastising the person who had offended her, Patsy appeared to blink back tears. "Well, that's a horrid thing to joke about," she reproached him. "It's not as if we expect Jack to stay single for the rest of his days. But he'd hardly want to seek out another wife while he's grieving for poor, dear Sharon. Even to suggest such a thing is an insult to her memory!"

Not answering or attempting to defend himself this time, Frank Heflin seemed to shrink before their eyes. Though she disapproved of his drinking, Liz longed to put an arm around his shoulders. She held back, knowing he wouldn't welcome it.

Somehow Jack managed to catch her eye. The lead-in had been abysmal, decimating the careful arguments he'd planned. Yet both of them had guessed Patsy would take umbrage, at least initially. Even without Frank's faux pas to get her dander up, she'd have regarded it as a desecration.

At least Frank had given them an opening.

Go ahead... tell them, Liz prompted silently in response to his unspoken question. It couldn't be allowed to matter that Patsy had always hinted Liz was jealous of Sharon, and might think she was expropriating her dead sister's husband in response to that unhealthy emotion.

Mutely conveying his gratitude and admiration for Liz's pluck, Jack reached across the butcher-block countertop and grasped her mother's hand. "Don't be so hard on Frank," he said. "The fact is, I've been thinking along the same lines myself..."

The color drained from Patsy's face. "Jack...you wouldn't!" she exclaimed.

Continuing to hold her hand as if maintaining a bridge
of touch between them would help her understand, Jack
elaborated. "Liz has agreed to see this through with me,"
he said. "With your blessing, we'll be married before the
week is out."

Motionless atop her bar stool, Liz stifled a rush of
misgivings. Must it be that soon? She'd barely gotten used
to the idea. Yet if they hoped to convince the adoption
agency of their sincerity, soon was probably best.

"Just so you know, and understand completely where
we're coming from, ours will be strictly a marriage of
convenience," Jack said reassuringly when Patsy didn't
speak. "I've promised Liz her freedom the minute the
adoption's final...an annulment, if it doesn't seem likely
to invite a rehearing. If it *does,* then an amicable divorce."

Still Patsy was silent, absorbing what she seemed to regard as the unthinkable. At last she turned to Liz, who all
but held her breath. "If I thought for one minute that you
and Jack have been sneaking around behind your sister's
back, making a fool of her while she was still alive, I'd
never forgive you," she said savagely. "You'd be the one
who died, as far as I was concerned."

Though Liz had warned him what she might think,
Jack was speechless.

"Patsy, you can't mean what you're insinuating,"
Rosemary said reprovingly. "Liz and Jack have never
given you cause to suspect anything of the sort."

For her part, Liz couldn't hold back an avalanche of
tears. The very premise of her mother's accusation was so
demeaning...so ridiculous! As if Jack would have looked
twice at her when he had her sister...or Liz knowingly
would have injured the twin she loved...

"Mom, I'd never do such a thing! You should know that," she protested on a quavery note. "I agreed to do what Jack asked me to because I love Kassie and I want him to be able to keep her." Her voice broke with emotion. "I want . . . all of us to keep her," she whispered.

By some miracle, the little girl who was at the heart of their dilemma came to Liz's rescue. Awakened by a bad dream or the unaccustomed voices that were being raised downstairs, Liz's namesake, Kassie Elizabeth, chose that moment to crank up a wail of unhappiness.

Immediately Jack started to get up. Meanwhile Patsy hadn't retreated from her suspicions. "I'll go," Liz blurted, jumping to her feet. "The rest of you can hash this thing out."

Upstairs, the pint-size occupant of the green-and-yellow nursery had pulled herself to her feet. Sobbing, she held tightly to the guardrail of her crib as if to a lifeline. Damp and sweaty, her hair clung in points to her forehead.

"Come here, pumpkin, there's a good girl," Liz crooned, her tears mingling with Kassie's as she lifted her and snuggled her close. "You had a bad dream, that's all. Auntie Liz is here now. She won't let anyone hurt you."

By the time Rosemary came up and joined them, Kassie had quieted. Her jet-black, silken hair had been gently dried and her diaper changed. Liz was seated with her in the rocking chair where she'd coaxed her to sleep an hour and a half earlier. Kassie's cheek rested against the front of Liz's sweater. Her little eyelids were drooping.

Lifting a finger to her lips, Liz got up, carried her niece back to her crib and gently tucked her in. Kassie didn't raise a whimper of protest. Bending over to impart a good-night kiss on the baby's forehead, Liz ushered Rosemary into the adjoining playroom, where they could talk in whispers.

"I just want you to know that I consider the way your mother talked to you downstairs totally outrageous," Jack's mother said, her strong Irish features flushed with the injustice of it. "Jack's gotten her to back down and admit she had no cause to think such things. But I doubt if she'll apologize. And I think she should!"

Rosemary's support meant more to Liz than the older woman could possibly realize. "Never mind," she shrugged. "I'm used to it. In her heart, my mom knows better than to think that way. At least, I hope she does. It's just that she's always been so protective of my sister."

Patsy's bias was clearly old news to Rosemary. "Well, it's a damn shame the way she treats you!" she exclaimed.

The important thing was Kassie. "Did Jack manage to convince Mom and Dad that what we plan to do is right?" Liz asked. "Because if he didn't, and they let the truth leak out..."

"I wouldn't worry. Kassie's their only grandchild...Sharon's claim to immortality, you might say. He rather explicitly pointed that out to them."

"So. It's settled." Liz was silent a moment, girding herself for what lay ahead. "I suppose it's safe to go back downstairs," she speculated.

So like Jack's, Rosemary's blue eyes twinkled as, abruptly, she found a dash of humor in the situation. "Relatively, I should think, provided you've got a Saturday-night special in your hip pocket," she joked. "I just want to say that the sacrifice you're making for my son and granddaughter is very generous. And let you know how much I appreciate it. I just hope you don't end up getting hurt."

Whatever the consequences for her, in Liz's opinion, her little niece was worth it. Deliberately misunderstanding what might have been an oblique reference on Rosemary's part to the possibility she had feelings for Jack, Liz replied that, though she'd miss Kassie like crazy after mothering her for six months, there wasn't any other option. "If I don't do what Jack's asking, I might never get to see her again," she pointed out. "And I really do love her so much."

When they went back downstairs, they found the situation had eased somewhat, though it was still a little tense. Soon, to Liz's relief, Frank and Patsy said good-night. Hugging both Liz and Jack, Rosemary left soon afterward.

With Kassie asleep, and Eloise and Mrs. Rivers off for the evening, they had the house to themselves. It was going to be awkward, living there with him, Liz realized. She wouldn't be able to flit about in her underwear the way she did at home, or let herself get too comfortable. Maybe if I bring work home on a daily basis, it'll help me get through this, she decided.

Having won the cooperation of both their parents, Jack was in an expansive mood. "We did it!" he exclaimed, turning both thumbs up as Rosemary's taillights receded up the drive. "Patsy was a hard sell, as you predicted. But even she was forced to agree with us. What d'you say we polish off the rest of this evening's wine to celebrate? By my calculations, we've got a couple of glasses left."

Liz would have felt guilty about putting her feet up and getting cozy with Sharon's widower after her mother's thinly veiled accusation. "I'll have one, if I can drink it while we do the dishes," she answered briskly. "But then I'd better be getting home. I have an eight a.m. meeting."

When Jack argued they could leave the mess for Mrs. Rivers, Liz wouldn't hear of it. What was the value of a night off, she demanded, when you had to do double duty in the morning? They were soon laboring side by side, placing leftovers in the fridge and stacking the dirty dishes in the dishwasher. By the time the latter appliance was grinding away full tilt, Liz found it all too easy to imagine what life would have been like if she'd dated him five years earlier, instead of leaving the door open for Sharon, and they'd ended up together.

Barring their tendency to argue, it would have been so cozy. As things had turned out, the life they'd have together for Kassie's sake would be an illusion at best. In six months, it would be over. Recovering from the trauma of Sharon's death, Jack would meet someone new and fall in love. She'd have to watch from the sidelines, pretending it didn't hurt.

If only I didn't want him so much, she mourned. *This would be a whole lot easier.*

She couldn't know it, but Jack was thinking similar thoughts. *How nice it'll be to have her under my roof, even for a few months,* he realized. Though he'd been married to Sharon for half a decade, he felt more comfortable with Liz than he ever had with her sister. He wished to God he'd persisted in asking Liz out five years earlier, instead of hitting on Sharon to show her what she was missing.

Liz was one hell of a classy woman—and in her own elegant but tomboyish way, far sexier than Sharon had turned out to be despite her forthright posturing. The subtle but rich perfume Liz was wearing had been driving him crazy all evening.

I don't want her to return to Georgetown tonight, he thought. *I want her to stay* here, *with me. Most of all,* when enough time has passed to make it possible, I want a chance with her. "Listen," he said, deliberately invading her space. "It's getting late. And you have an early meeting. Why not stay here and rest? You can sleep in Sharon's room...or one of the guest rooms, if you prefer. You'll be living here anyway, by the end of the week."

She needed time, enough time to get her emotional ducks in a row. Friday would come soon enough. "Thanks, but I'd better not," she told him firmly. "I don't have any work clothes with me, for one thing. I'll see you on Friday, at the courthouse."

They had to make their marriage appear as genuine as possible, for Kassie's sake. Aware it would raise eyebrows, Liz announced her intention of marrying her sister's widower at her firm the following morning, and got precisely what she expected. Within minutes, the gossip was flying thick and fast.

She wasn't particularly surprised when Mac Royer called her into his private office shortly before lunch. "What's this I hear about your getting married...to your sister's husband?" he asked.

She didn't want to lie to him. But she couldn't tell him the full truth, either. If she did, he'd be forced to choose between complicity in their plans and blowing the whistle on them. "I know it's soon after Sharon's death," she answered. "But Jack and I have always been fond of each other. And we want to do what's best for his adopted daughter. I suppose you've heard about her pending custody case."

If something was happening in Washington, Mac had heard of it. Always quick on the uptake, he grasped the situation immediately. His indulgent nod told her the veiled confidence wouldn't travel beyond his office walls.

Accepting Mac's offer of a few days' comp time to get ready for her move to Virginia, she spent the rest of the week in Georgetown, sorting and packing her things. She supposed she didn't need to take that much—office clothes and her favorite jeans, the legal briefs she was currently working on and her cosmetics should do it. She'd be stopping by her row house from time to time, maybe even spending the night there occasionally, whenever her work load got heavy. She could pick up any extras she'd overlooked then.

Deciding what to wear for her "wedding" turned out to be something of a headache. Since her union with Jack wasn't intended to last, or be real in anything approximating the usual sense, rushing out to buy something for the occasion seemed a little foolish. If she dressed like a bride instead of a businesswoman, she feared, Jack might realize she had more-than-sisterly feelings for him.

Then again, he might be oblivious. She was just Liz to him. His dead wife's sister. Kassie's aunt. His coconspirator. He probably wouldn't notice if she showed up wearing a paper bag with appropriate cutouts for her head and arms.

By Thursday afternoon she still hadn't settled on an outfit. Then a commercial for imported luxury cars, which featured a redheaded model in a pale blue suit with frog closings, flashed on her TV screen during the evening news, reminding her of a similar outfit that had been languishing in the back of her guest room closet for several years.

I probably should wear black out of respect to Sharon's memory, she mused, holding it up to herself in front of a full-length mirror and studying the effect. *But it really isn't my color. Besides, Mom won't be there to criticize.* Her aquamarine silk, on the other hand, did complimentary things for her fiery hair and pale but freckled complexion.

She was a bundle of nerves the following morning, running at least ten minutes late and aching at the exquisite irony of what was about to occur, when, in her aquamarine suit, she dashed between the tall white pillars that guarded the entrance of Loudoun County's venerable, redbrick courthouse.

Jack was waiting for her in the lobby. "Liz...you made it!" he exulted, crushing her in a bear hug and then stepping back a little to smile down at her. "You look gorgeous," he added as if he meant every syllable.

"Thanks. You're no slouch yourself," she admitted breathlessly.

He was wearing an impeccably tailored navy suit, white shirt and muted tie. His left hand, minus the wedding ring Sharon had placed there in a private ceremony five years earlier, held a miniature corsage of white rosebuds. He'd tucked a single bud in his lapel.

"These are for you," he said, offering her the corsage. "Here...let me pin them on."

He managed to prick his finger in the process, getting a drop of blood on her jacket. The roses covered it. Under the circumstances the flowers were hardly necessary, maybe even in questionable taste. Yet the gesture pierced her to the quick. He was doing his best to make things easy for both of them.

She'd be seeing him every day for the next six months or so—eating her heart out on a regular basis. Yet just being near him gave food and drink to her starving inner woman. He was so tough, so contrary and full of humor—handsome in the less-than-perfect way she loved, and whiz-kid intelligent. His gentleness with Kassie and with her, now that they were operating on the same wavelength for a change, evoked a vulnerability in her that scared her to death.

"Thanks for the roses," she said a bit shakily.

He smiled again. "You're entirely welcome. Rosemary called to say she'd join us. I guess she got held up in traffic. I hate to start without her, but Judge Weisberg is supposed to marry us at noon. And he's on a tight schedule."

They had to get the license first. The process took about twenty minutes. When at last they had it in hand, Jack recruited two of the courthouse secretaries to act as witnesses. The four of them were in Judge Burton F. Weisberg's oak-paneled chamber, ready to begin when, on the stroke of noon from the courthouse clock, Rosemary rushed in.

"Hello, Burt," she said, greeting the judge, whom she knew socially, with a light kiss on the cheek. "The same to you, darlings. Thank heaven I made it. I had a nine o'clock appointment I couldn't cancel in Rockville, and the traffic was dreadful."

Replying it was always a delight to see her, and remarking that they ought to have dinner sometime, Judge Weisberg suggested they get started.

I can't believe this is really happening, Liz thought as Jack took her right hand in his and moved a little closer so that their shoulders were touching. He's always been beyond my reach. And now I'm marrying him.

The civil proceedings were mercifully brief. Though Jack's answers to the time-honored questions were firm and resonant, the rejoinders of a man who clearly knew his own mind and was following its dictates, Liz spoke in a barely audible whisper. Once the judge, who knew them both, had to ask her to repeat, causing her cheeks to flush.

To her amazement, Jack had provided a pair of rings. Hers was wide, old-fashioned, made of yellow gold. She all but froze when he slipped it on her finger. The band Sharon had given him had sported beveled edges and a pattern of white-gold inlay. By contrast, the one he handed her to put on his wedding finger was plain—the kind that had always symbolized fidelity to her. How ironic, she thought, that I won't be able to hold him to anything of the sort.

At last the ceremony was over. "You may kiss the bride," Judge Weisberg advised, nodding in Jack's direction.

He'd never kissed Liz on the lips before. And he knew she wasn't expecting it. Rebel and iconoclast that he was, he decided to go for it. Shutting his eyes and tugging her to him with one strong hand firmly gripping the small of her back and the other resting between her shoulder blades, he covered her mouth with his.

The resulting explosion of feeling was powerful enough to topple the courthouse's time-honored cupola. Or at least, that was how it felt to him. Never had he experienced such a storm of hunger in his loins. Or drunk in such indescribable sweetness. The tremulous, half-reluctant nature of her response only made him want to push for more. We're husband and wife, he thought rebelliously. Never mind how it came about. I want to take full advantage of it.

From Liz's perspective, his tempestuous but tender assault nearly blew her away. This was Jack, her sister's widower, kissing her, not one of the nice but inadequate substitutes she'd dated. Jack, whose wry smile and casual touch had left footprints of longing in her heart whenever their paths had crossed. Jack Forsyth Mc-

Garry Kelleher, the man she loved beyond reason, who was now officially her husband.

Did he feel the passionate intensity he'd ignited in her? Or was it all part of the act—an attempt on his part to convince Judge Weisberg and anyone with whom that worthy jurist might compare notes later that their marriage was genuine?

What must Rosemary think?

Her cheeks blazing with embarrassment, Liz took a backward step. If Judge Weisberg found their reaction to each other cause for speculation, he didn't say so. Instead he shook hands with each of them, offering his congratulations and best wishes.

"I trust you'll excuse me if I hustle you out the door," he told them regretfully. "As I mentioned to Jack, I have to convene an important hearing."

Reiterating his thanks for marrying them on such short notice, Jack ushered Liz, Rosemary and the two witnesses out of the judge's chambers. "What do you say we all go to lunch? My treat," he proposed when they reached the hall, including the secretaries in his invitation.

Convinced she'd be at a loss, under the circumstances, making small talk with two women she knew only slightly, Liz was greatly relieved when the secretaries exchanged glances and announced they planned to do some shopping on their lunch hour.

That left her, Jack and his mother. "I know what," Rosemary said, in what was clearly an attempt to ease the awkwardness they all felt. "Let's go to the Green Tree. It's within easy walking distance. The colonial atmosphere's charming. And the food's superb."

Seated next to Jack, across from Rosemary in the dimly lit Green Tree Restaurant, Liz could barely taste her curried chicken, which had been made from a recipe once used by George Washington's kitchen staff. She supposed it was excellent. It was all she could do to manage an intelligent response whenever the conversation called for it. She was extremely quiet when they bid Rosemary goodbye an estimated forty-five minutes later beside her Cadillac, which was parked on King Street.

"If you don't mind," Jack said, breaking the silence his mother's departure had caused to descend on them. "I'll follow you to your house, and you can leave your car there. That way, we can ride downtown, to my office, together."

Liz shot him a surprised look. "What do you mean, your office?" she asked. "I don't get it. The farm's just minutes away and..."

"I want to dictate a letter to the adoption agency. Plus an amended brief for Judge Barnes, informing him the terms and conditions have been met. I'd like you to go over them with me, and cosign them both. All the files are there. My secretary can type them up."

Despite her new ring and a kiss that had rocked her to her foundation, their marriage had just one purpose. She supposed she'd better get used to it. "Okay," she conceded. "That makes sense."

At her Georgetown row house, Jack held out his hand for her keys and transferred her luggage to his Infiniti's trunk, which also contained a small, masculine-looking suitcase. Even quirkier than the questions *it* raised was his refusal to let her remove her corsage as they drove to his office building near Dupont Circle.

"What's the difference whether I wear it or not?" she argued, unwilling to sport it all over Washington. "We're hardly the typical newly married couple."

The glance he gave her was impossible to read. "I want us to look like newlyweds," he insisted.

His secretary's raised eyebrows when they walked in together made it clear he'd kept his wedding plans under wraps. Yet, thanks to the flowers they both wore, the woman couldn't help guessing something was up. The expression on her face reflected it.

A gray-haired, grandmotherly type, she knew Liz slightly as her boss's late-wife's sister and his opponent in several custody cases. "I see you've been consorting with the enemy," she teased, giving Liz a friendly if puzzled smile. "Meanwhile, the phone's been ringing off the hook."

"You'll have to make excuses for me, Frances. Liz and I just got married and we're planning an overnight trip to the Eastern Shore," Jack replied, causing both women's jaws to drop and Liz to blanch at his directness. "For the next half hour or so," he added, "we'll be holed up in my office. If you could bring in Kassie's file? After a bit, we'll need you to do some typing for us."

Chapter 4

She didn't really expect a honeymoon. Unwilling to start things off on the wrong foot, she decided to forgive Jack's brusqueness and shift to a professional mode. She was unemotional and quick on the uptake as, seated across from him at his mahogany conference table, she made several suggestions for minor changes in the rough drafts he was composing.

When they'd finished, he reread both documents aloud. "How do they sound?" he asked, peering at her through gold-rimmed reading glasses.

"Fine," she answered. "I think the matter-of-fact approach is best."

She was being awfully poised and matter-of-fact. Was it possible he'd been too high-handed with her? He'd do well to remember she wasn't a bit like her twin, who'd manipulated him shamelessly and run the full gamut of emotions in her arsenal whenever she'd thought it would be to her advantage.

"You've been fairly quiet since we came in here to work," he observed. "In fact, you've been quiet all day. You're not embarrassed over what we're doing, are you? Or distraught about being less than forthcoming with the court?"

Liz shook her head. "Not really."

"What is it, then?"

Did ordinary married people have this kind of discussion? She could only guess.

"I believe what we're doing is morally right even if, legally, it's indefensible," she said. "Kassie belongs with you. Us getting married just feels funny to me, I guess."

As a typist on her word processor, Frances Stanwyck was both swift and accurate. The documents they'd prepared were ready for them to sign in just minutes.

"Please see that these are delivered by courier this afternoon, Frances," Jack instructed, lightly draping an arm around Liz's waist when they'd completed the task. "And thanks. See you on Monday. Come in late, if you like. And have a good weekend."

It was four-thirty. Adopting a wait-and-see attitude, Liz didn't quibble when, seated once again in his sleek automobile, they drove south across the Potomac to Arlington through rush-hour traffic and pulled into a service station instead of heading west via George Washington Parkway. To her astonishment, Eloise McWhurter was waiting there for them in her modest sedan. She'd brought Kassie along, strapped into her baby car seat.

"Since we're going to spend the night at my beach cottage, as I mentioned to Frances, I thought Kassie could chaperone," Jack said in response to Liz's astonished but delighted look.

The weather was fine. Eloise had remembered to bring the baby's beach toys as well as her diaper bag, folding crib, miniature suitcase and various other paraphernalia. She or Mrs. Rivers had also rustled up a stash of groceries. It would be like a family outing.

"I can't think of anything I'd like better than Kassie's company at the beach," Liz responded, her mouth curving as she gave her niece a hug. "We're going to have a blast, aren't we, pumpkin?"

They arrived at Jack's cottage south of Ocean City around eight-thirty p.m. If Liz remembered correctly, he'd bought it at Sharon's urging a year earlier. Now she was seeing it for the first time. A weathered, fairly unpretentious A-frame situated in a cluster of similar structures, it had a deck that overlooked the dunes. To her surprise, it wasn't the sort of place she'd have expected her sister to get excited about.

Beyond the cottage, a boardwalk wound between grassy palisades of sand, offering access to the beach proper. Liz could hear the hiss and boom of the surf. It was almost dark—fair but cool as it was still April. The swarm of tourists that usually haunted the place on summer evenings and weekends hadn't gathered yet. Just a few hardy souls who liked the salt air and wind in their face had driven down from Baltimore, Washington and other urban spots to join the small local population.

From somewhere, Liz caught the scent of grilling meat. She was suddenly starving. I could eat half a cow, she thought. Meanwhile, they were still wearing their wedding clothes. Kassie, also fully dressed in corduroy overalls, a T-shirt and a light jacket, was sound asleep in the back seat.

"If you can tell me which suitcase you want, I'll carry our stuff and Kassie's things inside," Jack offered. "You can bring her. While you feed her some of her favorite chicken and applesauce, I'll get my hibachi going. That steak someone's cooking smells awfully good and it's making me hungry. Luckily I asked Mrs. Rivers to pack us a couple of T-bones.''

Though Kassie rubbed her eyes and whined a little over waking up in an unfamiliar spot, she soon settled contentedly on her Aunt Liz's lap for a wake-up drink of apple juice from her special sippy-cup. *How I love you, Liz* thought, resting her cheek against the child's shining dark hair. *I wish I could be your mom for always.*

A bite of supper, a little exploring with Liz holding fast to her hands as she experimented with wobbly, uncertain footsteps, and Kassie was ready to play contentedly on a flokati rug in the living room with her plastic blocks, miniature fire engine complete with bells and whistles, and a heap of other baby toys. Meanwhile, Jack had set up his hibachi on the deck. While Liz changed into jeans and a sweater in the cottage's guest room, keeping an eye on Kassie all the while, the delicious aroma of charcoal-grilled steak and sweet corn began to drift toward her nostrils.

At some point Jack managed to change, too. They ate on the deck under the gathering stars, relatively at peace with each other while Kassie mauled a chocolate-chip cookie and kept them company. Afterward, though the breeze off the ocean had grown a little stiff, Jack suggested they go for a walk. Kassie would be warm enough, snuggled into her heavier corduroy jacket and cap with earflaps. He'd tote her on his back in a strap-on baby carrier.

Despite his ardent defense of fathers' rights and his obvious love for Kassie, Liz had never seen Jack as the quintessential father. Now, as they strolled side by side on tightly packed sand a few feet from the surf, with the salt air fresh against their skin, she did. He looked relaxed, comfortably domestic and utterly *right* toting his beloved daughter in a baby carrier. For Liz, the discovery only deepened his magnetism.

On their way back, they came face-to-face with another couple who were walking the beach with their tow-headed son. The boy appeared to be about three years old. In a spontaneous exchange that must come naturally to parents, Liz guessed, they traded hellos and basic information about their little ones.

The husband volunteered that he was a computer programmer, while his wife was a junior high school librarian. "It gets kind of hectic at times with us both working," he said. "Sometimes we need to get away and just be a family. What do you folks do for a living?"

"We're both lawyers," Jack said.

"Wow," the ponytailed wife exclaimed. "That must be *really* high-pressure."

They said goodbye, with murmured comments that perhaps they'd meet again.

Back at the cottage, Liz gave Kassie a sponge bath, put on her pajamas and tucked her into her folding crib, which Jack had placed in the cottage's master bedroom. He was quickly at her side to kiss his little girl good-night. The warmth and tenderness with which he did it spoke volumes about his love for her.

When he and Liz returned to the living room, he offered to build a fire in the cottage's stone fireplace. "It's still cool enough," he said. "And a bit early to hit the hay, don't you think? I love to lie on the couch and stare into the flames ... just open my mind to whatever thoughts come up."

He probably did that with Sharon and made love to her afterward, Liz thought. Appropriating a Scandinavian-

style armless leather lounger and pulling an afghan over
her knees, she told herself it didn't matter. Sharon was
gone. Though it was still a mirage, they seemed almost
like a family. The couple on the beach had thought they
were. If miracles still happened, she might have a chance
with him.

At last it was time to say good-night. After banking the
fire with a poker, Jack gave Liz an unexpected kiss on the
cheek. "Good night. And thank you... for helping me
keep my precious little girl," he said with a slight break in
his voice.

"Ah, Jack..." Mellowed by the fire and their walk on
the beach, Liz had all she could do to keep from flinging
her arms around him. "Don't you know how important
she is to me, too?" she whispered.

Awkwardly he put one arm around her. "It's going to
work...you'll see," he told her, wishing he dared say what
was in his heart.

Unwilling to sleep in Sharon's room at Jack's Waterford-area farmhouse on a regular basis, Liz moved her
things into one of the guest bedrooms. On her first day
back to work, which involved an early, high-pressure
meeting with some of the firm's most important clients,
she decided to take a walk along The Mall to clear her
head and process the changes that had occurred.

The latter opportunity eluded her. As she strolled past
the turreted red sandstone Castle of the Smithsonian's
administrative office building, she spotted her twin's former college roommate, the very woman with whom
Sharon was to have stayed while attending her Lake Forest College reunion. Short, blondish, a bit chunkier than
Liz remembered from their high school days together in
Bethesda, the woman had a boy of about eight and a

slightly younger girl in tow. No doubt she was in town to visit her parents, who still lived in the Washington, D.C., suburbs.

"Joanie! Joanie Weaver!" Liz exclaimed as she sprinted after them, causing the woman to turn her head.

"Liz Heflin?" the woman said hesitantly, giving her a tentative smile. "It's been *years!* I didn't expect to run into you this afternoon!"

Introductions of her children followed. Her name was Campbell now. She was married to an orthodontist. "I'm so sorry about Sharon," she sympathized. "When I learned about her death, I was devastated."

Liz thanked her. "We all were," she said. "It must have cast a terrible pall over the reunion for you, with her planning to stay at your house and all. She told me how much she was looking forward to one of your old-fashioned gab sessions . . ."

The frown on Joan Campbell's face caused her words to trickle to a standstill. "What's wrong?" Liz asked. "Did I say something to upset you?"

Sharon's former roommate shook her head. "No. You didn't. At least not in the way you mean. I don't know how to say this, Liz. But Sharon wasn't planning to stay with us. To tell you the truth, she wasn't even scheduled to attend. I'm positive about that because I was on the reservations committee. Sharon sent her regrets. She wrote that she couldn't come because her husband was tied up with an important lawsuit."

Liz was speechless. Sharon had gone to Chicago. That much was certain. She'd died on the way. But she hadn't been planning to attend her college gathering for old-time's sake. What *had* she been up to, then? All manner of possibilities, some of them less than virtuous, leapt into Liz's head.

"I'm right, aren't I, that the reunion was held on the weekend of March 8?" she asked in her cool, lawyer's voice.

Joanie nodded.

"And that you're saying my sister never even sent in a reservation."

"That's right. She didn't."

A small silence lengthened between them as Joan's son tugged at her hand.

"I'm sorry if I've raised a bunch of questions for you," Sharon's friend added unhappily. "I'm sure there must be a logical explanation for the mixup. It's possible Shar changed her mind and decided to come at the last minute. She may have planned to pay her reservation fee at the door." She gave Liz a regretful smile. "It would have been just like her, wouldn't it, to show up unannounced on my doorstep?"

Though she wanted to, more than she could say, Liz couldn't buy Joan Campbell's theory. To her practiced ear, it didn't hang together. She'd last spoken to Sharon about her plans a week before her fatal Chicago flight and, at the time, her sister had seemed quite positive about attending. Even if her decision had been a last-minute one, she'd still had plenty of time to phone in a reservation and get in touch with her prospective hostess.

"I have to admit you're right," Liz agreed, reluctant to pursue the matter any further.

There didn't seem to be much else to talk about unless she wanted to bring up the topic of Jack's precipitous remarriage—to *her*. Remarking how prosperous and happy Joan looked and how adorable her children were, Liz murmured something about getting back to the office and wished her a pleasant stay in Washington.

Seated at her desk a half hour later with a blank legal pad, ballpoint pen and her notes from that morning's meeting in front of her, she couldn't seem to focus on the stack of letters she needed to draft. Instead of mentally tackling them, she found herself staring out her office window and thinking about the conundrum her sister's trip to Chicago posed.

Shar was up to no good...I'm sure of it, she thought miserably. I wonder if Jack knew and tried to shield us. Or if he's totally in the dark about this. Somewhat tentatively, she resolved to feel him out. To her way of thinking, asking him about it point-blank simply wasn't an option. A bald-faced inquiry might hurt or embarrass him—exacerbate a wound he was licking in private and didn't want to share with anyone.

Thanks to a last-minute conference in Mac Royer's office, she was fully an hour late returning to the farm that evening. When she brought her Acura to a stop near the kitchen entrance, she noticed a commercial carpenter's van parked a few feet away. Irish was barking furiously at the whine of an electric saw. When it stopped, she heard someone pounding nails.

Before she could investigate, Jack came striding out of the kitchen with Kassie in tow. "Liz...you're home!" he greeted her enthusiastically, as she planted a kiss on the baby's cheek. "Come see what I'm having built for Kass."

Still dressed in her beige silk suit, cream-colored blouse and mid heels, with her briefcase slung on a strap over one shoulder, Liz was forced to accompany him at once to the other side of the house. There, at a safe distance from the pond, beneath an overhanging cherry tree, he was having a sandbox built. A swing set and slide designed for toddlers had already been erected a few feet away.

"So...what do you think? Will she enjoy them?" he demanded with an infectious grin that made Sharon's death seem very far from his thoughts.

It was easy to see from the expression on Kassie's face that she found the swing set entrancing already. "Go!" she cried, employing her favorite new word as she attempted to wriggle free of Jack's arms and investigate.

"They're great," Liz answered, trying not to notice the attractive little laugh lines that bracketed his mouth as she held out her arms to the dark-haired youngster. "Come to Auntie Liz, sweetheart. I'll give you a push."

Buckled into her swing for safety's sake, Kassie was soon flying high and loving every minute. Intent on adding a dash of suspense and a pinch of giggles, Liz walked around in front and grasped her niece by the ankles. Tugging her a bit higher, she held her steady for a second and then let go. Sailing back, back, back and then returning to her in a rush, Kassie was laughing uncontrollably by the time Liz repeated the motion.

During the few short days they'd spent together since their somewhat prosaic wedding, Jack's rangy, red-headed sister-in-law had tunneled her way ever deeper into his affection. Watching her play with Kassie in a joyous, unselfconscious way that Sharon seldom if ever had evinced with the baby, he doubted she had an inkling of what he felt. Or even saw him in a romantic context.

The better part of valor at the moment is to wait, he reminded himself, appreciatively caressing her small waist and the curve of her bosom with his hot gaze. If you don't, you'll blow whatever chance you have with her. Despite the happiness that blazes up in her eyes whenever she's around Kassie, she's grieving for her sister. She expects you to do the same. It would never occur to her in a million years that relief would be your strongest emotion.

Liz waited until the carpenter had finished and they were washing up at the kitchen sink prior to eating supper before mentioning that she'd run into the former Joan Weaver on The Mall that afternoon.

"You remember her, Jack," she prodded when he didn't seem to recognize the name. "She's the former college roommate Shar was supposed to have stayed with in Chicago last month."

Though she watched him closely for his reaction, the revelation elicited little or no response from him. His answer, if she could call it that, was a faint, uncaring shrug.

Unable to get the incident out of her head, Liz decided to investigate. To her surprise, when she phoned several of her twin's friends the next day to ask if they knew what Sharon had planned for the weekend in question, they seemed reluctant to talk. Most made excuses and promised to get back to her, or pleaded that they'd been out of touch.

With some trepidation she decided to tell her mother what Joan had said. Maybe Patsy knew something she didn't that would set her mind at rest. Phoning Jack to say she'd be home late again that evening, she swung by the modest brick rambler where she'd grown up, on Elmhurst Lane in Bethesda, just off Wisconsin Avenue.

The day was unseasonably warm, and for once Liz's dad wasn't puttering in the garage with the door left open to catch the breeze. Walking around back and entering through the screened porch, she discovered him sound asleep on the porch glider with a paperback police novel and several empty beer cans on the floor beside his yard shoes.

Patsy was in the kitchen, doing her nails, as she reheated some leftovers in the microwave and watched "Shop Till You Drop" on television. "Liz...what are you doing here?" she asked, glancing up at her remaining daughter's step in the doorway. "You should have phoned ahead. I could have run over to the Safeway and picked up something. As it is, I have just enough fried chicken and mashed potatoes left over for me and your father."

The last thing Liz wanted from her mother was a sample of Patsy's cholesterol-laden cooking. A warmer welcome would have been nice, she thought.

"I can't stay," she said reassuringly, sliding into the kitchen's faux-leather upholstered dinette across from her mother. "I just stopped by to ask you something."

Having applied a second, smooth coat of bright red lacquer to her nails, Patsy capped the polish bottle. "And that is?" she inquired.

"Whether or not Sharon discussed any last-minute changes in her plans with you regarding the fateful weekend she flew to Chicago."

At the mention of her dead daughter's name, Patsy's eyes narrowed. Her interest in the television game show ceased. "Why do you want to know?" she demanded.

"I ran into Joanie Weaver, Shar's roommate at Lake Forest, on The Mall earlier this week. A week before she left, Shar told me she'd be staying with Joanie during her reunion. As you might imagine, I was somewhat surprised when Joanie volunteered that they'd never had any such arrangement."

Patsy was silent a moment, regarding her. "And you're curious what your sister was up to, is that it?" she asked.

When her mother put it like that, it sounded as if she was digging for something scandalous. In fact, she supposed she was, though she genuinely hoped she wouldn't find anything.

"Shar was my twin, Mom," she tried to explain. "Despite what you may think, I felt very close to her. I can't help wanting to know the details surrounding her death."

"In my opinion, you're barking up the wrong tree."

The microwave alarm went off and Patsy reached behind herself to silence it. "It's entirely possible Shar decided to go at the last minute and stay in a hotel," she said. "You know how spontaneous she was. The way you're digging into this, Liz, it sounds as if you're questioning her integrity."

Assuring her mother she wanted to think only good thoughts about her sister, and murmuring something about it being her turn to read Kassie's bedtime stories that evening, she tried to beat a hasty retreat.

Patsy wouldn't let her, without getting a dig in first. "You might ask us out to dinner some weekend," she suggested as Liz hovered, an unwilling prisoner, on her doorstep. "We'd like to see our granddaughter *once* in a while. If everything's on the up-and-up with you and Jack, as you say it is, you shouldn't mind some visitors."

On Monday, Jack came home with the news that Judge Barnes had set a rehearing in Kassie's case. It was to be an informal one, with herself, Jack, the adoption agency's director and its attorneys seated around the conference table in his chambers.

"I agreed to hold it day after tomorrow," he admitted, causing Liz's eyes to widen. "Larry Barnes is clearing his calendar preparatory to going on vacation. And I'd like to get it over with. As far as I'm concerned, we're ready. The amended brief we wrote on our wedding day says it all."

Nervous that somehow their marriage would be exposed as a sham, Liz dressed for her appearance at the Wednesday hearing in a sober navy linen suit and pintucked white blouse. Jack was similarly outfitted in dark blue, with a Brooks Brothers shirt. As a matter of course, both had worn their wedding rings. For the first time since they'd spoken their vows, Liz almost felt married to him as they sat side by side, trying to convince the opposition they deserved a chance to be Kassie's parents.

Judge Barnes was clearly dubious about their motives. But he didn't express his skepticism until the adoption agency's lawyers had stated theirs, and Jack had argued for their sincerity.

"Perhaps, Liz, you can tell us in your own words about your reasons for marrying Jack so soon after your sister's death," he suggested. "Is the marriage intended to last? Or was it entered into on a temporary basis to evade the adoption agency's requirements?"

Abruptly the onus was on her. Jack's adoption of Kassie would succeed or fail depending on how she described her participation in it. His hand tightened perceptibly on hers. She could almost feel him holding his breath.

She had a good reputation with Judge Barnes and now she used it to the fullest. "Jack and I have always been fond of each other as in-laws, friends and fellow professionals," she told him softly. "We're family. There are worse foundations for a life together, don't you think?"

When the judge didn't answer, she continued. "We share a deep fondness for his adopted daughter, as well. When my sister died, I worried that Kassie would lack a mother, the way the adoption agency is arguing. I also wanted to keep her in the family. After it began to look as if Jack's petition to adopt as a single parent might be denied, I proposed the idea of marriage to him. He agreed at once. It's our intention to make a life together... for our own *and* Kassie's sake.''

"The question is, do you expect that life to be permanent?" Larry Barnes interposed, clearly pleased by her candor.

Stifling a gulp, Liz nodded. "Yes, I do, Your Honor," she said. In the retelling, she'd switched the roles she and Jack had played in negotiating their marriage, sensing the idea would seem more ingenuous, coming from her. However, if *expect* could be construed as a synonym for *hope,* as it was in her thesaurus, she hadn't totally perjured herself.

The judge permitted a glint of satisfaction to show behind his steel-gray spectacles. "What say you?" he asked, turning to the attorneys for the opposing side. "Mrs. Kelleher has given us her word that her marriage to Mr. Kelleher is genuine."

"If you could give us a moment, Your Honor..."

Hastily the attorneys conferred with their client. Though the adoption agency director still didn't seem to trust them, Liz could feel him softening. She knew she was right a moment later, when one of the attorneys turned to the judge and asked if she'd be willing to submit to the same interviews and background checks Sharon initially had gone through.

"That goes without saying," Liz agreed.

Again there was a huddled conference.

"If the court accepts Mrs. Kelleher's statement, we're prepared to accept it, also," the lead attorney for the adoption agency conceded at last. "However, with a different prospective mother on the roster, so to speak, we view the proceedings as a different ball game. We propose the process begin again, with the adoption to become final, if all goes well, a year from this hearing date."

"You're saying a *year?*" The words slipped out before Liz could stop herself.

Judge Barnes picked up on her misgivings at once. "What's the difference, Mrs. Kelleher?" he asked sharply. "If your marriage is to be permanent, I can't see how a year's wait to sign the final papers could cause you or your husband any undue distress."

With difficulty Jack held his tongue. It was time for Liz to think on her feet.

"I...we...that is, there *is* no difference to my mind, Your Honor," Liz conceded hastily. "I'm just feeling the burden of continued uncertainty, I guess. There's been so much of that in this case, and in Kassie's young life already. I'm anxious for it to end and her future to be assured."

The judge nodded, seemingly mollified. "That's understandable," he said. Pausing, he looked at each of the litigants in turn. "If the parties hereto agree that Elizabeth Kelleher shall replace her sister as a petitioner for adoption of the child known as Kassandra Elizabeth in this case," he added, "with all due interviews and background checks to be conducted, and that a year's probationary period will be sufficient, then it will be so ordered by the court."

The adoption agency's lawyers turned to its director for his approval. With a trace of reluctance, he gave it.

"So ordered," Judge Barnes said, shooting Jack and Liz a congratulatory grin. "Since this is my last hearing before I go on vacation, I'd appreciate it if each and every one of you would conduct your postmortems in the hall."

As seemed appropriate and propitious for their future relationship, Jack and Liz shook hands with the adoption agency director and his two attorneys, one of whom was a woman who'd dated Jack a decade earlier.

"Congratulations on your marriage," she told him, her manner tongue-in-cheek. "You didn't stay on the market long."

"Thank you," Jack said magnanimously. "As you can see, Liz and I are very happy together."

Announcing they'd be in touch to set up the necessary interviews, the adoption agency contingent headed for the stairs. The moment they were out of earshot, Liz groaned and held a hand to her forehead. "I nearly blew it in there," she said. "I could have cost you the ruling."

"On the contrary, you were wonderful!" Grabbing her with both hands, Jack enfolded her. Impetuously he covered her mouth with his.

Like a nuclear reactor going into meltdown, she could feel herself collapsing into him. Whatever he wanted, she wanted. If he'd suggested they adjourn to a broom closet, just then, or the judges' washroom, she'd have been his willing conspirator.

Minus his judicial robe, and with a jaunty straw hat perched on his head, Judge Barnes chose that exact moment to exit his chambers by the back door. "Well, well, well," he said, looking inordinately pleased with himself. "This wasn't exactly what I had in mind. Go home and do it in privacy. That's a married couple's privilege, y'know."

Chapter 5

Kassie was theirs to keep, at least temporarily. As Jack dropped Liz off outside the building where she worked a short time later, his vigorous squeeze of her hand accompanied by what she knew were heartfelt thanks for the part she'd played in securing the adoption agency's commitment, her strongest emotion was one of relief for not having completely cashiered their hopes. Yet as she took the elevator upstairs to the fifth-floor suite of her prestigious law firm, a feeling akin to depression settled into her bones. So passionate, so elated, yet almost certainly insignificant in a man-woman sense, Jack's kiss had rocked her to the soles of her feet. It had reminded her—if she needed reminding—of her stubborn and limitless desire for him.

A year—a whole year! she groaned silently, sinking into the padded leather chair behind her desk and covering her face with her hands. I'm not sure I can manage to sleep down the hall and share morning coffee with him for twelve months running and not betray myself. Knowing our marriage will have to end—that he can never be mine on a permanent basis—will be like a thorn in my flesh, prickling my every thought.

Having cut back on his workaholic schedule when Kassie came into his life, Jack was already home by the time Liz returned to the farm that evening in a restless, almost melancholy mood. Seated Indian-style on the floor of the sun porch, where they'd been playing blocks and toy cars together and created quite a mess, he was encouraging the dark-haired tot he loved to release her handhold on a magazine table and take a few unaided steps to him.

"Liz...come see what Kass is about to do," he urged in response to her terse nod of greeting as she headed for the stairs.

In the long run, Kassie wouldn't be her child. She'd belong to Jack and the lucky woman who would replace Sharon in his life someday. As Kassie's aunt and his former sister-in-law, she'd be reduced to watching her grow and change from the sidelines. Torn by her feelings and her sense of being trapped in a situation that would test her perseverance to the limit, she needed a moment to unwind. Change into jeans. Give the tears of self-pity that had arisen from somewhere inside herself a chance to settle.

"Let me have a couple of minutes, okay?" she asked, starting up the steps.

Jack remembered how their kiss in the hall outside Judge Barnes's chamber had given him hope. She hadn't bitten his head off. Or told him to keep his mouth to himself. As a result, her lack of warmth—unexpected but so evocative of Sharon's behavior toward him—set off a chorus of unhappy echoes in his head.

"No problem . . . if you don't mind missing one of the defining moments of her young life," he snapped.

The cutting retort, which made her think of their more acrimonious exchanges in the past, hit her below the belt. He was so damned high-handed. You had to dance to his tune or get off the floor.

"I didn't realize I was giving up the right to a moment's respite at the end of a trying workday when I agreed to marry you," she shot back, striding into the living room with her Irish temper on the rise and her graceful, neatly manicured hands planted firmly on her hips.

The difference between her clean, confrontational style and Sharon's syrupy, underhanded manipulation made him want to hug her on the spot. He'd had it coming, baiting her on a day that had been exceedingly tense and emotional for both of them.

To Liz's surprise, his irritation melted like a Popsicle in July. "Kass almost took a step on her own a moment ago," he informed her sweetly, as if no harsh words had been spoken. "I'm trying to talk her into actually doing it. Wanna watch?"

She was seated beside him in the instant it took to hike up the hem of her skirt and arrange her long, shapely legs. "C'mon, Kass," she coaxed, keeping her hands folded in her lap so as not to confuse the child. "Walk to Daddy."

Flashing her a quicksilver smile, Kassie returned her gaze to Jack. Her almond-shaped eyes luminous with concentration, she seemed to gauge his demand and measure the space between them. Should she do what he was asking? Or shouldn't she? Her lower lip quivered as she tried to make up her mind.

"C'mon, sweetheart," Jack crooned, holding out his hands. "You can do it. Just take a step."

The afternoon had turned warm and Kassie was wearing a ruffly, short dress embroidered with bunches of cherries in place of her usual corduroy overalls. It revealed her dimpled knees and tender thighs. Frowning with the gravity of what she was about to attempt, she reached toward him and took a hesitant step while still clinging to the edge of the magazine table.

"'Atta girl," Jack praised. "Now, take another one."

A bright child, she appeared to understand what was expected of her. "Go-go-go," she coached herself under her breath and let go of the table. Two disjointed, awkward steps later, she was in his arms.

All the disparate emotions of the highly charged day they'd just experienced seemed to knot together in Jack's chest. "Kass, Kass...you're wonderful," he whispered, his voice sandpaper-rough with emotion as he enfolded her.

Watching, Liz felt her love for them both rise up in a flood. The glaze of tears that had misted her eyes earlier slipped beyond recall and she wiped at them awkwardly with the back of her knuckles. How incomparably lucky I am to be here, in this place at this time, she thought, suppressing a sniffle. Simply to be part of Jack's and Kassie's lives at such a moment. Whatever anguish I feel later, when my time with them is finished, will have been well worth the cost.

Sunday was Patsy's fifty-sixth birthday. In response to her strongly worded hint that she and Frank should be invited down to the farm for a visit with their only grandchild, Liz suggested they come for Sunday-night supper. This time, Jack allowed Mrs. Rivers to stay and cook for them when she volunteered, though she usually had Sundays off. The menu she chose consisted of Patsy's favorite Virginia ham, asparagus Hollandaise and candied sweet potatoes. Carefully wrapped presents from Kassie, Jack and Liz awaited her on the living room coffee table.

Afraid her mother would be on the lookout for signs of intimacy between her and Jack, and inclined to think she might manufacture some where none existed, Liz was scrupulously careful to keep her distance from him. Throughout the meal, which they ate in the farmhouse's yellow damask-lined dining room, she tried to remain focused on the table talk and keeping Kassie, who had begun to insist on helping to feed herself, from making too much of a mess.

At birthday dinners in the past, she'd sat across from her parents, alone or with her suitor of the moment, while Sharon had presided over the table as its hostess. Now she had taken Sharon's place, across from Jack, next to Kassie. How awkward and strangely guilt producing that felt. Despite her reason for marrying Jack, which everyone but Kassie at the table supposedly understood, she felt like a usurper. She was sure that was how her mother secretly regarded the situation.

Somehow the conversation limped forward to dessert—ice cream and a lavishly decorated cake accompanied by an uneven chorus of "Happy Birthday." When at last they finished, they adjourned to the living room so Patsy could open her gifts. Though Kassie's silver-framed studio portrait of herself was rewarded by a grandmotherly kiss on the baby's soft cheek, and Jack's expensive travel case from Saks earned the praise it deserved, Patsy's reaction to Liz's lavender-flowered robe and matching slippers was a tepid thank-you and watery eyes.

"Remember the blue robe Sharon gave me three years ago?" Patsy said after a moment, setting the gift to one side on the sofa. "She had such exquisite taste, didn't she?

I positively wore it out.'' She swallowed as if fighting a lump in her throat. "It seems . . . so strange . . . so utterly wrong that we're here celebrating, while she's lying in Waterford cemetery.''

The silence in the room was deafening. To her horror, Liz watched huge tears slip down her mother's cheeks.

As Frank did his awkward best to comfort his wife of many years, Liz exchanged a helpless glance with Jack. It had been just two months since Sharon's death—slightly more than a month since they'd buried her. They both knew Patsy had a right to grieve—that the merciful numbness which partially blunted the initial pangs of loss would be wearing thin. Yet Jack couldn't help fuming.

I can't believe the way Patsy treats Liz, he thought. She ought to be damn glad she's got such a terrific daughter left. He considered his mother-in-law's selfishness in losing control in front of Kassie nothing short of criminal. Her dark eyes wide, the baby was staring at her adopted grandmother with a worried look on her little face.

With Mrs. Rivers remaining on duty, Kassie's nurse, Eloise, had taken the opportunity to visit her mother in Alexandria that evening. One of them would need to put Kass's pajamas on, read her a quick bedtime story and tuck her into bed. More than he could say, he wanted to snatch that privilege for himself—get out of the pressure cooker Patsy's behavior was creating for a few minutes. However, he cared too much for Liz to leave her in the lurch.

"Liz . . . why don't you take Kass upstairs and get her ready for bed?" he said. "I'll hold down the fort here for a few minutes.''

She took him up on the suggestion like a shot, remaining upstairs until Kassie had curled up, thumb in mouth with her favorite blanket, and her dark lashes had drifted lower to touch her cheeks. With no further excuse to absent herself, Liz retraced her steps to the living room.

Jack was in the process of inserting a tape in the video cassette recorder as she walked in. The expression on his face told her they weren't out of the woods yet. "Your mom asked to see the video we took on her birthday five years ago, shortly after Sharon and I were married," he said in an expressionless voice.

To her dismay, Liz remembered the occasion very well. Three months pregnant, Sharon had begun to show. Clearly believing she'd landed a prize in Jack, she'd gloried in hosting her first family event. Meanwhile, Liz had still been in shock over her sister's marriage to him. Her regret over not agreeing to date him when she'd had the chance had been overwhelming.

Aware her reluctance to satisfy her mother's whim was probably written all over her face, she sought the refuge of an oversize wing chair. "Don't you think seeing the video will just make you feel worse, Mom?" she asked her mother gently.

Patsy was adamant. "It's my birthday," she argued plaintively. "And I want to see my baby."

There'd be no getting out of it. Hunkering down, Liz prepared for the worst. A moment later, their vulnerable, five-years-younger faces materialized on Jack's twenty-five-inch TV screen. Patsy's glowed with pride at Sharon's catch. For her, it was clear, marriage to a prominent lawyer pulling down a six-figure salary had vanquished any qualms she might have had about how Sharon had acquired her wedding ring.

For her part, Sharon appeared smugly satisfied with the situation in which she found herself. Liz felt a stab of pain in the vicinity of her heart as she watched her sister rest a hand on Jack's arm and smile prettily up at him with the little dimples everyone admired so much flashing beside her mouth. While Sharon was alive, Liz had fought mightily not to covet what she'd believed to be her sister's bumpy but ardent relationship with Jack, while wishing the twin she'd loved like a second self every happiness. The pain of her struggle had kept her from darkening their door unless she simply couldn't get out of it.

Patsy's birthday get-together during the first days of their marriage had been one of those command performances. Though she'd come to terms with the situation sufficiently to be looking forward to having a little niece or nephew to love, it had been difficult not to envy the shape of Jack's unborn child growing inside her sister's body. Her irrational but real guilt later, when Sharon had miscarried and failed to get pregnant again, had been boundless.

As she looked at it now, she thought her own somewhat somber visage on her father's amateur videotape had a haunted, almost bruised look. She prayed to God Jack couldn't read its secrets—that he wouldn't guess at the conflicting emotions that had torn her apart or the immense yearning she still had for him. Once he was privy to her feelings, it would be impossible for her to remain under the same roof with him.

To Jack, the Liz of the video looked as she always did to him—bright, sexy, capable, a tad melancholy and out of reach whenever she stood on the sidelines observing her family in action. Flinching inwardly at what he considered the sickly, trapped-looking smile on his own face, he remembered the emotions of that occasion as sharply as if Sharon had dropped the bomb of her pregnancy on him hours earlier.

He'd gone to bed with her just once before their marriage—the night Liz had turned him down for a date. Afterward, he'd thoroughly regretted his foolishness. Cozened into it by the way Sharon had continued to phone him and issue difficult-to-refuse invitations, he'd taken her out a few more times, then let her down easy, claiming a difficult case had begun to consume most of his waking moments.

When she'd shown up at his office a month later, looking ominously prim and serious, and demanded a word with him behind closed doors, he'd feared she was one of those obsessive females who chased a man and clung to him when he had no real affection for them. The truth had been far more daunting—on a par with being sentenced to life in prison for a crime he'd unknowingly committed. To his horror, Sharon had claimed pregnancy as a result of their one-night stand, citing failure of the birth control for which she'd volunteered to take full responsibility.

"The baby's yours, all right," she'd told him emphatically when he'd expressed reservations with a sinking heart. "I haven't fooled around with anyone else for months and months. I think you'd better marry me, Jack. My folks are extremely religious and family oriented. They aren't going to permit me to have an abortion. Or settle for halfway measures."

She'd been twenty-seven at the time—well past the age of consent. If he'd known then what he knew now, Jack thought, he might have fought the inevitability of becoming her husband. Divorcing her after she'd miscarried the child she'd used to nail him, in light of her threat to take the farm away from him and ruin his reputation, hadn't seemed worth the cost. Married to Sharon or free of her, the woman he'd begun to want more than any compensatory form of riches would remain forever beyond his reach. When finally he'd bribed his wife into agreeing to adopt a child, something he'd ironically begun to crave...

The video came to an abrupt end, causing a scrambled, grayish pattern of static to appear on the screen. "That's it," Jack announced with relief, pressing the Rewind button.

He nipped in the bud a suggestion from his still-weepy mother-in-law that she might enjoy watching another video featuring her dead daughter if he was feeling up to it. "Liz and I each have early court appearances in the morning," he fibbed, extracting the tape when it had fully rewound and turning off the set. "If you'd like to take this tape home with you and view it again at your leisure..."

Clutching the tape and her husband's arm as he helped her down the front steps and toted her birthday presents to the car in a Hecht's shopping bag, Patsy managed to leave Liz's gift behind on the sofa. She and Jack noticed it when they turned away from the door after waving good-night.

Liz's sigh denoted a mixture of disappointment and acceptance. "Guess I'll have to *mail* this present to her," she said with a shake of her head.

The warm grip of Jack's hands on her shoulders sent a shiver of pleasure skidding down her spine. She quickly assured herself the gesture didn't mean anything. In his tough-guy way, Jack was simply commiserating with her over her mother's behavior. His words—which she didn't feel comfortable validating—only seemed to confirm her assessment.

"Sharon's gone," he said forcefully, his fingertips biting into her flesh through the thin fabric of her blouse as if to emphasize that point before releasing her. "It's time Patsy stopped playing favorites."

* * *

June blurred into July. The weather grew warmer and more humid, with occasional late-afternoon thunderstorms. Jack's kitchen garden was filled to bursting with ripening tomatoes. A timid walker at first, Kassie began toddling with a vengeance.

To Liz's relief, she made it through her first interview with the adoption agency's chief social worker—a pinch-faced woman who regarded her skeptically through wire-rimmed glasses—and a subsequent home visit, during which she gave Kassie a tub bath and prepared her lunch. There'd be more interviews and home visits to come, of course. However, it was beginning to look like she was mommy material.

It was hard not to pretend her marriage of convenience to Jack wouldn't turn out to be a prelude to something deeper. He was forever bringing her homegrown bouquets of flowers or draping an arm lightly about her shoulders as he made a point. She doubted he had an inkling of the effect his spontaneous gestures had on her. Though they'd become friends in a way she'd never dreamed possible, he wasn't in love with her. She was too different from her sister for him ever to feel that way.

Meanwhile, for some reason, watching the home video on her mother's birthday had only sharpened her curiosity about Sharon's relationship with him—and the mysterious trip to Chicago she'd been in the process of taking when she'd crashed to her death.

One afternoon, after arriving home at the farm in mid-afternoon and noticing from an upstairs window that Eloise was absorbed with supervising Kassie's play in an inflatable kiddie pool, she got up the nerve to go through the drawers of her sister's antique dressing table and quickly arrived at a glimmer of the truth.

For a married woman, Sharon had kept a lot of different men's names and phone numbers in her address book. None of them were those of family friends insofar as Liz could remember. Tellingly, none had women's names jotted after them. Sifting through them, Liz paused over one name in particular, that of a certain Ken DeKooning. She was positive she'd seen it before, inscribed in the guest book at Sharon's funeral service.

A further search in the same drawer turned up a cocktail napkin with the words "I love you, Shar—Ken," scribbled on the back with a blurry, felt-tipped pen. Clearly Sharon had kept it in defiance of the possibility that Jack would find it. Perhaps she'd even relished the notion. Heartsick over finding what she'd half feared to find, Liz couldn't help remembering how her twin had cheated on her steadies in high school. Yet in those days Sharon had always destroyed or covered up the evidence.

Surely she meant to destroy the napkin, but didn't get around to it before her death, Liz thought, attempting to cast the evidence in a more acceptable light. Now that task had fallen to her. Unwilling that Jack should be hurt by finding out that Sharon had been having affairs behind his back, she shredded the napkin into little pieces and flushed them down the toilet.

Getting over the discovery herself was another matter. For all her faults, Sharon had been Liz's twin. She couldn't seem to shake her morbid curiosity about Ken DeKooning and her sister's relationship with him.

The phone number listed beside his name in Sharon's address book, which Liz dialed from work the following morning, turned out to be that of an insurance company with offices in an elegant, relatively new complex a short distance from her own. Deciding not to request Ken

DeKooning's extension, Liz hung up when the reception-
ist answered.

Leaving her firm shortly before quitting time, she
walked over and tipped a concierge in the lobby to point
out Ken DeKooning to her. Goose bumps prickled her
arms when the name inscribed in her sister's address book
turned out to belong to the anonymous dark-haired man
who'd come alone to Sharon's funeral and stood in the
dining room afterward, nursing a drink without speaking
to anyone.

Their eyes met and, for a moment, Liz imagined a glint
of recognition in his. It was quickly hidden. With the decisive steps of a man who realizes himself to be the object
of another's pursuit or unwanted inquiry, he pushed
through the lobby's revolving glass door and blended into
the late-afternoon throng of office workers headed for
cars, buses and Metro trains via the city's teeming side-
walks.

Making up her mind in an instant, Liz hurried after
him. She tailed him for a block or two, then approached
when he paused at a red light.

"Excuse me...I'm Liz Heflin, Sharon Kelleher's sister," she said, stating her maiden name out of habit as she
rested a hand lightly on his arm and felt him flinch.
"You're Ken DeKooning, aren't you? I remember seeing
you at her funeral. I was wondering if I might buy you a
drink. There's a little Irish-run bar just down the street..."

The light changed. Meeting her eyes with obvious reluctance, Ken DeKooning sagged a little. "Why not?" he
agreed, falling into step with her.

They slid into a booth in the back of the Shamrock Bar
where, once they'd been served, they wouldn't be bothered by anyone. Liz ordered a glass of white wine, her
quarry, a gin and tonic.

"So," said Ken DeKooning, clearly hoping to cast their meeting in a casual light. "What shall we talk about?"

From her experience as an attorney, Liz knew there were some witnesses you led gently and some you subjected to the cold shower treatment if you wanted to learn anything of value from them. The man she suspected of being Sharon's lover fell into the latter category, unless she missed her guess.

"Some papers I found in my sister's dressing table at the farm in Waterford led me to believe you and she had an affair," she said bluntly. "Is there any basis for that assumption?"

Ken DeKooning's handsome features crumpled. He nodded, seemingly relieved, if mortally embarrassed, that she should know his secret. "We met at an early-evening program at the Corcoran," he supplied, apparently sensing Liz would require that information. "I didn't know she was married until I'd gotten in too deep emotionally to back out."

Along with the implication that, ultimately, Sharon's marital status had ceased to matter to him, his choice of words caused Liz inwardly to wince. She wanted the facts, shorn of intimate details. "How long were the two of you romantically linked?" she asked.

He took a fortifying sip of his drink. "Six months or so...until her death. We used to meet at my place... And her beach cottage near Ocean City whenever she could get away."

So, thought Liz. That's why she wanted the cottage. Maybe he could provide a rationale for Sharon's clandestine trip to Chicago, as well. Uncertain, now, whether she wanted to hear it, Liz forged ahead. "Sorry, but I need to know," she said in no uncertain terms. "Did the two of you have plans to meet the weekend of her crash?"

Tears of what appeared to be genuine grief glittered in Ken DeKooning's eyes, though they didn't spill. "I'm an insurance underwriter who works with large firms, primarily in the printing and publication field," he answered. "I was scheduled to travel to Chicago on business. She had a college reunion coming up in that area which would serve as an excuse for her absence. We arranged to meet. I planned to fly in from Atlanta, where I had a Friday afternoon conference..."

Falling silent, the man who sat opposite Liz in the uncomfortable little booth struggled visibly for control. After a moment he continued. "I was delayed," he told Liz with an anguished look. "I tried to phone the hotel where we'd booked a room to tell Sharon I was taking a later flight. To my surprise, she hadn't checked in yet. Then, at Hartsfield Airport, I saw news of the crash on television. It was her airline and her flight number. There weren't any survivors. Devastated, I called and canceled my Chicago meeting...flew home to Washington."

Heartsick over her discovery, Liz felt she needed to pose two additional questions before she could let the subject rest. "Was Sharon in love with you?" she asked, giving her witness no chance to withdraw from their tête-à-tête without answering. "Had the two of you made plans for her to leave her husband?"

Ken DeKooning hung his head. "No to both questions," he acknowledged softly. "Sharon didn't love me. I never deluded myself on that score. I wasn't the first extramarital lover she'd had, you see. And I wouldn't have been the last. But she'd never have left her husband for any of the men she played around with. According to her, Jack Kelleher was too successful and good-looking to throw on the scrap heap. As his wife, she could be and do and have virtually anything she wanted."

As she drove home to Virginia a short time later, Liz was both angry and incredulous. How could Sharon have been so contemptuous of Jack? To her, it boggled the imagination. Most women would give their eyeteeth for a man like him, she thought. In bitter fact, *I* would, if I thought for a second that my feelings would be reciprocated. She'd never tell him what she'd learned that afternoon in a million years, of course. It would only exacerbate his grief and totally infuriate him.

She was in the farmhouse kitchen, attempting to make beef Burgundy from Mrs. Rivers's excellent recipe while Kassie manufactured graham cracker and applesauce glue in her high chair, when Jack walked in, in arrears of his usual arrival time by several hours. To her sympathetic gaze, he looked exhausted and in need of pampering.

"Tough day?" she asked, wiping her hands on her apron.

He nodded, flinging down his briefcase on a sideboard and dropping a kiss on Kassie's forehead. "I spent most of it in court."

Apparently the case he'd been arguing hadn't gone well. Meanwhile, a bottle of burgundy stood open at her elbow. "How about some wine?" she suggested, moving to take a balloon-shaped glass down from the cupboard's top shelf.

"Thanks. I could use a boost."

His intense blue gaze partially obscured by thick, dark lashes, Jack watched her stand on tiptoe to retrieve the glass. As expected, her narrow, tailored skirt crept halfway up her thighs. He imagined himself cupping her seat with his hands and hauling her up against him. The mental image caused his desire to spring to life, hot and insistent.

Oh, how I could use some loving from her, he thought.

At Liz's urging, Mrs. Rivers had retired to her nearby log cabin residence to watch her prerecorded soap operas. Except for Kassie, they were alone in the kitchen. Positioning himself behind the baby's chair, where she couldn't see him without twisting around like a pretzel, he willed something compromising to happen between himself and the woman he so sorely wanted.

Unaware of the thoughts that were bubbling up like molten molasses in his head, Liz poured out his wine and stepped within reach to offer it.

Accepting the glass from her hand, he set it aside on the island counter without tasting its contents. "You can't possibly know what a comfort it is to have you here at the farm when I come home in the evening," he murmured in a husky voice, his hands settling at her waist.

Liz was undone by the unexpected move, which corresponded to some of her more heedless fantasies. Awash in a longing that shook her with its intensity, she couldn't seem to muster a word of protest.

Having jettisoned reason along with his guarantee of noninvolvement when he reached for her, Jack took her silence for assent. Like a hawk dropping from the sky to ravish its prey, or a tidal wave inundating everything in its path, his mouth descended on hers, half-crazed with concupiscence and the ineffable sweetness of actually possessing her.

Her nipples going as erect as miniature volcanoes against his chest, Liz melted into him. This was Jack, the man she'd loved too long, whose mere presence lit a room and had her pheromones steaming. Jack, whose strenuous tongue was pushing her lips apart in pantomime of an even greater intimacy. Deep within, her longing flowered into a screaming need to have him. With each second that passed, she sank deeper into a passion to be filled by him—one that threatened rapidly to slip beyond her control.

Never, during her lackluster string of relationships, had a man made her feel that way. Never had she wanted one so much.

She couldn't let herself tumble, not when it would be "just sex" to him, with her assuaging his erotic needs as a stand-in for her dead, faithless sister. "Jack...please!" she gasped, wrenching free of his embrace even as she longed to shake her fist at the tangled circumstances that had placed her in such a predicament. "You promised when you asked me to marry you...no clinches!"

He'd never promised her anything of the sort. What he'd *said* was that their marriage wouldn't be consummated. And it hadn't, yet—though on one level, at least, she seemed to want that as much as he did.

He supposed with her the lust they'd just shared was purely physical. "Whatever you say, Liz," he responded, dropping his hands and taking a step back from her. He only wished his erection would subside as easily. "Forgive me for forcing myself on you that way. Tell you what...if supper isn't going to be ready for a while, I believe I'll go into my study and make a few phone calls."

Jack kept his distance for several days. Then he came home even later on Clarice Rivers's night off to find Liz cooking for them again. This time the menu was mashed potatoes and meat loaf made according to her mother's recipe. Because of the hour, Kassie was already in bed. They had the kitchen to themselves.

Moodily evaluating what he considered his all but nonexistent chances with Liz, who was silently wielding the potato masher, Jack reached for the receiver when the phone rang. To his consternation, the caller was a man who asked for Liz. Having dialed her Georgetown number and received a referral message, he'd sought her out in Virginia.

Jack's hope it would prove to be a business call was dashed the moment Liz got on the line. "Brent Allerdyce!" she exclaimed with obvious pleasure, turning off the fire under the potatoes and settling atop one of the kitchen stools for a chat. "Where on earth are you calling from? You're kidding! What are you doing in Washington?"

The ensuing conversation—replete with little murmurs of interest and an occasional amused chuckle on Liz's part, not to mention lengthy silences during which she appeared to listen with rapt attention to remarks Jack couldn't hear—did nothing to lighten his mood.

No question about it, the man was one of her former boyfriends. With characteristic stubbornness, Jack declined to leave the room. Instead, he opened the refrigerator and extracted the cork from the partially empty bottle of Burgundy she'd opened the evening he'd accosted her behind Kassie's high chair. Pouring himself a glass, he sipped it sparingly on the stool across from hers as he brooded and watched her face.

Ultimately, her caller appeared to come to the point. In response, Liz hemmed and hawed. She glanced at him. "I, um, can't right now, Brent," she said evasively. "I've been staying at my brother-in-law's, helping him care for the baby since my sister died. Maybe next time you're in town..."

"Tell him you're *married* to your damn brother-in-law," Jack advised.

Pretending not to hear, Liz said goodbye to her friend and put down the receiver. During the course of her conversation, the mashed potatoes had stuck to the bottom of the pan. Left to its own devices in the oven, the meat loaf had dried out and acquired a thick, black crust.

Too bad I couldn't go out with Brent, Liz thought, surveying the mess their dinner had become with aversion—even if he's just a friend and, compared to Jack, he means nothing to me. It might have saved my sanity. I need time away...free from this pressure cooker of a house and the stress of living with Jack...a man I love but can't ever possess.

Half-expecting her to offer some sort of explanation as a common courtesy, Jack was indignant when she simply dumped the dinner she'd been cooking down the garbage disposal and offered to fix them sandwiches. He couldn't seem to contain his jealousy.

"Who was that...an old boyfriend?" he asked as she got out the ham, cheese and rye bread.

"What difference does it make?" Liz retorted.

Jack's dark brows knit together. "Just curious, that's all."

"Have it your way, then. He's an old boyfriend."

A tense silence pervaded the kitchen as she hunted for the mustard.

"Was he good in bed?" Jack asked, unable to stop himself.

Liz gave him a speaking look.

"Well, *was* he?" Jack persisted.

He wasn't going to leave it, was he? Oh, no. He had his reputation as a expert cross-examiner to think about!

"You might say so," she answered, deciding to stretch a point.

Her response didn't appear to please him much. Frowning on his stool, Jack took another sip of Burgundy. "Do you miss it?" he asked, an element of wistfulness creeping into his tone.

Assembling their sandwiches with more slapdash irritation than proficiency, Liz glared at him. "Miss what?" she demanded.

"Sex," he answered.

Though she didn't reply, she clearly considered the question outrageous.

"Well, *do* you?" he persisted.

About to explode, she gave him the rejoinder he seemed to want. "Yes, dammit!" she exclaimed. "I do! What did you expect?"

To her consternation, hot tears streamed down her cheeks. Jumping to his feet with every evidence of remorse, Jack put his arms around her. "Is it that guy?" he asked softly.

Her tears continued to soak into the snowy cotton of his shirt. "No," she blubbered, holding on to him as if to a life raft. "He's nothing to me."

Jack's low growl of satisfaction was sensual but oh, so nurturing. "Let me do for you..." he whispered.

A moment later, they were ravaging each other's mouths as if there was no tomorrow, and Jack was fumbling with the buttons of her blouse.

Chapter 6

For Liz it was as if a dam had burst, flooding the arid landscape of her separateness. Incredibly, it was *Jack,* not some pallid imitation she'd met at a Georgetown party— Jack of the laser blue glance and wry, self-deprecating grin who was causing unbelievably erotic sensations to flower by thrusting his tongue against hers. Jack, her sometime adversary, erstwhile brother-in-law and guiltily imagined lover, toying with her nipples so blatantly through the thin lace covering of her bra that the warmth he evoked transferred itself with the speed of light to the cleft between her legs.

At some point—she wasn't sure when—they'd crossed a barrier she'd thought too precipitous to breach. Now every neuron she possessed was firing on overload as she pressed herself against him.

Having sold himself on the notion that Liz was pining for what he imagined to be an active and satisfying sex life, but too principled to traffic with potential or former boyfriends while she was temporarily married to him, Jack was more than willing to make it up to her. Once they were lovers, he hoped, she'd stop viewing him as an occasional courtroom opponent who had happened to be her late sister's husband and begin to see him as a man she could want.

"Will you let me love you?" he begged, his firmly chiseled face so close to hers that they seemed to breathe with the same breath.

Liz nodded, swept away by the intensity of the moment. "Don't...spare the horses."

She wanted him, too—as fiercely as he wanted her. Jack's covetousness swelled to bursting.

They were alone in the house except for Kassie, who was fast asleep. Mrs. Rivers had settled in her cottage for the night. For the second time that week, the baby's nurse had gone to visit her sick mother in Alexandria. She wouldn't be home until late. Nobody but them would know if they crossed the boundaries they'd set for themselves.

"Come to bed," Jack muttered, kissing Liz's nose, her cheeks, her eyelids with libidinous tenderness.

They were three-quarters undressed by the time they reached his room, after stumbling up the steps in each other's arms while simultaneously attempting to remove every impediment of clothing. It was still light enough that he didn't need to switch on a lamp. There'd be ample illumination with which to register every shudder, every exquisite goose bump.

As they watched each other with bated breath and dilated pupils, Jack shed his jockey shorts while Liz removed the minimal lace scrap of her bikini panties, baring her natural redhead's nest of curls to his gaze. Unimpeded, his desire thrust forward, impressive and beautiful. Hesitantly she extended a hand to touch it. His involuntary reaction and corresponding sigh of pleasure nearly blew her away.

Meanwhile, Liz's shy but straightforward sexuality was sending Jack through the roof. On fire to possess her, yet determined to bring her the greatest possible fulfillment, he lowered his dark head to kiss her nipples, drawing them to taut, wetly engorged peaks.

"You have such a gorgeous body," he praised, his voice rough with hunger as he ran his fingertips from her excited buds to her smooth inner thighs, then reached around to firmly grasp her buttocks. "I want to ride you like a Cossack. Prostrate you with pleasure. Leave both of us gasping."

It was what she wanted, too, even if she was nothing like the lover he'd lost—a slim colt of a woman instead of a lush, blond temptress. I'm alive and Shar isn't...it can't be helped, she thought half-coherently. Besides, Sharon wasn't worthy of him. With boundless acceptance and a keen appreciation of the privilege that had fallen into her lap, she'd be a willing vehicle for his pleasure, the furrow of his contentment.

Seconds later she'd abandoned all scruples based on her sister's prior claim—even as she let the necessity for birth control slip from her head. Deferring his own satisfaction, Jack had eased her back on the bed and knelt between her legs to insert his tongue in her velvet folds.

Convinced she'd known need before, she realized she hadn't come close. Nothing, not even Jack's open-mouthed kisses or the flagrant adulation of his fingertips, had prepared her for his incendiary caresses in that most sensitive and private of places. Springing to erotic life, the nub of her femininity quivered with mounting urgency as he pushed her past the brink of helplessness.

Inevitably the dense, insistent spiral of feeling he was inducing reached its breaking point. Fluttering like a bird in a snare, Liz broke free of all restraint. Waves of shudders claimed her as, involuntarily, she arched her back from the bed and dug her toes into the mattress.

Her cries of ecstasy were like mother's milk to Jack. "That's it, darlin'. Make it last," he coaxed approvingly, feathering little kisses against her pelvis, the silken, gooseflesh-prickled skin of her thighs.

At last she quieted. Awash in relief and pleasure, she realized her mental image of making love to Jack hadn't been fully realized. True, she'd been to the summit of his loving. But he hadn't accompanied her.

Had his memories of Sharon gotten in the way? The way he'd barely been able to watch that video...

"Jack..." she lamented, a note of uncertainty creeping into her voice as she held out her arms.

Had he failed to satisfy her in some way? Or was she having second thoughts about what they'd done together? In response to what he took for her urging, he moved upward on the bed so that they were face-to-face. "What is it, love?" he asked.

"You didn't...come into me...."

The little furrows she liked so much deepened beside his mouth. "Yeah, I know, babe. I wanted to please you first..."

Her hair was a Titian halo against his pillows. In the slowly fading light, her hazel eyes glittered like topaz. "You did. Oh, you did," she confessed. "But that doesn't mean..."

Liz wanted him inside her. Now. She didn't want to wait. In his most erotic daydreams about her, Jack had envisioned them overdosing on lovemaking. With burgeoning arousal, he'd spun fantasies of them pleasing each other, resting, and then doing it again. Even sleep hadn't put an end to their pleasure in the scenarios he created. Drifting off, they would open their eyes again, low on energy but still ravenous for each other. Barely able to stagger across the room, they'd begin a third round of coitus in his armless rocking chair, which would lend support to their exhausted back-and-forward motion.

To him, Liz's wish to continue making love immediately smacked of the same divine craziness. This time, we'll go all the way together, he promised himself.

Wild to have her after five miserable years spent living with the consequences of his biggest mistake, while the woman he wanted hovered just out of reach, Jack laced his fingers through Liz's so that the vulnerable interstices between them were touching. Planting a series of heated little kisses on her mouth, he positioned himself for entry. In that moment of long-deferred fulfillment, the necessity of protecting her from the child he could give her never entered his head.

It was the furthest thing from her thoughts, as well. Jack Kelleher, the man she'd loved for half a decade without the slightest hope that anything would come of it, was poised above her like some passionate archangel. Half-shuttered beneath dark lashes, his eyes burned like ingots. She could smell the sumptuousness of his yearning in the invisible but wildly potent pheromones that seemed to stream from his every pore.

Prevented from guiding him manually, she lifted her lower body from the bed to help. She quickly discovered the gesture was an unnecessary one. She was too open, too damp with longing for his access to be anything but effortless. Within seconds, he was inside, home at last in the sheath of her womanhood, gripped by her strong interior muscles.

Sweet heaven, but she was deep—far deeper than Jack had projected in his wildest imaginings. And yet he filled her. The thrill of possession all but sweeping him away, he was on the verge of losing control. Somehow he managed to get himself in hand. "I have all of you, darlin'," he whispered, his voice so distorted by passion that she almost didn't recognize it.

An involuntary confession escaped her lips. "Yes. Oh, yes...it's what I've always wanted."

Jack's exhilaration increased a thousandfold. Liz felt as he did. After so many years of wanting her—aching simply to touch her in a way that spelled affection across the great divide his marriage to her sister had created, they'd become one person, a single man-woman entity pulsing to tides as ancient as humanity, deeply satisfying to the heart. The sparring and avoidance that had marked their past relationship notwithstanding, he'd always guessed it could be that way with them.

With a little grunt of satisfaction, he began to move, drawing them into a rhythm so instinctive and elemental she felt the depths of her soul connect to his and all the mating pairs of the universe. Drenched in pleasure, it portended a deeper, more implosive bliss to come. When it unfolded, her feminine instincts sensed, it would unite them with all creation.

How long they warred thus sweetly in Jack's big bed, Liz couldn't have said afterward. She only knew that, though time poured out like honey, her heart seemed to race. With each second, each exquisite contact, the bonfire of their passion blazed higher. Above her face, Jack's was a mask of rapture approaching the infinite.

It was their first time together. The ecstasy of having her wouldn't let him last. With the thought, huge shudders gripped him. Despite her earlier release, Liz joined

him in seconds. As she'd known it would, the resulting
conflagration annihilated their separateness. Their cries
incinerating the dusk, they clung to the heights, then
drifted down together.

It seemed the antithesis of everything they'd done together that they should simply go to sleep. Yet that was
just what occurred. Loose-limbed and free of tension
from the most powerful climax he'd ever experienced,
Jack rolled off her. Drawing her head against his shoulder, he pulled up a coverlet.

Liz yawned deeply but didn't open her eyes. Safe for the
moment on Jack's side of the chasm that usually separated them, she didn't want conversation from him. Or
declarations of love that didn't fit the tangled emotions in
his heart. With her bones approximating mush and her
every cell swimming in contentment, all she wanted were
a few warm kisses, the comforting presence of his hard,
tall body next to hers. Jack gave her both.

She didn't wake at the quiet closing of Eloise Mc-
Whurter's car door when the nanny returned from Alexandria around midnight, or stir at her light footsteps on
the stairs. Thoroughly spent from Jack's loving, and more
deeply asleep than she'd managed to be in months, she
barely moved in the unfamiliar bed beside the man who
was her legal husband.

It was only around seven a.m., when Mrs. Rivers arrived from her cottage to make breakfast, and the hazel-
nut-scented aroma of brewing coffee drifted up the stairs,
that she awoke and recalled with a dizzying rush what had
taken place. Beside her, sprawled comfortably on his
stomach, Jack was snoring gently. Neither of them was
wearing a stitch. It was her fondest dream—turned into

her most vivid nightmare by what she believed was his lingering love for her sister.

A breathless survey of the room located the undergarments they'd shed before climbing into the sack together. Both her bra and bikini panties lay in a little heap at the foot of the bed with Jack's undershorts. But where were her skirt and blouse? His slacks and shirt? To Liz's relief, she saw them, lying at the edge of his deep-toned Oriental rug, just inside his bedroom door.

Making a bad situation worse, they'd left that door open to the upstairs hall. At its opposite end, she could hear Kassie chortling to herself as she played with her favorite crib toys, one of which involved the ringing of a little bell.

Accustomed to returning home after dark from her trips to Alexandria and making her way upstairs without switching on a light, Eloise probably hadn't spotted them yet. However, that could change in a heartbeat. At any moment the nanny was likely to appear, fresh-faced and brimming with her usual energy, to scoop Kassie up from her crib, put on her coveralls and T-shirt and carry her downstairs for breakfast.

Unless Liz got a move on, the nanny would catch them *in flagrante delicto.* Under the circumstances she didn't trust herself to field discovery with nonchalance. Slithering out of bed as unobtrusively as possible so as not to disturb her bedmate, Liz gathered up her possessions and—wriggling into her crumpled outer garments—scurried for the guest room.

The full significance of what had happened the night before didn't hit her for several minutes, until she was safely ensconced in the guest room bath, beneath the shower's vindicating spray. In their haste to have each other, she and Jack had made love without protection.

Apparently he'd assumed she used something. For her part, she hadn't thought of inserting her diaphragm, which was back in Georgetown, in any case!

During none of her infrequent liaisons with boyfriends had she ever committed such a blunder. I could be pregnant, she thought with a sinking feeling in the pit of her stomach—the way Sharon was five years ago. *I could be carrying Jack's baby.*

Thanks to a history of irregular menses, she didn't have a clue whether or not their faux pas had occurred during a fertile period. Only time would tell the story. Logic-obsessed lawyer though she was, she tried to tell herself the risk was small. Except accidentally, when they were still dating, Jack hadn't managed to get her sister pregnant, though in recent years it had been an announced goal with him. Sharon's claims that he'd been the one at fault for their failure to conceive argued against unforeseen consequences.

She was probably in the clear. Yet as she hastily donned a taupe linen suit and peach silk blouse that fastened down the front with tiny covered buttons, she realized pregnancy wouldn't be the worst result of her improvidence. She'd always wanted a child—Jack's more than anyone's. No, the worst possible consequence of what had happened was that now he might guess how she felt about him. In her opinion, which she took for gospel, he was still crazy about her dead sister. The most she could hope for would be to play second fiddle to Sharon's memory.

When he'd made advances to her the previous evening, he'd simply needed someone. How on earth was she going to face him—let alone manage to live with him in the same house until Kassie's adoption was final? How to pretend it didn't matter, that the incident had been one of simple lust for her, as well, when the pain of his indifference would be written all over her face?

Stepping out into the hall with her car keys in hand and briefcase slung over her shoulder, she gathered Jack wasn't up yet. The door to his room remained three-quarters shut, the way she'd left it. His shower wasn't running. No baritone mangling of some indeterminate show tune emanated from his private bath.

Desperate for a fortifying cup of coffee, she decided to risk letting Clarice Rivers fill her wide-bottomed commuter mug before jumping into her car and heading for downtown Washington. By then, Kassie was cooing in her high chair as Eloise helped her eat breakfast. Despite Liz's furor to be gone, she paused for an extra moment to kiss the baby's silky head and speak several love words to her.

She nearly jumped a foot when Jack entered the kitchen in his bathrobe—a medium blue terry number that revealed his long, muscular legs and a hint of hairy chest as it accentuated the blue of his eyes.

It was immediately clear to him that she'd retreated from their intimacy behind a very substantial brick wall. He'd have to approach her carefully. "Good morning," he remarked to all and sundry, declining to single Liz out for special notice as he bent to give Kassie a hug. "I trust everyone slept well."

Both Eloise and Mrs. Rivers answered in the affirmative. Noncommittal, Liz fiddled with her briefcase. From her perspective, his offhand manner only made the situation more awkward.

"Gotta go," she murmured to no one in particular, refusing to meet his eyes. "I've got an early hearing. Have a good day, you all."

It wasn't until after she'd left, driving off in a cloud of dust, that Jack thought he realized what the problem was. The night before, he'd failed to offer her protection.

The day proved a miserable one for Liz. Nothing, not Mac Royer's unusually fulsome praise of the way she'd handled a recent case or the unexpected bouquet of flowers she received from a female client, could alleviate the gnawing self-criticism that festered in her gut. What an idiot she'd been to let Jack make love to her! Committed to sticking out her marriage of convenience to him until Kassie's adoption was final, she found herself constitutionally unable to do something as uncomplicated as returning to the farm for dinner. What on earth was she going to do? She didn't have a clue how to handle the mess she'd made of things.

For tonight, at least, she decided, she'd sleep in Georgetown. If she phoned Clarice Rivers with some excuse before Jack got home from work and the housekeeper relayed the message, maybe he'd take the hint and refrain from coming after her. She could only hope.

Inserting her key in the familiar brass lock of her brick row house on O Street shortly after six p.m. was the psychological equivalent of going to ground for a wounded animal. She wanted to fling her arms around her wall of family photos for comfort, curl up in a ball beneath her favorite afghan on one of the ivory couches that flanked her living room fireplace.

One thing she *wasn't* was hungry. Deciding on a drink and a bath, in that order, she went to the kitchen and poured herself a Scotch, then carried it, ice cubes clinking, up the circular iron staircase to her second-floor bedroom in order to strip.

Far from feeling violated by her experience in Jack's arms, her body tingled with a warm sense of womanliness. The sensation was almost wanton. Catching a glimpse of her expression in the pier glass that stood to the right of her dressing table, she had to admit her description was just. At last she knew what love could be like at its most fulfilling. Too bad it had turned out to be a dead-end street.

As she stood there, all but immobilized, the first fat raindrops of a predicted thundershower struck her windowpanes. With a little groan, she headed for the tub and turned on the tap. Several minutes later, as she lounged shoulder-deep in a sea of scented bubbles with her Scotch glass balanced on one knee, the phone rang. Though her heart leapt, she refused to answer. It's probably Jack, she thought with a yearning little stab of pain in the vicinity of her heart. Then again, maybe it isn't.

Whoever it was, she didn't want to talk. By tomorrow, she hoped, she'd be ready to take on the world again. When it came to Jack, on the other hand, she needed time—plenty of time and several more lengthy bubble baths before she could build the requisite shell around her heart.

A short time later, the phone shrilled again. This time, her caller waited past the fourth ring and the message machine clicked on. "Liz? Are you there?" Jack's voice pleaded from her bedside table. "If you are, *please* pick up. We have to talk."

"Not on your life," she muttered, hugging herself. If she knew Jack, and she thought she did, he'd want to reassure her, partly from guilt and partly out of self-interest. He was a decent guy, and he wouldn't want to hurt her. Plus, if she didn't come back, he stood to lose Kassie.

While she wouldn't let the latter catastrophe happen, she had to protect herself.

"Liz?" his voice asked again, before the message machine clicked off.

Setting her Scotch glass on the floor beside the tub and shutting her eyes, Liz sank deeper into her bubbles and courted mindlessness.

She was fully dried off some forty-five minutes later, wrapped in her favorite fuzzy, blue robe, which predated her graduation from law school, and scrounging in her kitchen cupboards for something chocolate, when the doorbell rang. *Oh, no!* she thought, realizing afresh how bullheaded Jack was. Dear God, please don't let it be him. I don't think I can face him!

Jack noticed her downstairs lights were on, her car parked at the curb. Unless she'd called up a former boyfriend and gone out on the town for the evening, which hardly seemed in character, she was home. And awake. She simply wanted nothing to do with him. Well, dammit, he wanted to see her! Continuing to bear down on her small, elegant door buzzer with all the tenacity he possessed, Jack let the rain that was still coming down in buckets plaster his dark hair to his forehead.

"Liz," he yelled. "Answer your damn door, will you? I know you're in there. We have to talk."

A moment later he started pounding.

It was pouring out. He'd be drenched. Meanwhile, Liz's neighbors would be disturbed and scandalized by all the noise he was making. Taking a few steps into the living room, Liz hugged herself. Haloed by a street lamp, his plastic-raincoat-clad shape was visible through one of the leaded sidelights that framed her front door.

She'd have to answer, or somebody would call the cops. Then again, maybe she could persuade him to see reason. "Go away, Jack," she shouted in turn. "I have nothing to say to you tonight. If you want, I can phone you in the morning."

It wouldn't do. He needed his arms around her—*tonight*. "Liz... open this door, or I'm going to break it down," he threatened.

He was a respected attorney, an officer of the court, and she knew for a fact that he was just blowing off steam. Perversely, something softened in her at the words. Shaking with trepidation over the scene that was likely to follow, she walked to the door and undid the bolt.

He was in like a shot, wet as a half-drowned mutt, tugging her to him as the water that ran off him in rivulets dripped onto her expensive hall carpet. Before she could utter a single word of protest, his mouth was ravaging hers. Plunging into the front of her robe as if he owned it and her in the bargain, his fingertips massaged her nipples with exquisite tenderness.

Between her legs, a flower of longing opened, hot and inevitable as a hibiscus captured by time-lapse photography. It was to be like this, then? Denied his love, which was still the property of her dead, unworthy sister, she was to be at the mercy of his libido, which for the moment was focused like a laser beam in her direction? Unable to oppose her own bone-deep craving, Liz allowed her arms to creep around his neck.

Seconds later he'd scooped her up in his embrace and carried her into the living room, depositing her on one of the couches where they'd sat facing each other as they'd hammered out their agreement to wed temporarily for Kassie's sake.

"Take off your robe...I'm going to make love to you," he announced, peeling off his raincoat and unfastening his belt.

"What if... I don't want to?" Liz countered shakily.

"You know damn well it's what we both need and want."

She ceased all protest as he shed his shirt and trousers and kicked off his expensive loafers. He wasn't wearing underwear. Or socks. His desire jutted forward like a cannon barrel. Caught in the grip of her need for him, Liz let her robe fall back from her shoulders.

This time he'd brought protection. A look passed between them as he assumed it, acknowledging the risk they'd taken the night before and its possible consequences. What happened was nobody's fault, Liz told him silently. If you hadn't taken responsibility tonight, I might have defaulted again. When it came to him, she realized, her reputation for caution flew right out the window.

Tonight, she knew, there'd be no preliminaries, no sweet initiation. A moment later Jack was inside her, filling her to bursting. His hard, tall body pressed hers into the sofa cushions. Less than twenty-four hours had elapsed since their coming together in his big bed. Yet as they proceeded to ravish each other without quarter, it was as if they'd merged after decades of drought and denial—so voracious they couldn't afford to waste a second.

Forged in longing and a plethora of emotions neither could articulate or consciously sift through, their climax was shattering and all encompassing. As they separated afterward, Liz wanted to weep. Though her knowledge of Sharon's faithlessness had stifled the qualms she'd had about making love to Jack, she believed he knew nothing of them. Ergo, though his body desired hers, he was still a grieving widower. If Shar were to walk through the door this minute, she tortured herself, there wouldn't be any contest.

Overcome by desperation and suddenly embarrassed by her nakedness, she wrapped herself in her favorite afghan.

Jack sensed her retreat instantly. "Go ahead," he invited. "Let me have it."

She didn't think she could bear an exchange of recriminations. "If you recall, our marriage was to be a temporary one, entered into for Kassie's sake," she reminded him gently. "You said I'd be eligible for an annulment. While that possibility has gone by the board, thanks to both our behavior, I think this kind of thing should cease. You were my sister's husband, and she's only been dead a few months. What we've been doing isn't right...or respectful."

Aching to tell her of Sharon's betrayal, Jack couldn't bring himself to do it. He didn't want Liz's pity. Now that he was free, he just wanted her to love him. "Sharon's dead and we're alive," he said, then tried to soften his approach at the film of tears that glistened in her eyes. "Whatever we do or don't do won't bring her back...that's all I meant," he added, moving over on the couch to put his arms around her.

Inevitably the bonfire that seemed to lie banked between them, ready to ignite at the slightest look or touch whenever they were together, roared to life again. Jack's attempt to comfort Liz was transformed into a quick stumble up her spiral staircase to her bedroom, where they joined in lust and ecstasy after a hasty pause during which Liz inserted her diaphragm for safety's sake.

As before, they went directly to sleep afterward amid her tangled bedsheets, drained of their tumultuous yearning but with nothing of substance resolved between them.

Liz woke around one a.m., jolted from slumber by an uneasy conscience or a dog barking somewhere in the neighborhood. Half-buried in the pillow next to hers, Jack's face wore a look of boyish innocence. Despite the shadow beard that had darkened his jaw, the sweep of coal black lashes against his cheeks made him look as vulnerable as a ten-year-old.

Now that she knew him better—knew firsthand the Jack who so lovingly cherished Kassie as well as she knew the formidable, take-no-prisoners attorney so capable of trashing her courtroom arguments—she realized what a truly special man he was. The sad fact is, I love you with all my heart, Jack Kelleher, she whispered silently. So much so that it blows me away.

Tempted to smooth back an unruly lock of hair that had fallen forward over his brow, she stayed her hand as he stirred and muttered something in his sleep. Though she was able to catch just a few words, they were enough to send her hopes plummeting.

"Sharon," he mumbled, "You *can't*. I love..."

The garbled dream fragment only confirmed what the thinking woman in her held to be true and shouldn't have obliterated from consciousness: the fact that the man she loved still loved her sister.

So what did you expect? she reproached herself. Shar's been dead for just a few months. Though Liz's twin and the man she loved had weathered some pretty stinging arguments during the course of their marriage, from what she'd gathered, he hadn't known about his wife's infidelity. There wasn't the slightest evidence to suggest he'd ever stepped out on her. Why wouldn't he feel devastation over her loss?

Make that desolation and a frustrated sexual drive in search of satisfaction, Liz amended with a little stab of heartbreak. I just happened to be handy.

Getting out of bed, she barricaded herself in the adjoining bathroom for a silent but wrenching spate of tears. Despite a tiny but unrelenting germ of aspiration in her gut, which argued Jack might develop those feelings for *her* if she hung on long enough, she wanted to throw up.

When she emerged, after washing her face with a damp washcloth, taking a couple of aspirin for a splitting headache and putting on a pair of pajamas she'd left hanging on the bathroom door prior to her move to Virginia, Jack was still muttering in his sleep. Meanwhile, it was a fairly chilly morning for summer. Her favorite robe was still in front of the living room fireplace, where she'd left it. Nothing else would do. Padding down her circular iron stairs, she wrapped the robe about her and huddled in a secondhand Eames chair she'd bought herself for her most recent birthday, to stare bitterly at the trappings of her life before Jack and wonder if she could readjust to it.

For his part, Jack had been dreaming about Sharon. In the scenario his unconscious mind had produced, Liz's twin had somehow managed to recover from her injuries. Appearing at his Waterford-area farmhouse, she'd demanded they take up married life again. Aghast, he'd refused, earning her scorn and fury when he'd admitted he was in love with Liz.

The nightmare had continued for a while, with more arguing between himself and Sharon. At last, while mentally grasping his late wife by the shoulders to prevent her from throwing Liz's personal effects out of the house, he'd awakened to find himself in the latter's bed—alone. Their heated lovemaking several hours earlier came back to him in a rush. Had Liz rejected him again? Wrapping an oversize towel from the bathroom around his hips, he went downstairs in search of her.

"Liz...there you are!" he said, his relief more genuine than feigned when he located her. Daunted by her somber expression, he tried the ghost of a smile, a blue-eyed twinkle. "I didn't know *what* to think...that you'd run off to the farm to get away from me, I guess."

The claim was so contrary to what she could be expected to do that she realized he was trying to make a joke. Well, she didn't find it funny. Keeping her fingers crossed that she wouldn't burst into tears and cover herself with ignominy, Liz launched into the speech she'd been rehearsing.

"What we've been doing is a mistake. It has to stop," she said as calmly as she could. "Despite the way I behaved, I don't believe in casual sex between people who will continue to be related, thanks to the enduring link of a child they both love, but have no intention of remaining a couple..."

To Jack, her carefully articulated statement sounded as if it belonged in a legal brief, one she'd authored in her head as she'd kept vigil in her chair, instead of scribbling it on a yellow tablet. She seemed to mean every word.

"I have no intention of hanging around, filling in for my sister as your bedmate," she added when he didn't respond.

Her characterization of their intimacy hurt. Hit below the belt, Jack assumed his tough-guy image. Though he ached to change her mind—make her see that his supposed devotion to Sharon was so much horse hockey, he had to think of his baby daughter first. Whatever his pain, he had to make sure Liz would stand by him through the adoption process.

With a moment to reflect, he was also becoming a little angry with her. "Okay, if that's how you want it," he agreed tersely. "What happened between us was probably a function of biology and proximity. I promise to back off... keep my hands to myself, if you'll stay the course for Kassie's sake."

His remarks, which he longed to retract the moment they left his mouth, only drove the stake of what Liz firmly believed to be unrequited love deeper in her heart. Unwilling to return to the farm until she could come to terms with her emotions, she promised not to abandon Kassie's cause. However, "I need some time away from being cooped up with you in Virginia," she said. "I've decided to stay on here in Georgetown for a couple of weeks."

She wouldn't be back until she absolutely had to return in order to keep from derailing Kassie's adoption. He didn't suppose she'd let him drag her home by the hair, caveman style, when he hadn't so much as hinted at the depth of his feelings for her, or revealed her sister's defection.

He couldn't bring himself to do the latter, though it would be the linchpin of his case. "Okay," he said again, beginning to hate the word. It occurred to him that he probably looked like a fool, standing there wrapped in her peach-colored towel. "I'll pick up my stuff and get dressed in the bathroom, if that's all right."

Liz's nod, as she stared past his shoulder, seemed a thousand miles distant. She was in the kitchen, firing up her coffeepot, when he popped his head in the door for a quick farewell.

"Kass is going to miss you," he reminded. "Don't be a stranger."

* * *

Liz's absence from Jack's life stretched to a week and then two. Though most of her newer summer work clothes were still in the guest room there, along with her favorite makeup kit, she'd managed to grab her briefcase on the morning of her flight from Virginia. She had the essentials, or what had passed for them, if you discounted the man and baby girl she loved. Each time she came close to caving in and going to them, she hesitated. She didn't want to subject herself to Jack's wiles until she'd summoned the strength to handle them. Yet she worried that Kassie would find her absence confusing. What on earth was she going to do?

After beginning to count on Liz's warm, enticing presence around the house, Jack spent the corresponding period of time in neutral gear. As the days passed, he chafed at her absence and the necessity of leaving the terms of their cease-fire up to her. Somehow, he had to talk her into returning to the shelter of his roof so he could put things right.

It was like a shot of adrenaline, then, when Mrs. Rivers informed him the adoption agency had phoned to set up another home visit. Deciding he felt lucky enough to roll the dice, he called the agency social worker back without first consulting Liz.

As expected, the woman wanted to set up a time and date.

"How about Friday around eleven?" Jack suggested. "Naturally, I'll have to check with my wife, because she has a busy career, too. But I doubt if it'll be a problem for her."

Friday morning was fine with the woman assigned to Kassie's case. "I'll pencil it in on my calendar," she agreed.

Preoccupied with the excuse she'd given him to insist Liz return to the farm at once, Jack blinked at the sudden wild card he was dealt.

"I've, um, been wanting to ask you about something, Mr. Kelleher," the woman said hesitantly. "It's a bit delicate, so I thought we might discuss it first over the phone. During my last home visit, you and your new wife were sleeping at opposite ends of the upstairs hall. At least, she kept her clothing and personal effects in a room situated at some distance from yours. I was forced to report it under 'unusual domestic arrangements.' As a result our director wants me to verify that the marriage *is* one in fact, not just a sham, entered into for the adoption's sake."

I'll bet he does, Jack thought, stifling a whistle. Well, you can tell him for me there's been consummation. Naturally he didn't speak the words aloud as he explored the woman's query from every angle, seeking ways to turn it to his benefit.

A moment later he came up with one that would put him and Liz on a much more intimate footing. I can't wait to get her reaction when I tell her about this, he thought, a wry grin tugging at the corners of his mouth.

Somehow he managed to keep his surge of optimism under wraps. "I can understand your director's concern, Miss Stevens," he said genially. "But he needn't give the matter another thought. As you probably noticed during your previous visits, my home has his-and-hers master bedrooms with a pair of connecting baths. The current Mrs. Kelleher didn't want to move her things into her late sister's closets and bureaus until we could redecorate."

"Um, I see." The social worker cleared her throat. "Has that been done?" she asked.

"It's in the works as we speak," Jack hedged, wracking his brain for the name of Sharon's former decorator.

Chapter 7

Liz had just returned to her office from lunch when her secretary put Jack's call through. "Your husband's on the line, Mrs. Kelleher," the cheerful, part-time college student informed her.

As far as the secretary knew, Liz's union with Jack was on the up-and-up, though she'd appeared a bit startled when Liz had announced she was marrying her sister's widower so soon after the funeral. The little frisson of longing and embarrassment Liz always experienced when someone addressed her by her married name passed through her.

"Thanks, Carolyn," she replied, punching the appropriate button on her console. "Hello, Jack. What can I do for you?"

She didn't have to wait long for an answer. "We're in a pickle, Liz," he said. "Kassie's case worker wants to come out Friday morning for a home visit."

Resolutely pushed down since their last encounter, her feelings for him sprang to renewed life at the sound of his voice. "I, uh, don't see why that would be a problem," she managed. "I can just come out. I'm sure no one here will object if I take the morning off."

She listened in dismay as he related the woman's query about their sleeping arrangements and his off-the-cuff response to it.

"I've got a decorator coming out to the farm at six-thirty this evening with samples of in-stock draperies, bedspreads and the like," he said. "If necessary, her firm can supply us with Oriental rugs and even several pieces of furniture on short notice. We have to decide whether we want her crew to strip the walls and paint, or work with the existing wallpaper."

He was using the pronoun *we* as if he fully expected her to move into the room when it was finished—take up residence again at the farm until Kassie's adoption was final, and sleep in the room next to his. Though the prospect didn't bode well for her vow not to be compromised again, she had to admit she'd find it somewhat more appealing if Sharon's stamp could be removed from the walls, draperies and furniture.

"I'm going to need help getting your sister's stuff packed up and out of there," he added. "Do you think maybe you could come out tonight, talk to the decorator with me and hang around to help me clear the decks?" Pausing, he cleared his throat. "Maybe even stay for the duration, as we first arranged?"

If Jack goes through Sharon's things, Liz thought, he may turn up more evidence of her infidelities. And even if he doesn't he might plunge into grief when he handles her clothing and personal effects. Anything could happen . . .

As she mulled over the possibilities, the silence on her end of the line was deafening to him. At least she hadn't vetoed his suggestion that they return to their original agreement. "Kassie misses you," Jack said, attempting to fill the conversational gap while playing on her sympathies. "We all do, if you want to know the truth. If you'll give our bargain another chance, I promise to keep my distance."

Liz loved and missed Kassie, too. And, though she wished it were otherwise, seeing Jack was better than not seeing him. Though they'd remain apart in the conjugal sense, at least she knew what it was like to be rocked to splendor in his arms. Nobody and nothing—not Patsy's disapproval, if she'd known of their intimacy, or her own common sense—could take that away from her.

"I suppose I could," she agreed after a moment.

Jack's hopes soared despite the ambiguity of her commitment. "That'd be great, Liz," he said feelingly. "Listen...I need to tell you something. Eloise and Mrs. Rivers think you've been spending a few weeks at your firm's California office."

"What in the world would make them think that?" Liz asked, though she had a fair idea.

His response was a bit sheepish, but hardly apologetic. "You might say I gave them that impression," he admitted. "I felt bad about it at the time. But now I'm glad I did. Kassie's social worker is likely to question them about our relationship."

From her vantage point in Georgetown, Liz realized things would go back to being the way they'd been before Jack had harassed her about a phone call from one of her former boyfriends and then persuaded her into making love to him. Meanwhile, though they probably couldn't help wondering about the motives behind her marriage to

Jack, Eloise and Mrs. Rivers would be too polite to say anything about it—even to each other. Questioned by someone from the adoption agency, they'd stand behind their employer. The myth of a happy, if hastily patched-together family would be perpetuated.

Liz returned to the farm around six-thirty that night, a bit hesitantly, but packing a garment bag and duffel from Georgetown prominently festooned with leftover airline tags that substantiated Jack's claim. Her reunion with Kassie was a free-for-all of hugs and kisses. Contrary to her fears, her little niece didn't display the shyness children her age reserved for strangers. Instead, she insisted on occupying Liz's lap to play with a plastic nesting toy while Liz and Jack hurriedly downed the sandwiches and tropical fruit salad Clarice Rivers had prepared for them.

"You look great," Jack said between bites, gazing at Liz over Kassie's silky, dark head. "Energized by your absence, though I hate to admit it. Is that a tan I see on your face and arms? Or have your freckles just inched a little closer together?"

She couldn't help smiling at his teasing despite the awkwardness she felt. He was the man she loved. The fact that he didn't love her, even though she had such heated memories, was no excuse for grumpiness.

"Both, I guess," she said. "I've started running again...in two-mile stints, four times a week...and catching some sun on the patio outside my...er, room."

At Kassie's insistence, Liz read the precious toddler several stories before Eloise ran her bath. When she exited the baby's room, Jack and the decorator he'd hired were already coming up the stairs.

Spreading out the fabric and paint samples on Sharon's rose-sprigged coverlet, the energetic, fifty-something woman glanced from Jack to Liz and back again. "How extensive do you want the transformation to be?" she asked. "Not counting this evening, we've got just three days to work with."

Jack deferred to Liz.

Overcome with misgivings at the prospect of obliterating her sister's presence in the room, Liz reminded herself she'd probably have to sleep there for months. She didn't want to feel as if Sharon were looking over her shoulder every minute, or wake up each morning amid the profusion of cabbage roses and ruffles her sister had favored.

Besides, though she liked the color peach in modest quantities, she wasn't a "pink" person. Yet the basic decor, with its wood floors and dark cherry furniture, fairly cried out for pastels. "Is there some way we could change the room to make it appear a bit more tailored . . . give it a soft yellow-and-white color scheme without getting rid of this great four-poster?" she asked. "The love seat, with its white moiré upholstery, could stay, as well. There's a wonderful chest of drawers in the guest room we could exchange for the dressing table."

After discussing the problem at length, they decided to have the decorator's crew strip the walls of their flowered wallpaper and apply a soft yellow paint. Pale yellow sheets and a goose down comforter with a white-on-white duvet would transform the bed, along with some knife-edged throw pillows in yellow, blue and an Oriental print combining the two colors along with tiny touches of apricot. Any hint of ruffles would be banished. The decorator knew of a blue-and-yellow Oriental rug that would complete the scheme. Liz could bring some artwork from her Georgetown row house.

The tab would run into the thousands of dollars. However, when she questioned it, Jack assured her it would be worth every penny.

"Everything we talked about will actually be completed by Friday morning?" Liz asked the decorator doubtfully as she and Jack saw her to the front door.

The woman nodded. "Amazing, isn't it, what can be had for a price?" She laughed, clinking her cloisonné bracelets.

After she'd gone, Jack suggested they pop open a couple of beers and head back upstairs. "We've got to get the closets and drawers emptied out tonight," he reminded, "what with the wallpaper-removal crew scheduled to show up first thing in the morning. I stopped at a place near Tyson's Corner on my way home from work and picked up some storage boxes."

Reluctant as she was to begin the task, yet perversely drawn to it because of the awakening that might result, Liz agreed to help. She realized someone would have to empty the dressing table. Jack may as well do it, she thought, half-hoping and half-dreading that he'd find the same evidence she'd found of her sister's faithlessness. Though part of her wanted to spare him the pain, the Liz who'd tracked down Ken DeKooning and strong-armed him into having a drink with her argued persuasively that it was time for a reality check. Maybe the truth would ease Jack's grief, not exacerbate it.

"I'll take the closet," she offered, deciding to let fate determine the outcome. "You know, we ought to give Shar's clothes to charity rather than store them, though my mother wouldn't like it. Most of her things are in fairly good shape."

"Fine with me." Taking a swig of his beer, Jack set about emptying the drawers of his late wife's dressing table.

Her heart in her throat as she slipped Sharon's blouses and sweaters from their padded hangers and carefully folded them before placing them in one of the cartons he'd picked up, Liz braced herself for a muttered "What the hell?" or a sudden, telltale silence and cessation of all activity. To her surprise, Jack unceremoniously dumped the contents of her sister's dresser into storage boxes without giving them a moment's scrutiny. She was still hard at work in the closet when he carried them off to the attic.

As the redecorating activity commenced the following morning, temporarily disrupting Jack's household, he kept his promise to Liz. His demeanor toward her was friendly but above reproach. Each night when she returned to Virginia from her Washington office, she was amazed at how much progress had taken place.

By Thursday evening the decorating crew had finished. Jack had signed off on the project and paid the staggering tab with his credit card. As she transferred her clothes from the guest room to her sister's former walk-in closet, Liz had to admit the room retained none of its former ambiance. Its glowing walls, soft rug and discreet Oriental touches suited her to perfection. Even the furniture they'd kept had been integrated in a new, more pleasing arrangement.

Patsy's going to be furious the next time she visits, Liz thought, flopping down on the bed when she'd finished her task to absorb the room's effect. She'll consider what we've done a sacrilege.

Let her, said a little voice that seemed to come from deep inside herself. *The decision was Jack's ... and yours ... to make.*

A moment later her mental meanderings were interrupted as Kassie veered from a trek to the nursery with Eloise into Liz's new room and tried to climb up beside her on the big bed.

"C'mon, sweetie ... your Aunt Liz is tired just now," the nanny coaxed, attempting to dissuade the determined youngster from her goal. "Besides, you've got applesauce on your chin. We need to wash your face."

The duvet was white. Brand new. And by her lights, fairly expensive. Grabbing one of the tissues she'd placed in a yellow-and-white ceramic dispenser on the night table, Liz helped her little niece finish climbing up and gently wiped her mouth.

"Let her stay with me awhile, Eloise," she said. "I've missed her." She turned to the baby. "What's this, darling? A doggy puppet? Does it say *arrrf-arrrf?*"

She and Kassie were ensconced in the center of the big four-poster, dissolving in giggles as an imaginary man composed of Liz's right index and middle fingers dared the baby's doggy puppet to capture him with its mouth, when Jack paused outside the open doorway to watch them. How right they look together, he thought, unnoticed as Liz bent to kiss Kassie's cheek. My sweet baby and the elusive, redheaded woman I've promised not to touch. If only we could be a family in the usual sense.

As he walked on to his room and sank down in a leather lounger by the window with a case file he needed to read in his lap, he couldn't remember a similar scene with Sharon in the maternal role. But then Shar's mothering of Kassie had been mostly superficial.

* * *

After their sprint of preparation for it, the agency visit the following morning was almost anticlimactic. Smiling with approval at the way she carried it off, Jack hung back and let Liz handle most of it. It was she who led Ariel Stevens, Kassie's case worker, out to the yard to demonstrate the play equipment Jack had installed, and gave her a tour of the newly decorated bedroom she occupied.

As they'd expected, the adoption agency case worker asked to interview the baby's nanny and Mrs. Rivers. The latter was in the process of making Kassie's favorite raisin cookies, so she conducted the interview in the kitchen. Ariel Stevens was all smiles when she emerged, with a care package of the same in her briefcase.

Both Liz and Jack, who had been waiting on the living room couch while Kassie built block towers on the coffee table for their entertainment, got to their feet.

On previous occasions, Jack had been notified of the case worker's findings only after the agency director had gone over them. Still, he couldn't stop himself from asking, "What's the verdict?"

This time, it seemed, he wouldn't have to wait.

"I may as well tell you...my evaluation of Kassie's care and home environment is A-plus," Ariel Stevens said, her smile broadening as Jack put one arm around Liz's shoulder. "You and Mrs. Kelleher have absolutely nothing to worry about."

With Jack honoring his promise to keep his hands to himself yet always seeming to turn up at her elbow, they settled into a routine. A few days later Liz's firm got caught up in a maelstrom of legal work for a senator who was being sued by a former campaign aide. Though her specialty was divorce and custody cases, with some corporate law thrown in, and the senator's problems were being handled by another division of her firm, she found herself working around the clock, helping to conduct interviews and research legal precedents.

At last the flurry of activity subsided, and she had time to arrange a lunch date with Rosemary. They met at the Corcoran Gallery of Art's main-floor restaurant, surrounded by potted palms, echoing footsteps and massive marble pillars. With garden salads and oat-bran muffins on order, they were ready to sip their iced tea with lemon, and chat.

As always, Kassie was first on the agenda. Once the baby's latest sayings and most adorable behavior had been reported, they spent the next five minutes or so discussing a Maryland political matter that had been claiming most of Rosemary's attention.

As she listened to her friend's complaints, nodding sympathetically in all the right places, Liz thought of the cutting remarks Jack had made the morning they'd parted at her Georgetown house. She wondered what his mother would make of them. Was he really the sort of man to dismiss a powerful, almost soulful coupling as "biology and proximity"? Or did he have a hidden, more sensitive nature?

She couldn't ask, of course. It would have been the height of indiscretion to confess that she and Rosemary's son had become lovers, then backed off from each other.

"So what are you going to do about Tom Hynes?" she asked, naming the politician Rosemary had been complaining about, and encouraging her to continue.

Something about the remark must have alerted Rosemary that Liz's interest lay elsewhere. "Enough about the mess in Anapolis," Jack's mother said as their salads arrived and they took exploratory bites. "Tell me how you and my son have been getting along."

Liz was startled, to say the least. But then Rosemary had always been a little psychic. "Okay, I guess," she managed after a moment.

The tepid endorsement caused one of Rosemary's carefully shaped eyebrows to shoot up. "And that means?" she asked, her keen blue gaze trained like a laser across the table.

Eager to talk about Jack without revealing anything she shouldn't, Liz responded with shrug. "I don't know," she said evasively. "What it sounds like. You know how we've always been at each other's throats." Pausing, she asked with a little shake of her head, "What makes him tick, anyway?"

"Well," said Rosemary, meditatively biting into a piece of marinated tomato, "he reminds me a lot of his father. He'll cover up his feelings, tough out a difficult situation. Do and try anything, no matter how offbeat or risky, in order to get what he wants. He's also subject to moods. He can say the damnedest things and not mean them. Why do you ask?"

Liz made a project of buttering her muffin. She decided to change the subject. "Promise you won't say anything about our conversation to him?"

Setting down her knife and fork, Rosemary mulled over the request for a moment. "All right," she agreed, her face a study in curiosity.

"I went through some of Sharon's things prior to the redecorating I told you about on the phone," Liz revealed. "I found some pretty strong indications that she'd been seeing other men. Since then, I've talked to one of them and he confirmed my suspicions. Shar was on her way to Chicago to meet him when her plane crashed."

To Liz's astonishment, Rosemary didn't seem that surprised. "I'd always suspected as much," she said. "I gather you haven't said anything to Jack about it."

Liz shook her head. "I'd never do that. In my opinion, he still loves Sharon. If he ever found out what she was doing behind his back, he'd be devastated."

Again Rosemary's response was unexpected. "I'm not so sure," she commented thoughtfully. "For some time, I've guessed that there were problems. It might be a relief for him to talk about them with someone he trusts."

Though she wished it were otherwise, Liz couldn't accept the notion. Bludgeoning her way into the role of Jack's confidante would only bring him hurt and drive a new wedge between them, to her way of thinking.

She blushed beet red a moment later when Rosemary confided a secret wish that Jack's marriage to Liz would become one in fact, instead of a mere legality. "I'd never have said this while Sharon was alive," Jack's mother told her. "But I always thought the two of you were right for each other."

Given all the overtime she'd put in, Liz decided to take the rest of the afternoon off. It had been some time since she'd visited her parents. Except for Kassie, I'm all they've got since Sharon died, she thought. I really ought to go.

This time, as she pulled into the drive, her father was busy in his garage workshop. As usual, he didn't have much to say. Though she didn't seem all that overjoyed to see Liz, either, Patsy made a pot of coffee and cut them each a slice of cake. It was only when her mother slid into the kitchen booth opposite her and fixed her with a baleful stare that she realized she'd committed some major transgression.

"I bumped into a friend of Sharon's and Joan Campbell's the other day," Patsy said. "You remember Melanie Saunders, I imagine."

Sharon, Joan and Melanie had been cheerleaders together. Racking her brain, Liz couldn't remember breathing a word about Sharon's extracurricular activities to anyone. Had Joan been talking to Melanie? Had the latter put two and two together?

"If you recall, Mom, both Sharon and I were in her class," she answered.

She could tell immediately that the calm approach wasn't going to cut it. "Melanie says you asked Joan a bunch of questions about Shar's trip to Chicago," Patsy informed her with pursed lips. "Sounds like the third degree to me. What was it all about?"

Unwilling to hurt her mother and doubtful Patsy would believe her even if she laid the facts about Sharon's adultery on the table, Liz tried to pass her curiosity off as a natural outgrowth of missing her sister.

Patsy wouldn't hear of it. "I'm not accusing you of anything," she said in a sharp voice. "But it's fair to say you were always a little jealous of your sister, especially in high school. It seems to me..."

"I was *not* jealous of Sharon, Mom," Liz interjected, adding silently, *though I had a perfect right to be where you were concerned.* "I loved her very much. We were *twins,* for God's sake!"

Her mother continued as if she hadn't spoken. "Poking around for dirt about your sister so you can distort Jack's memory of her does her a grave injustice...just as living under his roof does, in my opinion, despite your stated reason of doing so for Kassie's sake. I hope you're not scheming to make him love you, when he's grieving for your poor, darling sister."

Already sufficiently wracked with guilt for loving Jack and sleeping with him, Liz pushed her cake plate away and walked out of the house without so much as a fare-thee-well. *It was always Sharon, Sharon, Sharon with Mom when we were growing up,* she thought bitterly, getting into her Acura and heading for Virginia. *The same goes for Dad. I was strictly an also-ran. Why, oh, why, couldn't they manage to love us both?*

Maybe she *had* been a little jealous. She might as well face the truth. It struck her that her prowess in sports and her sterling record in law school might have been attempts to impress her parents so they'd love her equally. She was also aware that, if Patsy accused her of digging up dirt, she must have known some existed.

From the moment she walked in the door, Jack could tell something had spoiled her mood. Her eyes and nose looked vaguely pink, as if she'd been crying. Instead of stopping to play with Kassie as she usually did, she went straight upstairs.

"What's wrong?" he asked, following and waylaying her in the doorway between their adjoining baths before she could strip to her underclothes.

She couldn't give him the unexpurgated version of what had taken place because that would betray her sister's secrets. "I stopped by to see my folks after work," she admitted, not quite meeting his eyes as she washed the day's dirt and makeup off her face and brushed her hair vigorously back from her forehead.

An overpowering desire to comfort her welled up in Jack's heart. *I could kill Frank and Patsy for the way they treat her,* he thought, longing to take her in his arms but deciding not to go for it. *Their behavior toward her is nothing short of criminal.*

"Don't let them get you down," he said, the kind of tenderness he usually reserved for Kassie resonating in his voice. "I've seen firsthand what kind of parents they can be, and you deserve better. The only thing I can suggest is to let other people love you in their place."

Liz threw him a quixotic look. Exactly whom did he have in mind? The former boyfriend whose call had set off a chain reaction in their lives? Or some unknown guy she might chance to meet? Whatever the case, she doubted he could see *himself* in that role.

"That's easier said than done," she advised crisply. "I suppose I ought to give you Patsy's take on our living under the same roof, for what it's worth. She called it a 'grave injustice' to Sharon, no pun intended."

She looked so wounded, yet so stubbornly determined to rise above it. For a hot second Jack was on the verge of spilling his feelings for her. Fearing that, despite their passionate lovemaking, she didn't share them, he restrained himself. The last thing he wanted was to drive her away again before he could change her attitude. If she left a second time, the going might be permanent.

"Ah, Liz..." he whispered, daring gently to rub her back between the shoulder blades as a substitute for what he'd have preferred to do. "Don't feel so bad. We're doing what's right for Kassie."

Coming from him, the supportive gesture almost caused her to lose it. "I know we are," she said shakily. "I know we are."

Jack's light but expert back rub turned into a little pat. "Cheer up," he directed. "Mrs. Rivers has made her famous lobster casserole and lemon meringue pie for our supper. Plus, this weekend we're invited to a party in Middleburg."

* * *

It was a safe bet that Jack's friends and clients in the wealthy, stylish community that lay at the heart of Virginia's hunt country had questions about their marriage, coming as it had on the heels of Sharon's funeral. Since most of them were likely to be well informed, the sort of people who kept up with the latest news and gossip from Washington, they probably knew what there was to know about Kassie's case, as well. And why wouldn't they? It had been in all the papers and on television.

Why care what they think? Liz told herself late Saturday afternoon as she headed upstairs for a bath after a day spent planting mums with Kassie's help and giving the baby a series of rides on Jack's garden tractor. If they don't approve of what we're doing, they can say so to our faces. Patsy had, and the effect—though painful—hadn't been fatal.

Following a lengthy soak in the sunken Jacuzzi tub she'd inherited on her return to the farm, she dried off, put on bikini panties and a minimal strapless bra, and stood in front of the mirror to do her makeup. In the next room, she could hear Jack's shower running. Having seen him naked—gloried in the sight of gleaming muscle and the dark, uneven seam of hair that pointed downward from his chest to his generous attributes—she could imagine all too well how he looked beneath the spray. Just the thought of it was enough to arouse her longing for him.

It was time to decide on a dress. According to Jack, the party, which would consist of cocktails and dinner, was a twenty-fifth anniversary celebration. It was likely to be a somewhat formal affair.

Having stopped by Georgetown the previous afternoon to pick up several possible outfits, she meandered over to her closet. Should she wear the vanilla "baby-style" crocheted top and crystal pleated trousers that were the essence of comfort? Or the electric blue *peau de soie* cocktail dress with thin spaghetti straps, which boasted its own little jacket and had always made her skin look rather pale?

In the end, there wasn't any contest. She reached for her third option, a sexy, clinging, semitransparent silk tank dress in a pale cocoa shade which was sparingly decorated with muted silver sequins and matching embroidery. The cresting wave pattern of its understated embellishment looked as if it had been inspired by a famous Hokusai watercolor. When she'd worn it to a reception at the French Embassy a year earlier, it had drawn raves. One of the senior attachés, a Philippe Noiret look-alike, had dubbed her Ondine and insisted she was a red-headed mermaid.

The question was, what would Jack think?

Aware she was courting the kind of trouble she'd professed not to want, but unable to stop herself, Liz put on the tank dress over its matching opaque slip, and smoothed them down over her hips. In the pier glass she'd moved over from the guest room along with the pineapple-patterned dresser she'd elected to use, the dress's flirty, slit skirt floated about her ankles, calling attention to the flashes of leg it exposed.

She was in the living room, sipping a lemonade and laughing at Kassie's antics as Eloise pretended to chase the baby with outstretched hands, when Jack appeared. Handsome as the devil at midnight in his perfectly tailored dinner jacket and evening trousers, he paused at the bottom of the steps to stare at her with narrowed eyes.

"Is this dress all right?" Liz asked after a moment, when he didn't comment.

The unintended irony of her question prompted his mouth to turn downward slightly at the corners. "Believe me, it'll do," he answered, almost as if he wished it wouldn't. "Are you ready to go? We seem to be running a little late."

As they drove the eighteen miles or so that separated his Waterford-area farm from Ashton Grove, the multimillion-dollar horse-breeding estate belonging to Phyllis and Brad Humphries, Jack wished he'd passed up his Infiniti sedan for a convertible. It would have been worth it, he thought, just to see Liz's unruly curls and sparkling, diaphanous scarf blow about her face.

He'd never seen her look more beautiful. Though it might be the dress, which resembled nothing so much as a mermaid's glittery sheath of scales as it clung to her body, he didn't think so. Instead, he decided, it would be her divinely allotted imperfections, like her ultralong legs, wide but innocent mouth and all-over spangling of freckles which would make her the most lusted-after woman at the party.

If only he could lay some sort of claim to her—one that ran deeper than their temporary marriage vows and her renewed promise to stick around until Kassie's adoption was final—he wouldn't feel such reluctance for her to meet new men, one of whom might attempt to take her away from him.

Gracious to a fault, petite, blond Phyllis Humphries took Liz under her wing the moment they arrived and made a point of introducing her around. As a result she and Jack got separated. Covertly glancing about as she stood and chatted with a group of people she'd just met, Liz was aware that several of the female guests—one of whom had attended Sharon's funeral—were flirting outrageously with him despite the fact that, officially, he was unavailable.

There's nothing you can do about it unless you want to make a scene, she reminded herself. Anyway, you don't have the right. She decided to enjoy the party—simply to forget Jack's admirers and the likelihood that a number of the guests were probably gossiping about their hasty marriage. Calling into play the social skills she'd polished as a member of her prestigious law firm and an occasional participant in Washington's upwardly mobile singles scene, she laughed and chatted, exchanged jokes and political tidbits with her new acquaintances.

Gradually she became aware that a handsome, fifty-something media magnate and former ambassador to Australia named Graham Conner had become a charming and attentive fixture of the shifting group that surrounded her. By coincidence or perhaps in response to a subtle hint from him, Phyllis Humphries had assigned him to be her dinner partner.

The man was definitely interested. From his vantage point at the table, where he languished in the grip of one of Sharon's more aggressive former pals and could hear but snatches of their conversation, Jack watched Graham Conner pull out the stops in an attempt to charm his beautiful wife, and tried to evaluate her reaction to him. He couldn't tell if she was having a wonderful time as she conversed with the man, or was simply faking it. It certainly seemed as if she was laughing a lot. He wanted to stay her hand each time she pushed back her hair with what he considered a sexy gesture.

Following a champagne toast and the cutting of the anniversary cake, the get-together in the dining room broke up. People wandered into the library for a brandy or out onto the terrace to gaze at the stars. Some begged for an impromptu, full-dress tour of the stables, while others perused their hosts' imposing collection of California impressionists.

About to join a group engaged in the latter pursuit, which happened to include her erstwhile dinner partner, Liz felt Jack's hand on her arm. "Ah, there you are," she said, smiling up at him.

To Jack the comment seemed to imply that he'd been avoiding her, when in fact the opposite had been the case. "If you don't mind, I'd like to leave," he told her summarily, adding, "It's been a tough week."

It was the first Liz had heard of it.

"Sure you're feeling okay?" she asked, when, after waving a general goodbye to the other guests and paying their respects to their hosts, they got into his sleek, black sedan and headed for the highway.

Jack scowled. "Why wouldn't I be?"

They didn't say anything more until they were almost back to the farm. Then, "That media friend of Brad Humphries certainly took a shine to you," Jack grumbled. "Are the two of you doing lunch?"

As a matter of fact, Graham Conner had asked. And Liz had wriggled out of it without offending him. Could Jack possibly be jealous? She shook her head, denying it. "You know how busy I am."

The issue seemed only half-resolved as they went into the house, checked on Kassie and parted company in the upstairs hall to disappear into their separate rooms. Stripped once more to her bra and panties, Liz was in the process of removing her makeup when she heard a loud *"Ouch!"* from Jack's adjoining bath, followed by an angry stream of invective.

Hesitantly she tapped on the connecting door between their baths and, when the swearing didn't stop, opened it.

A washcloth wrapped about the index finger of his right hand, which appeared to be bleeding, Jack was grimacing with pain and disgust at his own clumsiness.

"What happened?" she asked.

"I've cut my damn finger!" he exclaimed, distractedly stating the obvious. "And I can't seem to stop the bleeding!"

He was wearing just his undershorts, but she'd seen him in less. "Here . . . let me help," she offered, trying not to notice how sexy he looked as she slid her rump onto the counter to rummage in his medicine chest for first-aid supplies.

As she dabbed hydrogen peroxide on the cut, which was minor, and then blew on it to ease the sting, Jack recounted how the accident had occurred. Favoring a straight razor for his heavy beard, he'd left it on his vanity counter before going out, then nicked his finger when he belatedly attempted to put it away.

"There, now," Liz said gently, almost as if she were comforting Kassie as she applied an adhesive strip. "Hold it upright for a few minutes until the wound starts to knit."

She was an angel of mercy, binding up his wound with such tender seriousness. Yet in her scanty, revealing underwear, with her back to the mirror and her long legs dangling, she was also a temptress who exacerbated his most passionate desires.

He was only mortal despite his promise to behave himself. "I know something that would make me feel a hell of a lot better than a Band-Aid," he said in a husky voice, pulling her into his embrace.

Chapter 8

She'd wanted him madly, with a persistent ache, ever since they'd left the party—as he seemed to have wanted her. So what if he didn't have love on his mind, merely a need to satisfy the lust of proximity and biology, as he'd described it that awful morning in her Georgetown living room? She loved him, anyway, and always had, from the moment she'd set eyes on him half a decade earlier. She probably always would. With the kind of knowing that springs from deep in the cell, she recognized him as her missing half, the yearned-for *other* poets and philosophers spoke about.

Guided by the wisdom of the body instead of her lawyerly, cautious head, she spread her thighs and wrapped her legs around him. Jack sighed as if, somehow, she'd filled him, whereas he was on the point of filling her. Their mouths merged in a ravenous kiss that only elaborated their hunger.

It seemed the height of idiocy that they were still partly dressed. Struggling to carry out the intention in her embrace, Jack dragged his shorts from his hips and reached into an adjacent drawer for a foil packet that contained protection. Opening it with the aid of his teeth, he put it on. As he did so, Liz twisted to free her left leg from her bikini panties and shoved them as far as she could down the other, so that they dangled from her right ankle like a signal flag.

Seconds later, Jack was inside her and her knees were gripping him. Only then did he push down her strapless bra partway to excite her nipples with his fingertips as he lovingly kneaded her breasts. By the time they started to move, the half-crushed bandeau of underwiring, stretch lace and silk illusion decorated her rib cage beneath her bosom like some clownish accoutrement, serving only to push her fullness higher, for his mouth.

It mattered not a whit to either of them how ridiculous they looked, he favoring his bandaged finger and she with her half-shed garments still clinging to her body. What counted was the thrust of his longing inside her, which seemed to reach infinity, yet managed with each renewed plunge to graze the most sensitive locus of her feminine self.

For Jack, the mute tyranny of their passion was like a goad. After the evening's torture of watching a handsome, eligible man make subtle advances to her, no words of proposition and assent had been required. Each had wanted what they wanted. And gone for it in a hot second, when circumstances had placed it in their grasp. We *need* each other, dammit, he thought half-coherently, hauling her more tightly up against him as his mouth devoured hers. Deeply...fully...rutting here on the edge of my vanity or wherever our passions take us.

He loved her more than life, more than anything except his baby daughter. She was like food and drink to him, as indispensable as light and breath. The mirrored door to the medicine cabinet stood open at an angle to the mirrored walls of his bath, causing the image of their fusion to ricochet from surface to surface, and suddenly he realized he was surrounded by multiple images of Liz with her head thrown back, in the throes of passion, gripping him for all she was worth. Like a satyr of old, with his bunched buttocks driving their insatiability, he was plumbing her to the utmost.

The unexpected, erotic glimpse pushed him past the vestiges of control he was exercising for her sake. With a shout of ecstasy and utter helplessness, he gave way to the inevitable. Her explosion followed in seconds—primal, multi-dimensional, a pull-out-all-the-stops, Fourth of July finale that severed her every connection to worry and stress while strengthening her bond with all creation.

Flushed, tingling, their skin bumpy with gooseflesh as if they'd been stroked by a feather, they clung together like one person. In the chemistry of an instant, their bones had turned to water. Their electrical overload had discharged, leaving them quiescent, almost weightless, awash in contentment.

Sighing, Liz slid down from the vanity, but didn't forsake his arms. With a surge of gratitude, he held her. She hadn't retreated from him. Maybe this time they wouldn't have to suffer through a bitter parting, or fall to negotiating a return to their original arrangement in the kind of lawyerly language that rang a death knell for his hopes.

"Come to bed, darlin'," he whispered. "*Please.* Let me hold you there."

I'd pass up heaven to do what he's asking, unless the two places were synonymous, Liz thought, taking off her bra at last and letting it fall to the floor before threading her arms about his waist.

Her wordless assent opened the door to fresh possibilities, though he wasn't physically ready to explore them yet. Planting blunt, tender kisses against her temple, her neck, the supple curve of her shoulder, he led her into his room and switched off the lamps. Gradually their eyes adjusted to the darkness. Its spread and summer-weight blanket pulled back by Jack's hand on their return from the party, his big bed waited to receive their pleasure and contentment.

Lying down against the cool sheets, they gravitated back into each others' arms. *What a luxury it is, just to lie here with him, waiting for the next round to begin or sleep to steal over us,* Liz thought, *instead of falling into a drug-like slumber to elude guilt. Drowning in regret and running for all I'm worth. Or making silent demands.*

He might never grow to love her the way she loved him. Or want her to stay, once Kassie's adoption was final. He'd never spoken a word on the subject. Unsure how to deal with such possibilities, Liz wondered how deep his affection for her sister had actually run. Though he and Sharon had maintained separate rooms and had their share of troubles, Liz had always assumed they'd shared a passionate relationship. Yet now that she was gone, Jack seldom spoke of her. During their own passionate interludes, her sister had seemed the farthest thing from his head.

A poignant echo, Rosemary's characterization of her son over lunch returned to Liz's thoughts. "He'll cover up his feelings, tough out a difficult situation," she'd warned. With renewed vigor, Liz wished she could tell him the truth about her twin. But she knew the words to do it would never pass her lips. Hurting him, unless it involved leaving him to save her own sanity, just wasn't in her vocabulary.

Ironically, though she couldn't know it, Jack was having similar thoughts. Liz will never believe me if I say I love her, he told himself, tracing the slim but muscular shape of her arm and letting his hand stray to her breast. It would sound so callous, coming on the heels of Sharon's death and our five-year marriage. Angry on Shar's behalf, she might wonder if I'd discard *her* emotionally as well.

Revealing Sharon's treachery would be the easiest thing in the world for him. Yet conversely the most difficult. He'd just have to say the words, talk Liz into believing them. But he couldn't bring himself to take that step. The bond between them was too fragile yet—no match for the close ties twins developed in the womb.

Maybe someday the point would be moot. Meanwhile, he had her in his arms. Though their coupling against his bathroom vanity had temporarily drained him of energy, he could feel the always present flame of his need for her curling to life again. This time we'll take it slow, he decided, his caresses becoming more intimate. Sometimes that way's the best.

When Jack awoke the following morning and reached sleepily for Liz, his arms came up empty. A glance at the clock told him it was still early. He remembered belatedly that it was a Saturday. Odd, but he didn't hear any noises coming from her adjoining bath. Dammit to hell, he thought in sudden fury, throwing back the sheet and storming through their connecting door naked in search of her. We had consensual sex last night and the second go-round was utter perfection. Yet she's run off to Georgetown again.

As he'd expected, her rooms were empty. Yet she hadn't raided her closet. Or packed a bag. Her briefcase stood beside her night table, partly open as if she'd recently removed some papers from it. If she'd been running from him, she'd have taken it with her. Maybe she'd just gone for a walk.

A half hour or so later, when he entered the kitchen fully dressed, Mrs. Rivers relayed a message. "Mrs. Kelleher said to tell you her boss asked her to run into the office this morning," the housekeeper informed him. "She said she forgot to tell you about it last night."

When he phoned her at her firm, punching in her private extension, she answered on the first ring. "Sorry," she said before he could quiz her about the situation. "I forgot to tell you . . . Mac got home from California late last night, so we couldn't meet yesterday. He called ahead from our L.A. office and asked me to come in today to discuss a fairly important case he wants me to handle. I'd have mentioned it this morning but I, um, overslept. I didn't want to wake you . . ."

To Jack's listening ears, she sounded fairly impersonal. Yet she'd said nothing about "having to talk" or returning to their original arrangement. He could be businesslike himself, when his thoughts were occupied by legal matters. Maybe it didn't bode anything negative.

"Will I see you at the farm later?" he asked, trying to keep the question a casual one.

There was a slight hesitation on her part as she absorbed what she considered to be *his* impersonal tone. "I might have to stay and work on this thing a while," she answered. "Supposedly the client is coming in to talk to us around 11:00 a.m. But I should make it home for dinner. All right?"

* * *

Clad in his Saturday clothes, which made him look at least a decade younger than his fifty-seven years, Mac Royer arrived a few minutes later with a Thermos flask of coffee and a bag of donuts and waved Liz into his office. "The case I have in mind is right up your alley," he said, giving her one of his rare, lopsided smiles as she sank into the guest chair opposite him. "I know the young woman's mother from my high school days in Baltimore."

She guessed Mac himself was footing the bill. It sounded as if the case was important to him. It might even have landmark proportions. Her brain shifting into high gear, Liz was poised like a racehorse at the gate as she waited for him to continue.

It turned out that her client-to-be, a twenty-two-year-old junior-college graduate named Diane Erickson, recently had demanded that her former boyfriend, Todd Burroughs, the father of her two-year-old daughter, Samantha, contribute seventy-five dollars a month to the child's support.

"The story goes like this," Mac said. "Diane and Todd were never married. According to her, their relationship lasted just a couple of weeks. When she learned she was pregnant a short time later and informed him of that fact, he refused to take any responsibility for the baby. 'He told me I was on my own,' is the way she puts it.

"Diane had Samantha and went back to work full-time as a secretary to support herself and her daughter, which meant leaving the baby in day-care. That fact didn't seem to upset Burroughs, who stopped by to see his daughter once during that period of time, but didn't contribute to her upkeep.

"When Samantha was a year old, Diane returned to night school to finish her associate degree. She has now graduated with a 4.0 average and plans to attend the University of Maryland...on a rare full scholarship."

To Liz, Diane Erickson sounded like an exemplary client. *If she doesn't drink, sleep around and do wild parties, it shouldn't be a problem to help her get some child support for her daughter,* she thought. *So why does my sixth sense tell me it's going to be difficult?*

"You say Diane Erickson demanded child support from Todd Burroughs," she commented. "Did she file a legal motion to that effect? Is he gainfully employed? Or something of a loafer...?"

Mac leaned back in his chair. "Yes to your first question," he said. "She got a storefront lawyer to do it for a hundred bucks. As for your second, Todd Burroughs works part-time as a night clerk at a motel. Though the job doesn't pay much by Washington-area standards, he takes home more than enough to contribute $75 a month to Samantha's upkeep."

"Sounds pretty straightforward to me," Liz observed. "Your connection with Diane's mother aside, why does this case merit a Saturday conference?"

She was rewarded by that lopsided smile again. "Because it's going to land in the papers."

Liz raised an eyebrow.

"To everyone's surprise, though he resides with his widowed mother, Todd Burroughs had never told her about Samantha," Mac said. "When Margaret Burroughs learned she had a granddaughter, she wanted contact with her. And more. A retired postal clerk who receives disability payments from the government, she volunteered to care for Samantha full-time, and urged her son to fight for Samantha's custody...demand that Diane pay *him*."

It would be a fathers' rights case, Liz realized. There were hundreds of them around these days. She still didn't understand why this particular one would prove to be so sensational.

"Supposedly the grandmother has talked a big gun into representing her son for a reduced fee," Mac added. "From what Diane's mother has told me, the argument will be that Margaret Burroughs's care of Samantha will be preferable to Diane's, since she's available to baby-sit the child around the clock, whereas Diane will have to place her in day-care in order to attend classes."

"But...but...that's outrageous!" Liz exclaimed. "The mother's to be penalized for trying to better herself, in the process improving her daughter's economic welfare? Meanwhile, to date, Todd Burroughs has shown zero personal concern about whether his child has enough to eat, clothes to wear or a roof over her head. I have a feeling he's going along with his mother's proposal out of allegiance to her and a wish to punish Diane for her audacity in asking him for money, rather than any love he might feel for Samantha. With so many judges on the bench these days who look askance at working and student mothers..."

Mac nodded. "I knew you'd get the point."

From out of nowhere, a chilling thought struck her. "Who's the high-powered lawyer you spoke about?" she asked.

Mac's answer, "Ned Riley," relaxed her some, but didn't completely assuage her apprehension. "Ned had a heart attack a couple of weeks ago," she reminded her boss. "And as you know, he works alone. Is this thing going to drag on for months, while he recovers? Or will he get someone else to take over for him?"

"The latter, I should think," Mac said, biting into a donut. "Here's the case file so far. Diane will be here in half an hour. You'll want to look it over before talking with her."

Liz's interview with her new client, a fresh-faced young woman in blue jeans who brought her adorable, blond two-year-old along to the office, went well. Both modest and articulate, Diane Erickson gave every indication of being a responsible, loving mother. She was clearly shaken to the soles of her running shoes at the prospect of losing her daughter.

"Though it's only fair Todd should pay something toward Samantha's support, I'm willing to forget about the seventy-five dollars if he and his mother will drop their custody suit," she said, fear resonating in her voice.

After reassuring her young client that she'd give the matter her very best effort, Liz spent another couple of hours in the office, researching custody precedent. Some of the more recent decisions she turned up weren't especially comforting.

Beneath the new layer of concern she'd acquired over Samantha Erickson's custody, she was also fairly nervous about returning to the farm and facing Jack. Did he expect their relationship to continue on the intimate basis they'd revisited the night before? Given his behavior to date, she guessed, the answer was probably yes.

Her feelings, on the other hand, were a little more complicated. God knew, she loved him to distraction and wanted him—more with each day she spent under his roof. And that went double for each passionate lovemaking.

It was just that she couldn't be sure what would happen when the year she'd promised him was up and his adoption of Kassie was irrevocable. As things stood, she could still walk away and survive emotionally though it wouldn't be easy. Doing so after a year of making love to him would be a lot more difficult.

A glance at her watch told her it was nearly two o'clock. She still hadn't eaten lunch. Abruptly hungry, she left the office and strolled down the street to her favorite deli, where she ordered a tuna salad sandwich. After munching it at an outdoor table, with a bottle of mineral water at her elbow, she continued her walk with the object of visiting a nearby bookstore, then changed her mind when the sandwich seemed to lie like a lump of clay in the bottom of her stomach.

Returning to her car, she drove somewhat reluctantly back to the farm. Kassie was on the sun porch when she walked in, playing with her plastic blocks and nesting toys while Jack leafed through some files in a nearby chair.

"Hi," she said breezily, though she still wasn't feeling up to par. "What are you guys doing?"

As usual, the baby held out her arms to be kissed. Getting to his feet, Jack seemed to expect a similar privilege. When she didn't offer it, he bussed her affectionately on the cheek. "How'd your meeting go?" he asked, the blue intensity of his gaze at full voltage.

"Fine..."

Liz's one-word response trailed away as she glanced for the second time at the file he'd laid to one side on a wicker end table. The nagging worry that had settled in her gut that morning—helping to upset her stomach, or so she thought—returned in spades. Oh, please, she thought, throwing herself on the mercy of a higher power. Tell me *Jack's* not the attorney to whom Ned Riley handed over the Erickson-Burroughs matter.

To her horror, the man she'd grown to love so intensely proceeded to describe that very case from the father's point of view, adding that he'd be representing him.

"To tell you the truth, when Ned Riley asked me to fill in for him, I jumped at the chance," he confessed. "This case is going to attract a lot of attention. If we win, the victory will give fathers a new weapon in the fight for an equal chance at their children's custody, by tearing down the notion that mothers are the 'natural' or 'only' choice to provide nurture...even when their careers or educational pursuits prevent them from giving that nurture sufficient attention."

Liz wanted to wring his good-looking neck. This was the Jack who'd overwhelmed her with helpless fury in the courtroom five years earlier, prompting her refusal to date him. The one who, right or wrong, would seek to win by whatever means available.

"Who's to decide what's sufficient?" she demanded furiously, her hands poised on her hips. "*You?* It flies in the face of logic and fairness to suggest a mother should be penalized for seeking to better herself. Lots of single and divorced women work and successfully raise families."

"C'mon," Jack interposed. "That's the way of the world. Whoever can summon the best argument..."

Liz's fury was growing by leaps and bounds. "What a hypocrite you are!" she exclaimed. "You work, yet you expect the adoption agency to let you keep Kassie rather than give her to a stay-at-home mom or dad. I work, and you claim I'm an acceptable substitute for Sharon. Yet the fact that this fine young woman wants to get an education so she can earn a better living for her child means she's an inadequate mother? That's a crock of you-know-what!''

Like a fireman charging to put out a three-alarm fire without stopping to analyze what had caused it, Jack rose to the bait. ''Personalizing the issue by comparing it to our situation is hitting below the belt,'' he argued. ''So what if I have a double standard where my clients are concerned? Don't *you?* It's our job as attorneys to get them whatever they're fighting for.''

When she didn't answer, a horrible possibility dawned on Jack. ''Don't tell me...'' he postulated, hoping against hope that he was mistaken. ''You're representing Diane Erickson.''

She nodded without speaking.

Jack was heartsick. The case had a strong potential for driving them apart. As he sometimes did, he covered up feelings of vulnerability and confusion by going on the offensive. ''Well, well,'' he drawled with his infuriating smile of old. ''May the best man win.''

It was more than Liz could stomach.

Seconds later they both realized Kassie had stopped playing to gape at them with an expression of confusion and upset. The people she loved best in the world were arguing! To their mutual horror, two huge tears rolled down her cheeks.

''Ah, sweetheart...'' Remorsefully scooping up her little niece, Liz patted her on the back. ''Please don't cry. Your daddy and I both love you,'' she begged.

After a moment or two, Kassie seemed reassured. Smoothing the toddler's silky hair, Liz continued to glare at Jack, though she carefully lowered her voice. ''You can see for yourself what it would be like if we continued to live under the same roof while we work on this case,'' she told him with patched-together self-control. ''We'd be at each other's throats. Besides, it would constitute a conflict of interest. I'm moving back to Georgetown for the duration.''

Before he could formulate a comeback, she was handing Kassie to him and racing upstairs to pack.

On Monday morning, Liz met with Mac Royer and offered to withdraw from the Erickson-Burroughs case. Though she'd pursue Diane Erickson's interests to the utmost of her ability, representing her when Jack was the attorney for the opposition could constitute a conflict of interest, too. She didn't want to put the young woman's case in jeopardy.

"I have no problem with you continuing as Diane's counsel, so long as she asks you to do so in writing and Jack gets a waiver from his client," he replied. "I'm confident you'll do your best for her no matter what the personal cost."

Liz phoned her client a short time later. After explaining that she and Jack would be living separately until Samantha's custody was resolved, she asked how she wanted to proceed. The young woman was adamant. She wanted Liz to continue as her counsel. "I just hope representing me won't cause major family problems for you," she said worriedly.

Her emotions seemingly closer to the surface than at any time she could remember, Liz wished she could give her client a hug. "Any inconvenience to me would be minor compared with what's at stake," she affirmed.

The hearing would take place in just two weeks. As the days raced by, Jack had ample time to regret the arrogant words he'd spoken to Liz. He longed to phone her, drive over to Georgetown so they could talk in person. But he knew she'd construe such actions on his part as extremely unethical.

To make matters worse, he was still miffed at her for calling him a hypocrite—even though he supposed the label could be made to stick. I'll be damned if I'll change my courtroom demeanor and tactics...not to mention my focus on fathers' rights...simply to please her, he thought. If she has any feelings for me at all, she'll take me as I am.

For her part, Liz was close to despair whenever she had a chance to think about their situation. She was also physically off her feed as she prepared to argue for her client in the Erickson-Burroughs case, which had been scheduled for an early hearing.

It's miserable being at odds with Jack, she thought as she dragged her body out of bed the day before the hearing. Before Sharon died and plunged us into this mess, I was crazy about him. But I'd never have done anything to pursue it. Our lives were completely separate. Now the unanswered questions between us—and what I consider to be his complete lack of ethics—are tearing me to pieces.

Fixing herself some toast and black coffee, she sat at her kitchen table to eat and then went back upstairs to begin getting ready for work. The effort was short-lived. Her breakfast promptly reappeared, in less-than-palatable form, leaving her feeling drained and a little weak in the knees.

Somehow she'd managed to catch a summer flu bug. Of all the awful luck, she thought, feeling her forehead with the back of her wrist. At least she didn't have a temperature. Washing her face for the second time that morning and doing her best to camouflage a wan, somewhat drained look with makeup, she drove to the office to put the finishing touches to her battle plan. Known for his quirkiness and the cold shoulder he sometimes turned to what he considered feminist aims, Judge Barnes would be a tough nut to crack. Plus Jack would be a tough opponent. She wanted to be as ready as diligence would make her.

The following morning she was queasy again. To be on the safe side, she skipped breakfast. By the time she reached the courthouse, though, she was feeling better. In fact, she was beginning to get hungry. On the theory that it would fortify her for the coming ordeal, she washed down a chocolate donut with a carton of milk in the courthouse coffee shop.

Seeing Jack in the courtroom after a two-week estrangement made her even more nervous than she already was. He was wearing a severe-looking navy pinstriped suit that, in her opinion, made him appear sharp, quick-witted, invulnerable. His sober nod of greeting, which she decided owed more to common courtesy than anything approaching affection, caused a bereft feeling to settle in her gut. Returning it in kind, she huddled with her client.

She's not feeling well, Jack realized, his sympathy going out to her. It's going to put her at a disadvantage this morning. Sworn to defend his client's best interests, he vowed not to let it affect the way he argued his case.

After a slight delay, Judge Barnes breezed in, accompanied by an "All rise" directive from the bailiff, and took his seat on the bench. He gazed at Liz and Jack with obvious interest in the fact that they'd be opposing each other.

"Good morning, Mr. and Mrs. Kelleher," he said with a grin. "How has the institution of marriage been treating you?"

Their simultaneous but somehow shaky, "Very well, thank you, Your Honor," caused him to raise an eyebrow.

"Glad to hear it," he said briskly. "Have both the principals waived any objection to being represented by husband-and-wife attorneys?"

Both Liz and Jack answered in the affirmative.

Judge Barnes nodded. "Very well. Though it's somewhat unusual, there's precedence ... both in the courtroom and in the movies. Of course, *Adam's Rib,* with Spencer Tracy and Katherine Hepburn, was a murder case. What do you say we get started on the matter in question?"

Jack went first, advancing much the same argument he'd used on Liz the day she'd acquired the case. "My client, Todd Burroughs, is asking that the court award him custody of his daughter, whom he loves and wishes to raise, based on the fact that her mother cannot care for her adequately," he began.

Outraged, Liz raised an immediate objection. "During the first two years of Samantha Erickson's life, Diane Erickson was the *only* parent to care for the girl adequately ... or even at all," she argued. "She was the only parent to support her financially. She's done a loving, superb job, and ..."

"I'll allow a certain amount of latitude here, counsel," Judge Barnes interjected.

Tossing Liz a quick, unreadable glance, Jack continued with his statement. It was all she could do not to interrupt again as he argued that a single parent attending college or working full-time could not provide the same level of nurture as one who stayed at home.

"Granted," he said, "Todd Burroughs is employed part-time. Though it's likely his hours of employment will increase at some future date, in no case will he be forced to place his daughter in day-care, or hire a baby-sitter. His mother, Margaret, a fifty-two-year-old retired postal clerk with whom Mr. Burroughs resides, has gladly volunteered to look after her.''

Pausing, he added with great effect, "To the possible complaint that both parents would find it necessary to place Samantha in the care of a third party, we say that a grandmother's loving supervision is infinitely preferable to that of a shifting cast of strangers.''

Furious with him for casting aspersions on day-care, thus hinting that Diane Erickson had failed to provide optimum nurture for her daughter, Liz ticked off her arguments in turn. As a stranger to Samantha, Todd Burroughs's mother was the equivalent of a baby-sitter or day-care worker, and could not be regarded as a substitute parent. Quality of care counted, not the precise number of hours a child spent in a parent's company. Samantha was happy and emotionally healthy with her mother, as the psychologist's report she'd submitted with her brief would attest. Disrupting the bond that had been developing there since her birth could do her irreparable damage.

"In my opinion, the mother should be rewarded, not penalized for trying to better herself and improve her child's lot," she stated. "Todd Burroughs's sudden interest in his daughter's custody, coming as it does on the heels of Diane Erickson's request for child support, smacks suspiciously of revenge. His previous callous refusal to contribute a dime to her upkeep and demonstrated lack of interest in spending time with her don't bode well for a future in his custody.''

Thanking her for her remarks, Judge Barnes announced that he would like to hear from the principals, beginning with Todd Burroughs and his mother. Meanwhile, as she'd outlined her arguments, Liz's stomach had threatened to stage another upset. The necessity of disposing of her breakfast in private before she upchucked in public had reached the critical stage.

"Your Honor, could we approach the bench?" she asked in an urgent tone.

Shoulder to shoulder with Jack, though she refused to glance in his direction, Liz begged for a brief recess so she could use the facilities. "Sorry, your honor...I'm suffering from an attack of indigestion this morning," she admitted.

Giving her a thoughtful look, Judge Barnes granted her five minutes. "What's the story, Liz?" he asked tartly. "Stomach flu? Or bread in the oven?"

Chapter 9

The judge's question sent her flying, as if she'd slipped on a mental banana peel. Dear God! she thought in panic and amazement. Is it possible I'm pregnant? That the answer was yes, or could very well be yes, totally threw her for a loop. Already muddled and out of control, her once familiar life seemed to dissolve and rearrange itself before her eyes in a stunning and terrifying new pattern that was rife with joys and pitfalls.

Aware Jack had turned to gape at her—that he'd made a truncated little gesture with his hand, as if to grasp hold of her arm and demand the truth, she struggled to think on her feet.

"Flu, your honor," she fibbed in a weak voice. "I saw my doctor about it yesterday. With your permission . . ."

Following a hasty explanation to her client, she was hurrying from the courtroom.

Her first priority when she reached the privacy of a restroom stall was to rid herself of the offending donut.

Though she felt limp and trembling afterward, at least she could think a little more clearly. A quick revue of the past eight weeks confirmed what she should have realized earlier. She hadn't had a menstrual period since the time she and Jack had made love without protection.

Though she tried to tell herself it was all in her head, she'd never been that late. Neither a history of irregularity nor her recently renewed commitment to running as an antidote for stress could explain such a lapse of nature. Besides, the flu wasn't something that troubled you exclusively in the morning hours.

She was going to have Jack's baby.

Staring into the ceiling-high mirror that spanned a bank of white porcelain sinks, she met her own incredulous hazel gaze. Unless she was very much mistaken, there was a little person curled up in her womb, a minuscule, utterly dependent infant who could turn out to have Jack's mouth and her red hair. The discovery made her want to hug herself in awe and delight even as she shuddered at the problems that could result.

If Jack finds out, she realized, *he'll never let me go,* whether or not he ever learns to love me. I could find myself trapped in a marriage of convenience with the man I've always wanted, only to learn that he can never be mine in any meaningful sense.

The imagined scenario got worse. If she held him to his promise of an annulment or, barring that, a divorce, once Kassie's adoption was final, he was certain to demand custody. She'd find herself joined in a legal fight similar to the one Todd Burroughs was waging against his frightened former girlfriend. Abruptly terrified of Jack's legal prowess and already bonding with her potential child, though its existence hadn't been confirmed yet by a doctor, she couldn't bring herself to face the prospect.

She was due back in the courtroom in exactly one minute.

I'll run off to Australia and live under an assumed name before I'll butt heads with him over this, she vowed, applying a fresh coat of lipstick in lieu of battle armor. Like those of hundreds of other children, our baby's picture will appear on "missing" leaflets and the sides of milk cartons.

On her return to the courtroom, she noticed for the first time that a reporter from the *Globe* was seated in the back row, his ballpoint pen poised to take notes in a narrow, hand-held notebook. Had he been there from the outset? She could only guess. With all her strength she hoped his presence indicated the preparation of a long "perspective" piece on custody cases in general, not some hearing-specific article that would pit her effectiveness as an attorney against Jack's, beneath lurid, intentionally quirky headlines.

Meanwhile, the dark-haired lover who had probably impregnated her with his child was giving her a searching look. *Everything okay?* he mouthed when at last he managed to catch her eye.

She nodded firmly. "Ready to proceed, Your Honor."

Though she did everything right, getting Todd Burroughs to admit he hadn't visited his daughter since she was six days old and hadn't entertained the notion of fighting for her custody until his ex-girlfriend had demanded money from him, Liz had the sinking feeling that the balance of the hearing hadn't gone particularly well for her and her client.

Diane Erickson seemed to share her opinion as they talked afterward in the corridor outside the courtroom. "You were great, Mrs. Kelleher," she said worriedly, shouldering the backpack she carried instead of a purse.

"You got Todd to admit he's neglected Samantha from birth...that he was angry when I asked him for even minimal child support. So why do I think the judge is going to rule against us?"

"I don't know, Diane," Liz replied. "To be honest, I have the same fear. Maybe it was the way my husband kept hammering away at the precise number of hours you're able to spend with Samantha each week. Or the way Judge Barnes kept overruling my objections. I probably shouldn't tell you this. But... confidentially...he has something of an antifeminist leaning. All I can say is, don't worry about it until we get a ruling. If necessary, we can beat them on appeal."

The young woman, whose spunk Liz admired so much, seemed to shrink into herself. "And in the meantime?" she asked. "Would Samantha live with me? Or them?"

"With you," Liz said forcefully. If I have to, she thought, I'll use Jack's words in the brief he wrote attempting to retain Kassie's custody against him...shame him into stipulating that much. "I think we can safely say that the court will see reason in that regard," she added. "Whatever he may think about the issues at stake in this case, Judge Barnes is obliged to be sensitive to the damage that could be caused by moving a very young child from one parent to another and back again until the issue's resolved, particularly if one of the parents is a stranger to her."

Diane bit her lip. "I hope you're right," she said.

"Trust me." Liz gave the young woman's shoulders a squeeze. "Go on to your class now, and don't worry unnecessarily. Mac Royer has assured me that our firm will be behind you all the way."

While Liz and Diane Erickson had been talking, Jack had been standing a few feet away, conferring with his clients and exchanging a few words with the reporter whose presence Liz had found so upsetting. Keeping tabs on her out of the corner of his eye, he saw Diane Erickson start for the stairs and Liz vanish into the women's rest room.

When Liz emerged, he cut his conversation with the reporter short. "Wait up," he called as she started to leave. "I need to talk to you."

Infuriated by his courtroom performance, and with her newfound knowledge of the baby she believed she carried hugged close to her heart, Liz could barely wait to return to her office and phone her gynecologist for an appointment.

Correction—my *obstetrician*/gynecologist, she thought. "What about?" she asked with a distinct chill, turning to face him. "I'm in a bit of a hurry."

Hurt by her tone, he zeroed in on Judge Barnes's remark, at once, just as she'd expected he would. "There isn't any chance he's right about you being pregnant, is there?" he asked. "As you know, that first time . . ."

Though she wanted to melt at the eagerness in his beautiful eyes, Liz maintained her glacial facade. Jack had Kassie. It would be difficult enough to give *her* up, after taking her sister's place as that sweet toddler's mother. She'd be damned if she'd open the door for him to take the baby they'd made together away from her, too. At the ripe old age of thirty-two, she might never have another one.

"Not a chance in the world," she lied. "My period came last week."

The bitter tone of her response was anything but typical of her. She's upset about the way the hearing went, he thought. And I honestly can't blame her. She's got a very credible client. Every time I opened my mouth to knock her down a peg, I felt as if I were cutting my own throat.

"Look," he said. "Don't let's let a lawsuit come between us, all right? What do you say we get together at the farm tonight... fix ourselves a couple of drinks and put our feet up? Kassie and I have missed you a bunch."

Alcohol's the last thing I'm going to want or need for the next seven months, she thought. But that's hardly the point. I wouldn't sit around and have a soda with you after the way you cast aspersions on my client if you were the last man on earth.

"No can do," she replied. "This case isn't over yet. We have a ruling coming up on Friday. If it goes against us, I plan to appeal. And that could take quite a while. If it's all right with you, I'd like to go now. Some of us have to work for a living."

The gynecologist's secretary managed to fit her in the following morning at ten, thanks to a cancellation. Her legs spread in the stirrups on his examining table as he poked and prodded, Liz all but held her breath. I should be sorry this has happened, she thought. It's going to turn my life into chaos. Adversely affect my career. Maybe even force me to move away from the Washington area if I don't want a custody battle with Jack.

Yet she didn't regret it in the least. Though her pain over the necessity of leaving Jack in the lurch if she turned out to be pregnant hadn't been resolved—yet—by a credible plan for helping him keep Kassie, she wanted a baby more than she wanted air to breathe or water to drink. Maybe even more than she wanted him.

At last the physician finished checking her. "I suppose you're anxious to hear the verdict, Liz," he said with a smile, after giving her a chance to sit up and cover herself. "As far as I can tell, you're roughly two months pregnant and healthy as a horse. Congratulations."

"Th...thank you, doctor." Unable to control the happiness and fear that trembled in her voice, she tried to disguise them by cracking a joke. "I don't suppose you can tell if it's a girl or a boy yet."

The physician laughed. "I'm glad to see you've got a sense of humor. When your little one hits the terrible twos, you're going to need it. In all seriousness, the answer to your question is no. We can sometimes determine the sex of a fetus via ultrasound by the time you're four or five months along."

Pausing, he glanced at her left hand. "Our records have you down as single, Liz," he added. "But I see you're wearing a wedding band these days. Who's the lucky guy?"

About to blurt out Jack's name, Liz hesitated. "Whatever's said in this office is confidential, right?" she asked.

Her doctor nodded. "Absolutely."

"The fact is, I married Jack Kelleher, my late sister's husband. But I don't expect the marriage to last. I don't want him to know anything about the existence of this baby."

Her heart overflowing with both joy and anguish, Liz managed to go through the motions at her law firm until quitting time. Released, she headed home to Georgetown, oblivious to the jangle and stress of traffic. All day, in the back of her mind, a plan of action had been forming. She'd pour herself a glass of milk, make a sandwich and spend the evening hashing it out.

Parking in front of the mellow brick row house she'd have to give up for a time in order for her plan to work, she went inside and changed into her oldest T-shirt. A glance at her silhouette in the mirror before going back downstairs told her it hadn't been affected yet. But it would be, soon. She'd have to make her move quickly if she was going to make it.

Settled in her Eames chair, with the air conditioner running, Natalie Cole on the stereo, and her half-drunk glass of milk resting on a small triangular table beside her, she came to a decision. *I'll request a transfer to our Los Angeles office and remain on the West Coast until well after the baby's born,* she thought. *We can tell the adoption agency Jack will be closing his Washington-area practice at some future date and that we're both moving west. I'm going out first to look for a house, establish contacts, because my job is more flexible.*

She reflected that her parents wouldn't miss her and come running to see her in her new home. As for Jack, she could keep him at bay by threatening to tell the adoption agency the truth if he didn't cooperate.

Eventually he, her parents and Rosemary would have to know she had a child, of course. But that could be resolved by continuing the deception. When her son or daughter was a year to eighteen months old, she'd say she'd adopted him or her. Or undergone artificial insemination.

That meant denying Jack the joy of fatherhood that was rightfully his, and would mean the earth to him. Just the thought of it made her feel guilty. Yet she'd be damned if she'd face him in a court of law and ending up essentially losing the precious child who was growing beneath her heart.

God knew, Jack wouldn't mean to hurt her. Despite his bullheadedness and tough-guy attitude, she realized, he had a tender heart. It was just that fathers' rights cases were his specialty. He was committed to them. And his own emotions would be involved.

He'd want their baby and Kassie to grow up together as full-time siblings, on his farm in Virginia. She'd be left with shared custody...the chance to cuddle their child on weekends. It wouldn't be enough.

There was an alternative to deceiving him, of course—one her heart kept revisiting after it had been rejected by her head. She could tell him the truth and stay married to him. He'd insist on it under those circumstances, she realized.

Inevitably, if they continued to live under the same roof, they'd have sex again. Maybe even more children. But he'd never love her as he had her sister. For the rest of her life, or as long as she could stomach it, she'd be forced to live in a no-man's land, with her most cherished dream dangling just out of reach.

The following day she confided in Mac Royer, sparing him a recitation of the more intimate details. Sympathetic in the extreme, but nonjudgmental, almost like the father she'd always wanted but never really had, he listened but didn't comment when she revealed the deception she and Jack had practiced against Judge Barnes and the adoption agency in Kassie's case. Maybe he considered it justified, but he didn't comment.

Instead he remarked that the firm's California office needed someone with her expertise and agreed to help her work out the transfer. But he wasn't wholeheartedly in favor of it.

"I hope you know what you're doing, Liz," he said somewhat skeptically. "As a practitioner of family law, particularly divorce and custody cases, you must be aware that breaking up a child's home is a very serious matter."

"I *am* aware of that, Mac," she answered, leaning forward in her chair in an effort to convince him. "It's the kind of thing that's happening to Diane Erickson as we speak that I'm trying to prevent."

Shrugging, he didn't answer.

The subject was closed, she guessed. "By the way," she said, "if we lose on Friday, someone else will have to take over Diane's case. Appeals take time. Much as I might wish to, I can't afford to return to Washington in a maternity dress."

Jack was playing handball with a male friend at his athletic club near Foggy Bottom. Though he was usually the stronger player of the two, he was getting skunked. Finally, he'd had enough. "What do you say we shower off and have something cold to drink?" he suggested, his cotton tank top soaked with sweat and his dark hair plastered to his forehead.

The friend, Tom Miller, an affable, physically fit pushover of a guy who'd attended law school with Jack, happened to be one of the few people in the world who knew the particulars of his deal with Liz. He had some news of his own to impart when, with towels wrapped about their hips after showering off, he and Jack sat drinking chilled mineral water on a viewing bench outside the handball courts.

"Guess what, old buddy?" he said offhandedly, but with a big grin on his face. "Sooz and I are expecting another baby."

Jealousy pricked Jack in the most vulnerable part of his stomach. I wish to God Liz had gotten pregnant, he thought. Having a baby with her would be so thrilling I'm not sure I could stand it.

Throughout the Erickson-Burroughs hearing the day before, as he and Liz had tried make mincemeat of each other's legal arguments, he'd kept hoping Judge Barnes's outrageous question was dead on target. If it had been, he theorized, *maybe I could have talked her into staying married to me after our year is up. Hell, I* know *I could've.* In his heart, he didn't really believe it, though. The way things had been going between them, the prospect of a turndown was just too great.

Pushing down personal concerns, he clapped his friend on the back. "Hey, man..." he said with genuine enthusiasm and affection. "That's terrific! Congratulations! When's the happy event?"

The Miller baby would put in an appearance in mid-April give or take a week or two. With a three-year-old son who was the apple of their eye, Tom and Sooz were hoping for a daughter. They were thinking of buying a bigger house.

"So tell me," Tom said, perhaps noting Jack's distraction, the wistful look on his face. "How are things going with you and your 'missus'?"

His defenses down, Jack gave him an anguished look. "I've fallen in love with her," he said. "Hell, I've always been crazy about her. We went to bed together a few times, and now she won't have anything to do with me. I want it to be a real marriage, not just a setup to fool the adoption agency into letting me keep Kassie. But the sad fact is, I'm going to lose her..."

A brief story about the Erickson-Burroughs case had appeared in the *News-Press* that morning, detailing the arguments involved and noting that Judge Barnes would hand down a ruling on Friday. Apparently Tom had read it.

"I doubt the tack you took in court yesterday did you much good," he said. "Ever tell her you're crazy about her? That you can't live without her? Why not propose to her again, for real this time . . . buy her a nice diamond or something?"

A glimmer of hope piercing the dark cloud of Jack's despair as they returned to the locker room to dress, he gave his friend's advice thoughtful consideration. Maybe Tom was right. Though he and Sooz had endured their ups and downs, due to the fact that Tom's mother lived with them part-time, they got along like a house afire. The well-being their relationship generated fairly beamed from his congenial countenance.

I've already given Liz a gold wedding band, he thought, laying his plans as he buttoned on his shirt and knotted his navy-and-yellow-striped tie. Maybe I'll buy her a striking diamond solitaire to accompany my proposal.

Tuesday's cast of characters was back in the courtroom on Friday, glaring at each other across the aisle as they awaited Judge Barnes's ruling. That is, at least the principals were. Though Jack kept trying to catch Liz's eye in a friendly way, she refused to look at him.

Having skipped her usual healthy breakfast of fruit and cereal in favor of bottled water and a handful of soda crackers, Liz congratulated herself that she looked only a little green around the gills. I wonder how long this stage of pregnancy is supposed to last? she thought ruefully, then went back to worrying about Judge Barnes's decision. Beside her, she sensed, Diane Erickson was rapidly becoming a basket case.

The familiar "All rise," didn't come a moment too soon. As Judge Barnes took his seat, Liz felt an instinctive chill of apprehension. He was going to find for the father. She just knew it in her bones.

Her heart sank even further when he singled her out for attention. Something of a loose cannon on the bench, Larry Barnes had a deplorable tendency to schmooze with the losers before pulling the rug out from under them. "I trust you're feeling better today, counsel," he said, addressing her.

"I am, thank you, Your Honor," she replied with as much nonchalance as she could muster. "Rest and plenty of fluids did the trick."

"I'm glad to hear it." The judge smoothed the few remaining hairs on his mostly bald pate as he regarded the litigants. "I suppose we'd better announce our decision and note any exceptions, since I've got another hearing scheduled in half an hour," he said. "The fact is, I've found for the father in this case...."

As Diane Erickson began to weep, and the Burroughses hugged each other in delight, Judge Barnes elaborated on his reasoning. In essence, he'd bought Jack's theory that a grandmother's loving, full-time custodianship was preferable to leaving Samantha with her mother, who'd be forced to place her in day-care while she worked and attended classes at the university.

"I agree with Mrs. Kelleher that the mother is to be admired for trying to better herself," he said. "Her diligence and good grades are indeed praiseworthy. However, my primary responsibility must be young Samantha's welfare. In my opinion, a single parent faces an uphill, ultimately losing battle if they attempt to care for their child while attending college classes full-time and adding part-time work to their schedule. Unless a grandparent, aunt or uncle steps in, such a child must spend the bulk of its time with baby-sitters, day-care workers or other strangers . . . bereft of the love and guidance only a parent or other close relative can provide. There's a tendency to fall between the cracks.''

The decision was guaranteed to generate explosive comments from women everywhere. For Liz, it had the effect of casting her determination to leave for California in stone. I'll be damned if I and my baby will ever be caught in this kind of vise, she thought. But she couldn't give her personal problems much consideration at the moment. First she had to ensure that Samantha would remain with her mother until the case was heard by a higher court.

"Permission to speak, Your Honor," she cried, jumping to her feet with a determined look on her face.

The judge eyed her speculatively. "Proceed."

Viewed out of the corner of her eye, Jack's celebratory expression only fueled her anger at him. "Please be advised that our side intends to appeal," she said urgently. "I beg the court to allow Samantha Erickson to remain with her mother, at least until that appeal has been heard. At the age of two, she's never known another parent. If the Burroughses are given custody now, and the decision goes against them on appeal, the child may experience hardship and confusion. She could suffer permanent damage."

As she spoke, Todd Burroughs and his mother were tugging at Jack's sleeve. Inclining his head to receive their whispered comments, he addressed the judge in turn.

"We see no reason for delay in the transfer of custody, your honor," he said. "In our opinion, the court's decision is sound, and we don't expect it to be overturned. In fact, we regard opposing counsel's plea as a mere delaying tactic. We view her argument that the child will be damaged by the move as spurious. Whatever the final outcome of this case, we think it's time Samantha Erickson got to know her father and grandmother.''

Her redhead's temper inching hotter, Liz had all but reached the boiling point. How dare Jack suggest no damage would be done when he'd advanced that very argument in persuading her to marry him for Kassie's sake? It was utterly outrageous.

''There's precedent for my argument, Your Honor,'' she said, managing to keep her fury under wraps as she rattled off pertinent decisions in the cases she'd researched.

To her satisfaction, Judge Barnes took notes. It was a very good sign. Though he liked to legislate from the bench, he wasn't a revolutionary by any means. He could usually be persuaded to honor the decisions of his peers.

Apparently Jack hadn't done any similar research, counting on his own glibness and Judge Barnes's philosophical leanings to do his work for him, because he had no opposing case law on the tip of his tongue.

He voiced no further objection. Though Liz couldn't know it, his initial flush of elation had been followed by a sinking feeling. Brisk, decisive and under good control, Liz wasn't going to forgive him anytime soon, unless he missed his guess.

Meanwhile, the judge had been contemplating his options. ''Not hearing any further objection by the winning parties,'' he said at last, ''I hereby order that Samantha Erickson remain in her mother's custody until such time as the case has been heard on appeal, subject to reasonable visitation by the father.''

Still teary-eyed, but clearly more hopeful, Diane Erickson squeezed Liz's hand. A moment later everyone rose as Judge Barnes hurried off to a meeting in his chambers, and Liz and Diane exited to the hall. After a

quick word with the Burroughses, who seemed somewhat unsure whether they'd won or lost, Jack followed
them.

"Darlin', please," he begged, taking hold of Liz's arm.
"I need a word with you."

She shook free of his hand. "Later," she snapped.
"Can't you see that I'm talking to my client?"

He was instantly contrite. "Sorry," he said. "I'll wait
for you outside. I didn't mean to interrupt."

Liz spent several more minutes bucking up the young
woman she liked so much. When she felt she'd done so
sufficiently, she broke the news that she was transferring
to her firm's California office, effective immediately.
"Though I won't be able to continue as your counsel, I'll
be handing your case over to Karen Greene, a very capable attorney here in our Washington office," she said. "I
know you're going to like her. However, you're free to call
me whenever you want . . . run ideas past me or whatever.
Here's a card with my business number."

As promised, Jack was waiting for Liz on the sidewalk. "Come have a bite of lunch with me," he begged,
every hint of triumph at his conquest scrubbed clean from
his voice. "I want a chance to apologize. Talk about
where we go from here. And make you a proposition . . ."

She'd have to tell him what she was planning at some
point. This was as good a time as any, she supposed. It
was going to be horribly difficult—the toughest thing
she'd ever have to do despite her anger at him. Yet the
baby they'd made took precedence.

It was approaching eleven. If they didn't get moving,
they'd run smack into the lunch crowd. "Okay," she
agreed. "Since I have a couple of errands in the neighborhood, someplace close would be best."

Side by side, but not touching, they walked to a hole-in-the-wall eatery a block or so from the courthouse. Jack chose the most secluded table possible. It wasn't the kind of place he'd imagined them sitting in yesterday, when he'd plunked down a cool ten thousand bucks for Liz's diamond solitaire. But it would have to do. She might not give him another chance.

"What'll you have?" he asked, scanning the menu as a waitress stood by with pad and pencil.

Aware she needed to eat, though she didn't have much appetite, she decided her stomach could handle a grilled chicken sandwich. "Number seven, hold the mayo," she said. "With a large glass of milk."

It was the sort of healthy choice an expectant mother might make. Glancing at her, Jack decided he was prey to wishful thinking. "A cheeseburger for me, hold the pickle, with fries and a beer...whatever you have on draft," he told the waitress.

"I'm really sorry about the argument I used in my effort to get the Erickson girl's custody transferred immediately," he said once the woman was out of earshot. "When you started citing all those decisions, I thought of our conversation by the pond, the day of Sharon's funeral and how I'd used the same basic argument to talk you into marrying me for Kassie's sake."

It was going to be ten times as difficult to leave him if he insisted on being so contrite and reasonable. "I thought of that, too," she admitted softly.

"I know you did. I could feel your outrage beaming toward me across the aisle. And I realized I'd been acting like a royal jerk. Say you'll forgive me."

He hadn't broached the subject of the other infuriating arguments he'd advanced—denigrating Diane Erickson for getting an education, to name just one example.

Given enough time, she supposed, she could bring him around to it. Yet, that didn't change the essential nature of her dilemma. At the root of her despair was the fact that Jack didn't love her. Considering how she felt about him, she couldn't continue with their marriage on that basis. By itself, wild, glorious sex wasn't enough.

Now that they were going to be parents, the exit door was slamming in her face. She had to get out before he discovered her secret, or spend the next eighteen years battling him for their child's custody.

He was so wry. So sexy. So utterly wonderful in so many ways. Nobody would ever take his place.

"Of course I forgive you, Jack," she said gently. "I realize you thought you were doing the right thing."

Backhanded absolution or not, he would settle for it. "Then you'll come home to Virginia with me tonight," he said tentatively, fingering the velvet ring box in his pocket. "Kassie has missed you so. And I have too, darlin'...so much."

It was now or never. "I can't, Jack," she said, keeping her voice as low and even as she could, though her heart was breaking. "I've accepted a transfer to our California office, effective immediately. I'm packing up this weekend and flying out Wednesday."

Chapter 10

Patched together of hope, determination and the guts it would take to declare his feelings, the bright, imaginary edifice of a shared future Jack had constructed came crashing down about his ears with the poignancy of a twelve-story building kneeling to a demolition expert. His pride, the tenderness and need he'd almost dared to express, lay in ruins. Utterly devastated, he said the first thing that came into his head.

"You *can't* go!" he exclaimed. "Without you I'll lose Kassie! You promised me a year, for God's sake!"

It was still just *Kassie* to him. Liz would remain a means to an end, if they lived together for decades. Taking the presumed hit, she retreated even further into herself.

"If you recall, our agreement was for six months," she reminded him in a quiet, reasonable tone. "When you, the adoption agency director and Judge Barnes agreed to increase the approval period to a year, I wasn't consulted."

Thinking back to what he'd regarded as an unmitigated triumph, Jack had to admit she was right in a technical sense. "You could've said something," he argued, "instead of keeping your mouth shut and letting me think the revised plan was okay with you. You're a free person."

He wasn't going to lay the suffering they'd brought down on their own heads exclusively at her door. Much as she loved him, she simply couldn't cope with it. She had a wrenching cross-country move and the baby she was carrying to think about.

"I'm glad you realize that," she answered, maintaining a calm facade, though her heart was aching. "I'm not about to give up a promotion when there's no need to do so. You can tell the agency you plan to move your law practice to the West Coast and I've gone ahead to look for a house. Or that my assignment there is temporary. Tell them anything you want."

There didn't seem to be any possibility of dissuading her. Struggling to adjust to a radically altered set of circumstances he hadn't expected and couldn't control, Jack simply stared at her for a moment. "You say you're leaving on Wednesday?" he asked in a monotone, like a patient suffering from shell shock.

Liz nodded. Lord, but it was difficult to hurt him, even if his shock and pain had nothing to do with the way he felt about her as a person. Somehow, she had to get it through her head that their sexual escapades had been just that to him—biology and proximity, as he'd so succinctly stated. If he'd loved her as she loved him, and wanted her to stay for her own sake, she reasoned, he'd have told her so. Nobody had placed a muzzle on him.

"I need to come out to the farm this weekend to pick up my stuff," she said, aware such a visit would be exceedingly painful.

"And say goodbye to Kassie," Jack answered, torturing himself with the question *Why can't she love us both?*

Liz blinked back tears, unwilling to let them spill until Jack couldn't see them. "Yes," she agreed softly. "Yes."

They settled on ten the following morning.

"If I'm out working in the yard when you're ready to leave, you'll come say goodbye to me, won't you?" he asked.

So bereft sounding, yet mutely accepting, the request almost undid her resolve. "Of course I will, Jack," she said, longing to hurl herself into his arms. "Though we'll be divorcing in the spring, as planned, we'll always be friends and in-laws."

For the first time in many years, that night, Jack wept in the privacy of his room. He thought he'd never known such grief, not even when his father had died. Or such a sense of helplessness. Where did I go wrong? he asked himself—over and over again. Should I have told her the truth about my feelings, and how long I've carried them, only to drive her away out of moral outrage that I was denigrating her dead sister? Is there *nothing at all* I could have done to make things different?

The greatest irony of all, in his opinion, had been the heat and ecstasy of their lovemaking. Had it stemmed from simple need on her part, as he'd once described it so callously to her in order to cover up his own emotions? Or had she felt something more than physical release with him? Desperate to know, he doubted he'd have the courage to ask.

He was on the riding mower she'd used so many times to give Kassie a ride the following morning, when he saw her car come up the drive. Accustomed to parking behind the house during her sojourn at the farm, she turned right instead and headed for the circular turnaround that led to the front door. He supposed she didn't want to carry her things through the kitchen, thus laying herself open to Mrs. Rivers's questions.

Entering the house through the living room, Liz went in search of Kassie first. The precious, dark-haired toddler was in her playroom, having an imaginary tea party with cast-off plastic cups, spoons and bowls Eloise had appropriated from the kitchen. Eloise herself was seated in the rocking chair she used for comforting and story telling, mending a pair of Kassie's overalls.

"Aun'ie Liss!" Kassie cried, jumping up and rushing forward on chubby legs to cling like a limpet to her. "Up! Up!"

"Kass, darling..." Her heart overflowing with what it would cost to leave behind the adorable little niece she loved so much, Liz scooped her up and held her tightly as she gave her a kiss.

"Welcome back, Mrs. Kelleher," Eloise said with a smile, getting to her feet also. "It's good to have you home."

Briefly Liz closed her eyes as she rested her cheek against Kassie's hair. She's my first child—as she is Jack's, she realized. It's just that I don't have a prayer of keeping her.

"I'm not staying, Eloise," she said, setting Kassie on her feet. "I have to go back to California on Wednesday... for an indefinite period."

"Oh. I'm sorry." Plainly, the congenial, easy-going nanny didn't get it. "Kassie's going to miss you," she added. "Whenever a car comes up the drive around dinnertime, she rushes to the window."

With Kassie stubbornly following in her wake and then wailing when Eloise restrained her, Liz entered the bedroom she and Jack had so recently redecorated. The connecting door to the bathroom stood open, leading to Jack's private bath and the bedroom where they'd consummated their need for each other.

She couldn't afford to remember the sizzling, erotic details, or she might waver. Saving her cosmetics for last, she began to carry armloads of clothing and other items to the car. When at last the bathroom, too, was empty of her personal junk, she returned to the playroom for a last goodbye.

Predictably, her little niece clung for dear life. "Kassie go bye-bye, too," she insisted.

"Sorry, darling," Liz answered, fighting back tears. "I can't take you with me."

The toddler's wails were like shards of glass pricking her flesh as she ran downstairs and went in search of Jack. She found him in the rear yard, his dark brows drawn together in a frown as he checked the oil gauge on his riding mower. Straightening, he wiped his hands on a rag as she approached.

"Have you said goodbye to Kassie yet?" he asked, his beautiful eyes squinting in the strong sunlight.

Liz nodded. "It wasn't easy."

The mute evidence of tears streaked her makeup.

"Don't go," he said, letting the simple but urgent request stand in for the many things he longed to say to her but couldn't bring himself to utter.

I don't want to! Liz responded, deep within herself. What I want most in the world is you, me and both our children, happy together.

"I've promised Mac I would," she answered. "The firm's expanding its family law practice on the West Coast. I'm needed there."

I need you, too, Jack answered silently. Don't I count for anything? "If you must go," he said aloud, "the least you can do is give me a goodbye kiss."

Temporarily stripped of her defenses by her unwillingness to refuse him, she came into his arms, to be clasped and held so fiercely that she thought her bones must break. Seeking her mouth, he claimed it with desperation, like a man who was starving to death.

Seconds later she'd pulled back from him, shaken to the core. How can I leave him, she thought, when he's my light, my breath, my everything?

"Don't be a stranger," Jack said, breaking the spell, his unruly emotions back in check as he unintentionally sealed their fate. "If you're in the Washington area on business, come see us."

"I will," Liz promised shakily.

Four days later, with her Georgetown house shut tight for what she expected to be a year's absence, and with her personal effects traveling to California air freight, she was winging her way to Los Angeles, leaving Jack and the little girl she loved so much some 2,300 miles behind on the country's opposite coast.

Six months passed, with Jack swimming in a sea of loneliness in Washington and Liz forlorn but healthy in her rented, somewhat older town house just off Sepulveda Boulevard, on the edge of Bel Air. She'd found it through a friend from law school, whose cousin planned to spend a year in Bangkok, and it suited her purpose well. Soothing, impersonal, with lots of books and framed artwork, but nothing to remind her of Georgetown or

Jack's Waterford-area farmhouse, it offered comfort, simplicity, anonymity, a safe haven in which to await her baby's birth.

More focused on negotiation and compromise than winning at all costs, her work at the Los Angeles branch had turned out to be satisfying in the extreme. It and her growing bond with her developing infant had been her sanity's sole bulwarks as she tried to keep from imagining what Jack and Kassie were saying or doing at any given moment.

As for the baby—which an ultrasound test at five months had shown to be a girl with tiny, perfect hands and feet who was sucking her thumb—Liz had come to love her more than life itself. *I would die for her, if need be*, she thought. The trouble was, she loved Jack and Kassie, too—every bit as much. Despite the child in her womb, she longed daily to hold them in her arms.

With a month to go till her baby's birth, she was shuffling some papers on her desk preparatory to taking several months of maternity leave, when her secretary buzzed.

"It's a Ms. Diane Erickson, calling from Washington," the middle-aged woman said.

"Thanks, Lynn." Picking up the phone, Liz warmly greeted her former client. "How's it going?" she asked. "Any resolution to Samantha's custody suit yet?"

"That's why I'm calling," Diane answered excitedly. "The appeal was heard this afternoon. And I won! I get to keep my daughter!"

Liz wanted to jump up and down at the news. Justice had been served at last. "I'm so happy for you," she beamed. "If anyone deserves a lucky break, you do."

"Thanks," Diane said. "I won't disagree with that. Listen . . . I know you helped with the appeal from California because my attorney here told me so. I just wanted to say thanks. Because of you, Mac Royer and Karen, I'll get to raise Sammie myself instead of simply seeing her on weekends. Plus she'll receive the child support from her father that she deserves.''

To Liz's surprise and emotional confusion, Jack phoned her, too, a few minutes later. He hadn't called in months.

''Have you heard from Diane Erickson yet?'' he asked, his voice as raspy and deep as ever in her ear.

Their baby was kicking in utero, causing the part of her maternity dress that covered the bulge of her stomach to jump. Hearing from him had set her pulse to racing. Ordering it to throb at a more normal rate, Liz admitted that she had. ''She called just a few minutes ago,'' she told him.

''Well, I wanted to offer my congratulations. The most deserving litigant and the best attorney won. And by the latter, I don't mean Karen Greene, though she did an excellent job in your place. As she admitted to me, she was working from the brief you'd written, with your considerable help and consultation.''

Liz didn't know what else to say but ''Thank you.''

''You're entirely welcome,'' he answered. ''Win or lose, I believe in giving credit where credit is due.''

A small silence ensued in which neither of them said anything.

''How's Kassie?'' Liz asked finally.

The topic was safe enough, and Jack ran with it. ''Growing by leaps and bounds...another half inch since those pictures I sent you,'' he said. ''And talking a blue streak. She asked for the keys to the garden tractor the other day, so she could drive it herself.''

Liz couldn't help laughing as she imagined it. "What a sweetheart she is," she exclaimed with a little shake of her head. "And so intelligent."

"You know she's twenty-six months old already," Jack reminded. "We'll be celebrating the anniversary of her arrival next week. Any chance you could fly back for the occasion, since you missed her birthday in January?"

"I don't think so."

To his discerning ear, her response sounded a little too clear-cut, too immediate. What's going on? he wondered. It's as if she's afraid to see me. Yet, in the oddest way, he almost felt she *wanted* to.

He tried again. "We're lucky that, so far, the adoption agency has bought my explanation about your temporary assignment, and hasn't kicked up a fuss over Kassie's lack of mothering," he noted. "But that could change if you don't make it back for the final meeting, which will take place in about six to eight weeks. Both the director and Kassie's social worker might start to ask some embarrassing questions."

I can't go back to Washington pregnant, Liz thought despairingly. Or as a nursing mother with a brand-new baby in tow. "I just don't think it's going to be possible, Jack," she said with genuine regret, hoping he'd accept her explanation and wouldn't press. "I'm all tied up with a special project right now. I'm afraid you'll just have to handle it."

They said goodbye a minute or so later.

Something's up, Jack thought, leaning back in his executive-style chair and staring at the receiver. I wonder what it is. It occurred to him that Liz might be involved with someone else. But he didn't think so. Unlike Sharon, she was the kind of woman who'd honor her commitment, whether it had been undertaken for love or more pragmatic purposes.

Abruptly he thought of his planned six-day business trip to Seattle, where he'd been hired to consult regarding a multi-million-dollar lawsuit. He was scheduled to leave the following afternoon. Though the trip would cost him quite a bit more if he decided to change his itinerary at that late date and add a Los Angeles stop, he thought it might be worth it.

Making up his mind, he punched a button on his intercom. "Frances," he said when his secretary answered, "I need you to phone the airlines . . ."

In the back of his mind was the hope he could convince Liz to give their marriage another chance. Offering her a full partnership in his firm might do it. The realization of how Liz's viewpoint on divorce and custody cases would alter his practice prompted a smile. The fact was, it would become a lot more compassionate and humanistic, he thought. And that would be all to the good. If he could convince her to come back to him, pretty redheaded Liz *may reform and civilize me yet.* Somehow the thought delighted him.

Meanwhile, in Los Angeles, as she gazed out her office window and thought of him, Liz felt a funny little pain in the lower part of her stomach. Though it was followed by another one a few minutes later, she didn't worry. It was too early for her to deliver. This must be what Dr. Weingarten meant when he talked about Braxton-Hicks contractions, the "false labor" that helps dilate the uterus to prepare for the real thing and subsequent delivery, she reflected. Supposedly they can occur at any time during an expectant mother's eighth month.

* * *

Around two a.m. Pacific time, as Liz lay sleeping at her rented Bel Air townhouse, a whoosh of clear liquid spilled down her legs. Jolted awake by the clammy, wet sensation, she realized to her astonishment that her sheets were soaked. It took a few seconds for her to figure out what had happened. Her baby's amniotic sac had ruptured. According to the stack of books for expectant mothers she'd read, and the classes she'd attended with a neighbor acting as her delivery coach, the serious, hard labor of giving birth could be expected to begin at any moment.

"Oh, no!" she exclaimed softly, feeling at that moment as if she must be the loneliest woman on earth. "Please...not this. It's not time! My baby girl isn't finished yet!"

As the plea escaped her lips, the first labor pain made itself felt. Like a menstrual cramp, but harder, it began in her lower belly and seemed to work its way to her ribs before subsiding. While it lasted, she felt as if she needed to breathe, concentrate and focus. She didn't want to move or speak.

If only Jack were here, she thought, collecting herself and wriggling out of her wet bed to sit ungainly, in a dampish nightgown, in the chair beside her night table and dial the phone. Cristina Johnson, an aspiring architect who lived three doors down, answered on the third ring.

"It's me," Liz said urgently. "Can you come over right away? I'm going into labor."

Jack took off from Washington's Dulles International Airport on a flight bound for Atlanta, Georgia, at approximately 5:45 a.m. eastern time. He'd thrust a connecting ticket to Los Angeles, LAX, and on to Seattle late that afternoon into his inside jacket pocket. It was a Saturday. Below, the rolling terrain of northern Virginia was swathed in a light overcast.

Settling back in his first-class seat, he flipped open a magazine but didn't actually to scan the pages. He was going to see Liz, and he'd be arriving unannounced. The rest of his life depended on the kind of welcome she gave him.

It was 2:45 a.m. in California. Her contractions roughly eight minutes apart, Liz was preparing with her neighbor's help for a trip to the hospital. Thinking she had another four weeks of pregnancy to go, she hadn't bothered to pack a bag yet. Now everything she wanted to take with her had to be gathered at breakneck pace.

By the time Jack was changing planes, she was ensconced in a private, "family-style" labor-and-delivery room, complete with a television set, homey-looking cabinets and several posh easy chairs to offset the cold mechanical aspects of the fetal heart monitor, automatic blood-pressure cuff and various other equipment that was attached to her as she labored, sitting mostly upright, in a specially designed bed. The spacing of her contractions had narrowed by a minute or so. Nurses breezed in periodically to check on her. Seated on a stool at her elbow, Cristina patted her back, reminded her to pant and concentrate and handed her a kidney-shaped metal basin whenever she felt nauseous.

Jack's flight from Atlanta touched down at LAX twelve minutes early at 9:33 a.m. in a light drizzle. One of the first passengers to deplane, carrying just a nylon garment bag over his left shoulder, he was able to make it through the airport, hail a taxi and reach Liz's Bel Air town house in less than half an hour. Asking the driver to wait, he got out of the car and then sprinted for her stoop when the heavens opened.

Rain was falling in his face as he rang the bell. There wasn't any answer. Leaning on it again, he started pounding. "Liz," he yelled, "if you're home, please answer! It's raining cats and dogs out here, and I've come all the way from Washington..."

In response to the noise he was making, a window opened on the upper story of the town house next door. A sixtyish woman with her hair in curlers peered out. "Who you lookin' for?" she demanded.

"Liz Kelleher," Jack answered. "I'm her husband. She didn't know I was coming. Do you know where she is?"

A startled, vaguely worried expression on her face, the woman withdrew slightly to confer with someone who had come to stand behind her. From what Jack could tell, the other person seemed to be urging caution. More than likely, neither the woman nor her companion had ever heard of him.

"Don't know," the woman answered finally, addressing him again. "She left this mornin', early. They was carryin' a suitcase."

Jack digested the news without speaking for a moment. By now the rain was descending in torrents. His hair was plastered in slick, dark points to his forehead.

The word *they* had gotten his attention. Had Liz left on a romantic junket with another man? Gone off to a weekend legal conference? Or simply headed out at the crack of dawn to participate in a 12K run somewhere? Whether out of trust in her or a tendency to be optimistic, he couldn't get himself to accept the notion of a boyfriend. One of his other guesses was more likely to be accurate. Probably the "suitcase" had been a briefcase or a duffel bag.

Whatever the case, he doubted she would return before the departure of his Seattle flight. Giving the neighbor a wave of thanks, he returned to his taxi. Damn! he thought, attempting to brush some of the water from his hair after directing the driver to return to the airport. No Liz. And I've got a five-and-a-half-hour layover.

From two doors down, across the street, another neighbor had seen him, too. Throwing on some clothes and a raincoat, she ran downstairs to see if she could help. Unfortunately, Jack left before she could make it. Watching his taxi disappear, she went back to her own town house where her husband was watching television.

"I wonder if that was her baby's father," she murmured. "He kind of looked the part, y'know, from what I've imagined of him."

By the time Jack drove away from her door, Liz's pains were coming extremely close together. Sweat poured off her forehead as she gripped the sides of the bed/delivery table, panting in response to Cristina's relentless coaching. With an utter abandonment of self, she gave her body over to the birthing process.

Whenever she could snatch a moment's surcease, she glanced at the fetal monitor. The baby's blood pressure and pulse had increased slightly. *Don't be afraid, little girl... everything's going to be all right,* she told her little one wordlessly. *Your mommy can't wait to hold you.* Seconds later, huge tears rolled down her face. The child she was pushing forth into the world would be Jack's daughter, too. And she'd denied him the wonder of being present at that moment.

Having looked in on her several times earlier, Dr. Weingarten strolled in, checked her progress and patted her hand. "Time for me to scrub up," he said cheerfully.

"Hang in there, Liz. Don't finish the job before I get back. I want to be around for your daughter's debut."

Jack was back at LAX, drinking black coffee and perusing the *Los Angeles Times* in one of the busy airport's many restaurants, as the baby girl he didn't realize he'd fathered inched closer to birth.

For Liz, the pains were very big now—nearly seamless and all encompassing. Yet, in the end, it all seemed so easy. With Cristina at her side and Dr. Weingarten gowned, gloved and positioned to receive her infant, she threw everything she had into four or five excruciating pushes. Suddenly the baby's head was free. Another push, and her shoulders were out. Her slippery-as-a-fish little body followed in seconds.

Hot tears stung Liz's eyelids as her daughter's first quavery, outraged wails split the air. She was so beautiful! She has my hair, Liz thought incredulously, leaning forward to check out the vaguely peach-colored fuzz that dusted the baby's head. And Jack's frown. His forehead crumples in that exact way. It was too early by several months to tell whether the tiny girl would inherit her father's stunning blue eyes.

Another push, involuntary on Liz's part, expelled the afterbirth. Accepting the baby from Dr. Weingarten's hands after he'd checked her briefly, the birth attendant suctioned her airway, cut and clamped her cord and massaged her gently to get her circulation going. An injection of vitamin K followed to prevent any internal bleeding that might occur.

While Dr. Weingarten finished working with Liz, a sample of the baby's blood was taken so that several standard tests could be performed. An antibiotic ointment was put into her eyes to offset whatever germs she might have encountered in the birth canal. Finally, cleaned, weighed and swathed in a blanket and knit cap to raise her body temperature, Liz's precious six-pound, two-ounce infant was placed in her arms.

"She's a beauty, Liz," Cristina said. "Look at that tiny nose! She has such an adorable little chin . . ."

"You can say that again," Dr. Weingarten agreed, flashing Liz an approving smile. "For a preemie, she's in fabulous shape."

Liz's bond with the child she'd carried for so many lonely months was both profound and instantaneous. Tears of joy ran down her cheeks as she cuddled the baby to her breast and placed the most delicate of kisses on her cheek. An invisible river of continuity seemed to flow between her and her child, uniting her inextricably and forever with the tiny scrap of her flesh who'd so recently left her womb and would grow up someday to be wise and loving and independent.

"You'll never know how much your mommy wanted you, Arden Rose Kelleher," she whispered just loudly enough for the baby to hear. "It's as if my whole life has been reaching forward to this moment, so I could hold you in my arms."

And as for Arden's daddy? The empty place he wasn't there to fill seemed to throb like a hole in Liz's heart. Every little girl, Arden included, needed a father, just as Liz needed the man she loved. Yet now, more than ever, she understood the ratcheting pain and fear she'd glimpsed in Diane Erickson's eyes when the lower-court decision on Samantha's custody had gone against her.

What in God's name am I going to do? she asked herself. Jack has a right to know Arden, just as she's entitled to his nurture. It would be so magical if she and Kassie could grow up together. Yet I'd die a thousand deaths if I told Jack the truth and he took her away from me in a divorce and custody case.

The horns of her dilemma were like shards of broken glass, poised to sever an artery no matter which way she jumped. *You could go back to your marriage,* a little voice deep inside suggested as Arden grasped the index finger she offered and held it tightly through the mittened sleeve of her hospital-issue nursery gown. She knew that's what Jack would want under the circumstances. He might even grow to love her as she loved him. The inevitable coupling that would unite them again might come to be based on more than mere biology and physical longing.

Chapter 11

With a six-week maternity leave in which to get acquainted with her new baby, and Maria Velásquez, the twenty-three-year-old, documented Salvadoran immigrant she'd hired to be Arden's live-in nanny, on hand to help, Liz expected the transition to motherhood to be as smooth as she could make it. Even after her leave was over, she would be able to continue nursing Arden. With her office just ten minutes from her rented town house, she could pop home and do it on her lunch hour.

None of the problems that sometimes arose to plague premature babies, such as precipitous weight loss, occurred with Arden, and Liz was able to bring her home on Monday as scheduled. A quick call made on her first afternoon in the hospital had alerted Maria that she'd be needed right away. Dropping by the hospital to meet her new charge and exclaiming over her beauty in strongly accented English, the nanny had accepted Liz's spare key and moved into the Bel Air town house to prepare for their arrival. She was waiting in the doorway, all smiles, when Cristina delivered them.

Five days later, Jack returned to Los Angeles, having changed his ticket a second time at considerable expense. Once again, it was a Saturday. This time the weather was mild, sunny and beautiful, with nary a drop of rain in sight. He considered it a good omen. *Liz can't be gone two weekends in a row,* he reasoned, mentally justifying his plan of arriving unannounced. *If we can just talk, maybe we can mend whatever got broken.*

As he got into a taxi at the airport, bound for her place of residence, Liz had just finished nursing Arden. More tired than she'd expected to be as a result of giving birth and waking during the night to feed her daughter on demand, she was desperate for a nap. Yet she thought it would do Arden good to go for a ride in her new baby buggy on such a fine afternoon. Selflessly, she settled on the latter option.

"Why you don't let me take her, *señora?*" Maria offered as she started getting ready to go. "She'll fall asleep as soon the buggy starts moving. She won't know who's pushing."

Liz had to agree. With a full tummy, Arden was a sleepy-time pushover. "Okay," she said, stifling a yawn. "I could use a little rest."

Maria and Arden left shortly afterward, with Liz accompanying them as far as the stoop to give her baby a goodbye kiss. She'd been stretched out, relaxing on her bed with her eyes closed for approximately five minutes when the doorbell rang.

"I wonder who that could be," she thought with a frown, trying to decide whether or not she should answer it. No doubt it was some sort of salesman. She was about to shut her eyes again when the thought occurred to her that it might be Maria. Maybe the nanny had forgotten her key and come back for something.

She was astonished to find Jack standing there. *"You!"* she exclaimed, her brain in overdrive as she tried to evaluate the problems his sudden appearance might create. "What on earth are you doing here?"

Drinking her in with the avidity of a man who's been wandering in an emotional desert, Jack thought she looked thinner. Yet, in a way he couldn't define, her figure seemed more lush. A bit tired looking about the eyes, as if she hadn't been getting enough sleep, she'd acquired a stunning inner radiance.

Lord but he loved this stubborn, yet somehow vulnerable woman! "What does it look like?" he answered, longing to take her in his arms. "I'm visiting you. I had business on the West Coast, so I thought I might as well. Aren't you going to ask me in?"

He was so gorgeous, so impossibly wonderful, this tough-talking but tender, dark-haired man who'd contributed the necessary spark of life to help make her precious daughter. She doubted if there was another like him in all the world. Meanwhile, baby paraphernalia was scattered all over the living room. And she hadn't decided how to handle their tangled situation yet.

"Um, sorry...I can't do that," she said, prevaricating. "The place is a mess. Could we go out for a walk or something?"

She was wearing a chrysanthemum-printed, kimono-style top with matching wide-leg trousers—what he thought of as a lounging getup. Was she entertaining a man, one she didn't want him to meet? If so, despite their official status as married people, he didn't feel as if he had any right to intrude.

"Okay," he said, his hopes diminishing. "Want me to wait out here for you, on the stoop?"

Liz nodded gratefully. "If you wouldn't mind. I promise... I'll be right back."

A moment later, the door had closed in his face. *Lucky I checked my garment bag at the airport this time,* Jack thought regretfully. But he didn't have much time to fret. Liz returned in less than minute, clad in leggings, a baggy sweatshirt and tennis shoes, with her front-door key on one of those phone-cord-type bracelets around her wrist.

"Pardon the informality," she said, noting the quizzical lift of his brows as she gently steered him in the opposite direction from the little park where Maria had probably gone with the baby. "But it's Saturday, you know."

He tried a grin. "You know how lawyers are... as stuffy as penguins. I should have traveled in my jogging suit."

Two blocks over, the neighborhood ran to expensive, single-family homes with carefully watered lawns. As they strolled past them, beneath the shade of some tall eucalyptus trees, Jack told her the latest news about Kassie. The toddler was growing by leaps and bounds. She could count to six and recite the first three letters of the alphabet.

"She's even potty training herself," he recounted to Liz's amazement. "Of course, she's driving Eloise crazy, asking to go to the bathroom every other minute."

"I wish so much that I could see her," Liz blurted.

Afraid she missed the adorable two-year-old but not him, Jack decided to take the bull by the horns. "Come

back, then,'' he urged, offering her his heart on a plate.
''We both miss you.''

If only I could, Liz thought. It might work. Then again,
maybe she ought to postpone making momentous life decisions until Arden was a little older and her hormones
had stopped sky tripping like astronauts.

''It's possible I might be back in the Washington area
for a few days next month,'' she said. ''Mac has invited
me to attend a conference on negotiation the firm is
sponsoring. I didn't plan to come because of the...
because of all the work I have facing me here. But now...''
She let the possibility dangle. ''Now, I might.''

She'd almost said, *because of the baby*. I want to tell
him, she thought. So much it's eating me up. Soon...very
soon...I'm going to have to deal with what's fair and what
I really want.

''You realize, of course, that you'd be welcome to stay
at the farm,'' Jack said.

He yearned to add, *We're still married, you know. We
belong together.* But he didn't dare. She'd think he just
wanted to go to bed with her. While this was achingly true,
it wasn't his only motive. He wanted a life with her. If the
force of his affection for her was a deciding factor, she'd
have to love him back one of these days.

Liz didn't say anything for a moment. ''I might take
you up on that,'' she ventured at last, trying to picture the
four of them under one roof together. Unfortunately, the
specter of Diane Erickson's narrow escape in the courts
still haunted her.

Unintentionally they'd come full circle. They were almost back to her door when Liz spotted Maria, pushing
Arden's buggy. They were approaching from the opposite direction. I'm not ready yet for them to meet! she

thought in panic. *The truth is, I'm terrified of what he could do to me legally.*

If they came face-to-face with the nanny, who hadn't been forewarned, Liz knew, the jig would be up. Thanks to some fancy footwork, she managed to get Jack turned around, so that his back was facing in the nanny's direction. "How long do you plan to be in L.A.?" she asked hastily.

Jack wanted to kick himself. Instead of taking a couple of days off to court her properly, he'd settled for a stopover of just two and a half hours, thanks to some function he'd allowed his mother to talk him into attending on Sunday in Baltimore.

"Actually, this is a stopover I sandwiched in on my way back from Seattle to Washington," he confessed. "I have to be back at the airport in an hour and fifteen minutes. Since it's a thirty-minute cab ride..."

Ask me to stay, and I'll do it in a hot second, he begged her silently. *Please, babe. I want you to.*

Jittery over the impending collision of the man she loved and the baby daughter she'd kept a secret from him, Liz didn't ask him. "C'mon," she said, tugging at his hand and leading him across the street instead. "At least we have time for a cup of coffee. I know a great little bakery on Sepulveda Boulevard where they brew a killer hazelnut."

Though he'd noticed the young Hispanic-looking woman pushing a baby carriage toward them before Liz had claimed his attention, Jack had no idea of her significance. He allowed Liz to lead him away to the bakery, where they ordered and sat opposite each other at a little table by the window. Clearly she wasn't going to invite him into her house, and it meant a few more minutes with her.

At last, unable to draw out their tête-à-tête any longer, he got to his feet. "I suppose I'd stand a better chance of hailing a taxi here than I would on your block," he said tentatively.

No offer to summon one for him from her home phone was forthcoming. "You're probably right," she agreed.

Resigning himself, he paid the tab and held the door open for her. Seconds later an empty cab approached. Biting the bullet, Jack stepped forward to the curb and hailed it. "Do I get a goodbye kiss? I came an awfully long way for one," he said, standing so close that Liz could smell his after-shave as the cabby screeched to a halt.

Heartsick over the necessity of parting from him, she was on the verge of spilling everything and throwing herself on his mercy. Only the fact that she couldn't endure the thought of being separated from Arden kept her from going for it.

"Of course you do," she said breathlessly.

With a little rush, his mouth descended on hers. Sensual, urgent, yet achingly tender, his kiss seemed to sear her very soul. It awakened feelings in her that had ebbed slowly during her pregnancy and died out completely, or so she'd believed, in the delivery room. Just by being Jack, and kissing her with that subtle mastery of his, he'd brought them back in spades.

She was in no shape for a man and wouldn't be for another six weeks. But that didn't matter in the least. She wanted him to hold her and keep on holding her until night fell. *I love you, Jack! We made a baby girl to-*

gether! Please...don't go! her heart cried out, desperate to fill the silence her head was imposing on them.

Seconds later, he was getting into the cab and waving goodbye to her from the rear seat. Seizing the first opportunity that came his way, the cabbie darted into traffic. Ignorant of her love and their seven-day-old child, Jack started moving away from her.

Neither of us said anything about getting a divorce, though the year I promised him is almost up, she realized, hugging herself as he became a speck in the distance and then vanished altogether. As she turned away and headed home to Arden, she wondered what it meant.

Having attended a seminar given by a graduate of the Harvard Negotiation Project when she was seven months pregnant, and having done some other research on the subject, Liz took a pass on flying to Washington for the April conference Mac had invited her to attend. Though she'd thought about the prospect endlessly, she still wasn't ready to face Jack. Nor did she want to travel from coast to coast with a nanny and a month-old baby, plus all the baggage that would entail.

A second opportunity to do both came up sooner than she'd expected. In mid-May, shortly after she went back to work, she got an urgent call from Mac Royer. He needed her back in Washington, pronto. The assignment would last several weeks.

"I can't leave Arden," she objected immediately. "She's less than two months old. And I'm nursing her. I plan to keep on doing so for another four and a half months."

The warmth in Mac's voice bridged the physical distance between them, making her feel as if she were sitting in his office. "I didn't expect you to leave that precious baby," he answered. "While I realize it'll be something of a hardship, dragging your daughter, her nanny and a whole raft of stuff across the country and back again, this is a wonderful opportunity, Liz. One of Washington's fair-haired power couples is divorcing, and there are children involved. You may remember them...David Haynes and Mary-Cate Conyer."

Liz did indeed. The last time she'd seen them, very briefly at some Washington party or other, David had been the top aide to the Librarian of Congress, while Mary-Cate had been an up-and-coming State Department attorney. At the time, they'd had two sons and were expecting a daughter. Though they were both hard-working professionals, with demanding careers that caused them to complain they never had enough time for their children or romance, they'd seemed happy enough. What had happened to sour them on marriage and each other?

"David has stepped down from his position at LOC to accept a lesser job since Mary-Cate moved out, taking the children with her," Mac said. "He wants their custody. From the court documents that have been filed so far, his argument appears to be that he's always been the parent willing to work for less money and status in a more flexible job so the children's needs get met, while Mary-Cate keeps increasing her work load and decreasing the time she spends at home as she climbs the career ladder. In all fairness, that does seem to be the case. Recently, she was appointed attorney to the National Security Council..."

"Wasn't there a case a couple of years ago, in which the father made a similar argument?" Liz asked.

She could feel Mac's nod. "You have a good memory," he said. "The judge in that case, a woman, found for the father, surprising everyone."

In Liz's opinion, it wasn't so surprising. Children's needs had to be considered first. "Which parent are we representing?" she asked. "The mother, no doubt."

Mac had the grace to laugh. "How did you know?"

"Experience. And simple instinct." Liz drew a trio of smiley faces on her notepad—one for each of the Haynes-Conyer children. In a way, those kids are lucky, she thought. Unlike Arden, they have a chance to know both their parents. "It'll be a losing battle, you know," she added. "Why do you want me to take the fall?"

"Your expertise in negotiation," he replied. "If you play your cards right, there shouldn't be any fall to take. I don't want *anyone* involved in this suit to lose . . . not Mary-Cate, not David, especially not those kids. They were neighbors of mine, and I'm fond of 'em all. What I want is for them to get back together. I'm willing to pay your expenses from Los Angeles . . . hell, your whole entourage's tab at the Willard for a couple of weeks, if you can accomplish that. The case is bound to be high profile. If you can pull off what I'm asking you to do, it will probably land you a partnership."

Liz had dreamed of becoming a partner since joining the firm eight years earlier. Now that the longed-for triumph hovered within her grasp, she wasn't sure she still wanted it. Among other, more important matters, she had Arden to think about.

"That's very generous of you, Mac," she said. "But you don't have to break the bank. The woman who was renting my Georgetown house has just been transferred.

At the moment it's empty, though still fully furnished. We can stay there.''

Mac laughed again. ''You see? It was meant.''

She supposed he'd talked her into it. ''Okay,'' she said, ''if you'll spring for three first-class airline tickets, so I'll have a proper place to strap Arden's car seat, I'll take the case.''

''Done,'' Mac answered. ''I'll clear it with accounting.''

While he was speaking, a sudden thought occurred to her. ''Who's the opposing attorney?'' she asked. ''Jack?''

''I was afraid you were going to ask me that.'' Mac cleared his throat. ''As it happens, you're right on target. However, I want you to get that notion of 'opposing' out of your head. I know... with the lower-court loss to him in the Erickson-Burroughs case, not to mention your personal situation, whatever it is, the idea of beating the odds and knocking his socks off must be awfully tempting. When thoughts like that drift into your head, I want you to think of those children.''

On a cool, clear evening near the end of May, Jack stuffed his portable phone into the pocket of his poplin windbreaker and strolled down by the pond after reading Kassie her nightly allotment of stories, kissing her and putting her to bed. He was expecting a call from an important client in New York, and he didn't want to miss it. At least, the get-up-and-go lawyer in him felt that way. The man was another story. Pensive, moody, he reflected that he'd left a very large portion of his heart in California. If it weren't for Kass, he thought, his life would be little more than a desert.

Pausing beneath the massive willows that edged the pond to gaze into the shadowed, murky water, he recalled the windy March day, slightly more than a year earlier, when he'd proposed to Liz on that very spot.

Even then he'd wanted it to be a real marriage, though he'd known she'd be outraged if she even guessed as much. A year had passed. Sharon was still dead. And they'd gone on living. Was it too much to ask, once and for all, just to be happy?

Having been postponed with Jack's consent because the adoption agency director was out of the country, the final hearing on Kassie's custody would be coming up soon. Now that their old friend Judge Barnes had retired, he supposed the new Superior Court judge in the family division, Sandra Kaplan, would preside. Somehow he had to talk Liz into returning and playing the role of his loving wife, so his custody of Kass would be adjudged final. Or rather *their* custody. Somehow he had to convince Liz that being married to him was a role she didn't want to live without.

As he pondered some possible ways to do it, his portable phone rang. Pulling it from his pocket, he said hello, fully expecting to hear his New York client's somewhat brash, preoccupied tones. To his astonishment, after letting *him* initiate all communication between them since her departure for California, Liz was on the line.

"I'm in D.C., Jack," she said. "Staying at my house in Georgetown. And lawyering for Mary-Cate Conyer."

Another lawyer from her firm had signed the original petition. It was like having the world handed to him on a plate, then snatched away in an instant. "Liz, darlin'," he said in distress. "You know I'm representing her husband."

Her voice was as calm and unruffled as the pond's surface as she answered him. "I know. Mac told me," she said. "I don't consider it a problem."

He could feel the chains falling from his hopes. Still, his instincts, which he trusted, warned him to be careful. Hadn't it been directly after her loss to him in the Erickson-Burroughs case that she'd decided to accept a transfer to California? In the upcoming matter, David Haynes stood to win big. The record showed he'd acted *in loco parentis* for his mostly absent wife, in addition to being a damn good father to his three children. Unless he missed his guess, it would be a piece of cake to win custody for David Haynes. The man deserved it. Unfortunately, Jack's success on David's behalf might ruin his own chance with the only woman he'd ever wanted.

"So... when are you coming out to the farm?" he asked, probing her willingness to get close to him again. "As you probably remember, it's beautiful out here this time of year. Kassie's running full riot, digging in the flower beds and hiding from Eloise in the orchard. The little dickens leads her nanny a merry chase."

Of course Eloise can't take your place with her, he wanted to add, but held his tongue.

Silence answered him. Now that she was within driving distance, Liz was clamoring to see the silken-haired little girl she considered her daughter, too. Unfortunately, Arden had turned out to be a voracious eater, who wanted to be fed on demand. Though Liz could express breast milk for her and place it in refrigerated bottles for Maria to administer, as she had several times successfully in Los Angeles, she'd decided to reserve that stopgap measure for the Haynes-Conyer hearing.

That meant she'd have to take Arden and explain her to Jack. Unwilling to do that yet, if she was *ever* to do it, she needed to see something of him first, attempt to gauge his feelings for her and assess her risk.

"I'm dying to see Kass," she said. "But things are a little hectic here. Do you think you could bring her into town? That we could meet for lunch somewhere?"

She still didn't want him at her house. What was going on? A risk taker always, Jack decided to call her bluff.

"I've got the same problem, I'm afraid," he countered. "Maybe we could arrange it after the hearing."

"That would suit me," she said.

Disappointed, he forged ahead, switching topics. "Meanwhile, we're eligible to complete the formalities of Kassie's adoption at any time, now that Edward Kranz, the adoption agency director, is back in the country," he announced, hoping her thoughts wouldn't turn immediately to divorce as a result. "I was going to phone you about it tomorrow. Since the Haynes-Conyer thing doesn't go before Judge Kaplan until the first part of next week, would you be available tomorrow or Friday?"

She was aching to see him, despite the emotional tumult it would entail. "Absolutely," she answered, making no mention of the dreaded D word. "Just set up a time with Kranz's secretary, and let me know."

They said goodbye on a bittersweet note. I'll bring Kassie to the hearing, Jack thought, switching off his phone—use her shamelessly, if I must, to get Liz back. A moment later he thought better of it. He wanted to maintain the fiction that his wife had visited back and forth from California as frequently as possible since her transfer. And, after a nine-month separation, his bright-eyed two-year-old might not remember her.

In Georgetown, Liz stared at the receiver she'd just placed in its cradle. A knot of yearning settled in her chest as she cuddled Arden. *To hear me talk, it sounds like I don't give a damn what happens between me and Jack, and that's far from accurate,* she thought. *It's just that emotional vulnerability to him would involve telling him the truth. And I'm still terrified of finding myself caught up in a battle for Arden's custody.*

For the first time since she'd learned of her pregnancy, a competing train of thought, arising from the conciliatory plan she was evolving for the Haynes-Conyer case, made its presence felt. It was entirely possible she and Jack could work things out without clawing at each other's throats—maybe even revive their marriage on a more promising basis. Though she'd have to pick her way with care, she decided to try and find out if she stood a chance.

"You'd like to have a daddy as well as a mommy, wouldn't you, little girl?" she whispered, dropping a loving kiss on her baby's forehead. "Well, I'd like to have a husband, too, despite the fact that you're my universe."

She just needed to believe there was a chance Jack could love her for herself.

Jack set up their appointment at the headquarters of Children From Across the Sea, or CFAS, for Friday morning at ten. Liz was waiting for him in the building's downstairs lobby when he arrived.

"Hi," she said, melting into his embrace and then withdrawing again into her separateness. "You're looking wonderful. I thought it might be better if we went upstairs together."

"The same goes for you. Thanks for waiting," he answered, placing a proprietary arm about her shoulders as they waited for the elevator.

She was wearing a pale, greenish-aqua suit that followed her curves, emphasizing her slim waist and the slightly more rounded dimensions of her breasts and hips. Her mass of red curls, which just brushed her shoulders, was sweet smelling and arranged in its usual tangle. Jack wanted to make love to her on the spot, right there in the lobby. Or hit the Emergency Stop Only button on the elevator. Thanks to the impending award of Kassie's custody, which took precedence, he managed to restrain himself.

Their meeting with CFAS officials, who had once tried to remove Kassie from Jack's care, was almost anticlimactic. The essence of cordiality, it was also somewhat cut-and-dried. A cool thirty-five minutes later, her permanent papers had been signed and delivered to them. They were back in the lobby, headed for the sidewalk.

"How about lunch?" Jack asked, unwilling to relinquish his hold on Liz. "There's a great new place just down the street."

Thrilling to the touch of his hand on her arm in a way that told her she was past her postnatal period of attenuated desire, Liz knew that, if Jack pressed the issue of intimacy, she'd tumble. The passionate woman in her was craving exactly that, though the issue of telling him about Arden hadn't yet been resolved.

To her chagrin, perhaps in a subliminal bid for self-protection, she'd made other plans. "Sorry, I can't. I'm having lunch with your mother," she told him.

When Jack proposed that he join them, she advised with gentle, almost affectionate firmness that the occasion would be strictly girl talk.

The fact was, she'd determined to spill the beans to Rosemary Kelleher, whom she considered one of her best and closest friends, provided she could wrest a promise of utter silence from her first. She needed a listening ear— preferably some good advice—from someone! She could hardly confide in her mother. Besides, Arden was Rosemary's granddaughter, as well as her namesake.

They met at the Old Ebbitt Grill, on 15th Street NW, to hug fiercely in the lush Victorian bar area.

"God but you're a sight for sore eyes!" Rosemary exclaimed, standing back to have a look at her. "I'm sorry to say, life in California has been good to you."

"In one particular way, it has... very much," Liz admitted.

A frown ruffled Rosemary's usually serene countenance. "You haven't found someone else, have you?" she asked worriedly. "Because Jack..."

"In a manner of speaking, yes."

The maître d' was waiting to take them back to the open-air patio, where they'd reserved a table. Stifling her obvious dismay at Liz's remark, Rosemary followed meekly. However, she was anything but meek once he'd left them at a table to scan their menus.

"As your friend and confidante for years, I demand to know what's going on," Jack's stylish, self-directed mother said, leaning forward in her chair.

Liz leaned forward also. "You'll have to swear an oath of secrecy if you want me to tell you."

Taken aback, Rosemary didn't answer for a moment. Her healthy silver-streaked hair seemed to bristle with curiosity as she plainly weighed the drawbacks. "All right...I swear," she said at last with obvious reluctance. "I suppose all this secrecy is so I won't tell Jack."

"You might say so." Inhaling deeply, Liz plunged ahead. "When Jack and I were living together in Virginia last summer, we had sex a few times," she said. "The first time, we neglected to use protection."

"And you got pregnant!" Rosemary exclaimed.

Nervously Liz shushed her. "It's true," she admitted. "You don't need to shout it from the rooftops."

Jack's mother was clearly beside herself with excitement. "And the baby?" she demanded, remembering to lower her voice to a whisper.

"I gave birth to a daughter at the end of March," Liz said. "Her name is Arden Rose Kelleher. She was named partly in your honor." Opening her leather shoulder bag, Liz took out a sheaf of photos she, Maria and Cristina had snapped. "I made you copies of some pictures," she added. "If I give them to you, I expect them to be covered by our agreement, okay?"

Reaching for the photos with one diamond-studded, perfectly manicured hand, Rosemary paused in mid gesture. "Liz, you've *got* to tell him!" she said in an anguished tone. "Surely you must know what it would mean to him!"

"I can guess," Liz said wryly. "Since we're talking off the record, I may as well tell you that I love Jack very much. I have for years. Sadly for me, he was married to my sister. He seemed to love her. As you know, following her death, we got married so he could keep Kassie. It was to be a temporary union of convenience...one we would dissolve once he'd been awarded her final custody. Since that happened this morning..."

Flipping avidly through Arden's snapshots, Rosemary was only half listening to her. Nonetheless, she looked up. "This child is absolutely beautiful," she said with something approaching awe in her voice. "Young as she is, I can see some of Jack in her. And you, too, of course. She has your hair. And fair complexion. When do I get to hold her?"

Liz smiled, warmed by her friend's wholehearted praise of her daughter. "Anytime you like," she said. "When we finish lunch, if you want to come over."

Still engrossed in the baby's pictures, Rosemary accepted her invitation on the spot. A moment later their waiter came and they ordered salads. Giving them a last, hungry look, Rosemary put the snapshots in her purse. "What's stopping you?" she asked with her famous directness. "From telling Jack, I mean. If you love him, and you know how much he'd want the baby..."

"Don't you see?" Liz's question was replete with the ongoing heartache she felt. "From where I stand, I've got two choices, maybe three. Go back to a loveless, one-sided marriage with him, because that's what he'll insist on, for Arden's and Kassie's sake. The fact that we'd probably have sex again...maybe even more children...would only make it more difficult.

"On the other hand, if I divorce him and he finds out about Arden, he'll fight me for her custody. I've watched other mothers go through that hell, and I want no part of it. I don't want to lose her."

"What's the third option?" Rosemary said.

Liz was almost sorry she'd mentioned it. Yet she truly wanted to know what Rosemary thought. "Hanging around and daring to hope he might come to love me, I suppose."

At that Jack's mother shook her head. "Smart as you are, darling, and you're awfully smart," she said, reaching across the table to take both of Liz's hands in hers, "you don't have a clue about my son and his feelings, if you're tempted to rate that option last. What do you say we forget about those salads we ordered and just pay for them? I want to go home with you to Georgetown and hold my grandbaby."

Rosemary's advice, after a lengthy session with Arden in which grandmother and granddaughter appeared to bond instinctively, was for Liz to make a clean breast of things with Jack. "Though I can't vouch for him, and he certainly hasn't confided in me, I have a strong feeling you'll be pleasantly surprised to learn what his true feelings are," she said. "It doesn't mean a thing that he hasn't dared to articulate them."

Liz wasn't so sure. She was still mulling over her mother-in-law's advice on Monday morning, when she and her client met Jack and his client at the courthouse. At her insistence, they'd scheduled a reconciliation session before meeting with the judge.

As she expected, after conferring privately with Mary-Cate Conyer and listening to her unending stream of hostile remarks—which seemed to center on the strong belief her husband had been having an affair and would soon introduce a stepmother into the picture once the divorce was final—the session didn't go well. Holding the preponderance of her conflict-resolution skills in abeyance until such time as they might actually be useful, Liz suggested the couple think about what they really wanted. But she didn't press. The advice she had to give wouldn't have much effect until they were ready to listen to it.

Ultimately, after complaining of her husband's infidelity for the umpteenth time, Mary-Cate stormed out of the room. Glancing at Jack, who was watching her with a bemused expression, Liz gave a little shrug. "See you in chambers," she murmured, as if the outcome mattered not a whit.

As she followed her client out of the conference room, he couldn't help wondering what she was up to. Did she have a new strategy up her sleeve? Some sort of secret weapon?

The case was called in Judge Kaplan's chambers at four o'clock. Arguing for his client, Jack made an eloquent case for the father to be awarded custody.

"My client is best suited to raising the children of this marriage because he has more time to spend with them, and he's willing to spend it," he said. "Since the youngsters in question were born, he's been providing the bulk of supervision and nurture not covered by their schools and day-care service. As her career advanced, his wife came home later and later, to pop a TV dinner in the microwave for herself at, say, ten or eleven at night.

"Meanwhile David Haynes voluntarily cut back on his hours and then changed jobs altogether, the better to pick up the kids, help with their homework, fix dinner and tuck them into bed..."

In her heart, Liz couldn't help admiring the husband for the sacrifices he'd made. As a mother, she knew a baby could take an inordinate amount of time away from a fast-track career, and she was willing to make whatever adjustments were necessary for Arden's sake. She thought both parents in a marriage owed their children that kind of flexibility.

Without much to fall back on, she contended that the mother was best equipped financially to have custody. She could afford to hire the necessary help. Plus she was willing to modify her schedule whenever possible to be with them. The three children clearly loved her. She loved them back and, in the ways that counted, had been an excellent mother to them.

"There's also the matter of the husband's alleged infidelity, which speaks to his moral character," she said, having promised her client she would do so.

Jack immediately challenged the assumption. "I'm relieved to note opposing counsel's use of the word *alleged,*" he remarked. "My client categorically denies any extramarital liaison, though he admits to being friendly with the co-worker with whom he's supposedly involved."

The arguments continued that way for another twenty minutes. Finally the judge had heard enough. "Sorry, but it looks like I'll have to call a halt to this bickering for this afternoon, as I have another engagement," she said, consulting her calendar. "If everyone agrees, we'll meet back here tomorrow at three."

Grumbling about "the damn divorce dragging on and taking up all my time," Mary-Cate Conyer left the courthouse. David Haynes followed suit a moment later, headed in the opposite direction. About to suggest he and Liz go somewhere for a drink, Jack was startled by a strange, rattling sound as she picked up her briefcase.

"What's that noise?" he asked.

To Liz's dismay, she realized one of Arden's baby toys must have fallen inside. If Jack were to catch a glimpse of it, he'd ask no end of questions. Determined to keep their personal situation on the back burner until after the second round of negotiations she was planning to propose, on the theory that the techniques for conflict resolution she planned to introduce might have some influence on it, as well, she cast about for a logical, if untrue, explanation.

"Actually, it's a toy I picked up for Kassie on my way to the courthouse," she said.

Jack took the bait at once. "Why not come home with me tonight and give it to her?" he suggested.

Liz wished she could. But it wasn't possible. "I can't," she said, anxious to return home and have Arden empty her breasts of milk, as they were beginning to hurt. "I have another engagement."

Desperate for a way to get close to her, Jack did something that evening he almost never did. He phoned his mother for advice. "I can't get her to go out with me or drive down to the farm . . . not even to visit Kassie," he said. "What's more, she repulses any suggestion that I visit her at her house in Georgetown. She acted the same way in California. . . ."

Torn between wanting to help her son and keeping her promise to Liz, Rosemary attempted to do both. "I can't say much," she admitted, "because I was told what I know in confidence. All I can do is tell you to go over there and make her let you in. If I were you, I'd go *tonight*."

Astounded at receiving such a firm directive from a mother who had emancipated him at the age of eighteen and seldom interfered, Jack threw on his jacket and headed for his sedan, after first making sure Eloise would read to Kassie and put her to bed. An hour later, after defying most of the speed laws he'd encountered and pulling out all the stops, he stood on Liz's doorstep, ringing the bell.

Maria answered. "May I help you?" she asked in her softly accented voice.

Jack had a feeling he'd seen her before. But he didn't have time to puzzle over her familiarity. From the living room, where Liz was feeding Arden and had just disengaged her from the nipple she had firmly fixed in her mouth in order to switch sides, an infant wail of protest arose and was quickly silenced. His mouth dropped open, even as a zillion flashbulbs seemed to go off in his brain with blinding clarity.

Liz had conceived and given birth to his baby.

Chapter 12

Ignoring Maria's shy protest, Jack brushed past her and entered the living room. Seated cross-legged in her black leather Eames chair, with her bright, unruly tresses falling forward as she soothed an infant wearing some sort of ruffle-trimmed, stretch-terry garment, Liz looked like a modern-day Madonna. The unabashed swell of her breast as the infant suckled, the look of profound tranquility on her face, the baby's renewed contentment as it grasped a strand of her hair with its tiny fingers, stopped him dead in his tracks. A barbarian at the gate, he was gazing at love in its purest aspect.

Getting the baby settled at her other breast and adjusting the chrysanthemum-printed kimono top Jack had seen her wear briefly in California in order to cover herself, Liz looked up and froze. Incredibly, *Jack* was standing there, staring at her as if he'd never seen a woman nurse a baby.

She could tell at once that he'd figured out whose baby it was.

For what seemed a very long minute, neither of them spoke. At last Jack found his voice.

"Why didn't you tell me?" he said, the words dense with grief at his exclusion as he continued to stare at them. "You must have realized that I'd have wanted to know."

He hadn't phrased his question as an accusation, though he surely had the right. Pierced to the quick over the hurt she'd caused him, Liz didn't try to defend herself. Instead she told him the simple truth. "I was afraid that if you knew, you'd try to take her away from me," she whispered.

Jack digested the information for a moment. Did she plan to divorce him, then? It won't happen if I can help it, he thought fiercely. I want to cherish them both, for as long as there's breath in my body.

It sunk in that the baby was a girl. He had another daughter. "Mind if I come a little closer, so I can have a good look at her?" he asked.

Tears of guilt, uncertainty, relief and an improvident, almost selfless joy clung to Liz's lashes. At last he knew, as he should have known much earlier. Though she was still afraid of what might happen—of the custody suit he might decide to initiate against her, in the language of her mother's old-fashioned prayer book, the coming together of father and daughter was meet and just.

"Of course not," she answered softly. "Pull up a chair."

He came to sit on the Eames chair's matching hassock, which offered him the best access. His eyes were full of wonder, his physical attitude one of boundless reverence. We made her the night I got all bent out of shape over that phone call from one of Liz's former boyfriends and then made love to Liz, he thought in amazement. *Out of our passion and urgency,* she *came, one of God's angels, to dwell with us.*

"What's her name?" he asked.

The look of instantaneous, unconditional love on his face broke Liz's heart, even as his presence there, in the same circle of lamplight that contained her and their child, caused it to swell with happiness.

"Arden Rose Kelleher. The Rose part is after your mother. Go ahead and touch her," she suggested.

He realized she'd given their infant his surname instead of reverting to Heflin. It was a very good sign. Leaning toward mother and child, and feeling the unaccustomed clumsiness of his six-foot, two-inch frame as he did so, Jack stroked his daughter's velvety cheek with one gentle finger. How he loved her already! She was flesh of his flesh. At the molecular level in her amazing, perfectly formed body nestled his genetic inheritance, along with that of the only woman he'd ever wanted. With Liz's red hair in the offing and a chin he recognized as his own, she was herself and no other, though she'd borrowed from them both.

"You know I'll want to keep you and the baby," he said.

Liz wasn't surprised to hear it. For some reason, though he still hadn't said anything about loving her, his stated intention didn't sound as threatening as she'd once thought it would. "Let's not attempt to settle things tonight," she said, aware Arden had stopped nursing and was drifting off to sleep. "I'll need to put this little tyke down in her bassinet in a few minutes. Before that happens, would you like to hold her?"

Instead of pushing him away, Liz was inviting him in, after month upon month of deception. He wondered why. Had absence made her heart grow fonder? Or was she resigned to keeping their marriage intact so she wouldn't lose her precious child to him? She'd painted a fairly graphic picture of her fear in one guileless sentence.

He hoped he could assuage that fear and convince her to love him the way he loved her. His first step would be to give her time and space, instead of coming on strong, six-guns blazing, the way he usually did.

"You'd better believe it," he said, enthusiastically taking her up on the offer. "There's nothing I'd like better in all the world."

That wasn't exclusively true, of course, Jack realized as he watched her disengage her nipple from the baby's mouth and shift her slightly into a more comfortable position before covering up her breast. Like little Arden, he'd had that pretty pink nipple in his mouth and he'd thoroughly enjoyed its taste. He'd enjoyed other things, too, like plumbing Liz's moist depths and feeling her moan and writhe against him.

He wanted to feel those things again. And soon. But it was the baby's moment. Putting his sexual desire temporarily back on the shelf where it had gathered cobwebs since shortly after her conception, Jack prepared to bond with his daughter as Liz swaddled her lightly in a blue receiving blanket and placed her in his arms.

Far more powerful than he'd expected, the sensation of holding her reduced him to tears. "I'm not the kind of guy who cries," he blubbered. "I just can't help it. She's so utterly damn wonderful."

"I know." Getting to her feet, Liz bent over to give him a fleeting hug. "I did the same thing when I first held her in the delivery room," she confessed. "I still get teary-eyed sometimes, just looking at her. Of course, that's 'socially acceptable' for women. If you wouldn't mind looking after her for a minute, I'd like to take a potty break."

Alone in the room, with his baby girl entrusted to his keeping, Jack bent over to kiss her cheek. The steady rise and fall of her breath seemed nothing short of miraculous. So did a sudden, fluttery movement of her tiny, perfect hands, which had visible half moons on their fingernails.

His emotions swelling until they seemed to fill his chest, he made her a solemn promise. "I'm going to win your mommy over," he said. "We'll all live happily together with your big sister, Kassie, on our farm in Virginia. Kass is going to love you so much."

In very nearly the same breath, he vowed to take things slow. He wouldn't overwhelm Liz with protestations of love and dogged insistence that she move back with him at once, until he was sure she was ready to hear them. He wanted her to do it for the right reasons, because she loved him as he loved her.

A couple of minutes later, Liz was back. "I hate to put a stop to this, but I'd really like to tuck Arden in for a nap if not a decent night's sleep," she said with an indulgent smile. "At two months, she's still waking up around the clock to be fed. I get fairly exhausted sometimes, especially now that I'm working again. I try to get in a few winks whenever she does."

Asleep so peacefully in his arms, their daughter was wearing Liz out. Jack wished he could help. He supposed the most useful thing he could do at the moment would be to say good-night.

"I'd better be going and let you rest," he said, allowing her to take the baby from him. "We'll talk some more tomorrow, okay? After we get a decision in the Haynes-Conyer case?"

Liz nodded. "All right."

He wanted to kiss her good-night. Hold her tightly against his body, if her breasts weren't too tender. She was still cradling the baby against her shoulder, and he decided to restrain himself. "Good night, darlin'," he said, lightly encircling them both to place a lingering kiss on her cheek.

Returning to Judge Kaplan's chambers the next day at the appointed hour, Liz tried not to let the unrest in her personal life affect her judgment. She just couldn't help it if the look in Jack's eyes as he said hello set her heart to beating faster. Or if the love they shared for their baby daughter had kept her awake the previous night, recalling every move he'd made and every word he'd spoken in the hope of finding something to hope about there.

Mac was counting on her. So, too, were three innocent children, though they didn't know it, whose family was on the verge of collapse, not to mention two very unhappy adults who'd once loved each other and allowed their marriage to deteriorate.

After reviewing the events of the previous day, she was all but certain the wife would lose custody if the divorce proceedings went forward. Of course, thanks to the assignment she'd received from Mac, it was her responsibility to see that no divorce occurred.

Though she supposed in one way her hidden agenda could be construed as a dereliction of duty to her client, it had become increasingly clear to her that both the husband and wife still had feelings for each other. They were just buried under a mountain of hostility. Astonishing Jack and her own client, she asked the judge to put the case on hold once more so the litigants and their attorneys could try again to work things out.

The judge readily agreed. "It's always been my feeling that, where there's been love and there are children, a reconciliation is preferable," she said, giving Liz an approving smile.

"So...what's this about?" Mary-Cate Conyer demanded irritably as they trooped into a nearby conference room. "I don't have the time for this kind of runaround!"

"Or for anything else but work, work, work," David Haynes responded under his breath.

In answer, Liz put one finger to her lips as Jack watched with a bemused expression. She was about to put the principles she'd learned from the Harvard Negotiation Project graduate into action. "What I'd like you both to do, if it's all right with Mr. Kelleher," she told the sparring couple, handing out yellow scratch pads and carefully sharpened No. 2 pencils, "is to try and step outside your current situation and view it as well-meaning problem solvers. If you're willing to humor me, I'd like you to abandon the *positions* you've taken, and focus on your *interests* instead.

"For the moment, let's define those interests as what you'd most like to have happen if anything were possible, rather than limit them to the outcome of a divorce. I guarantee whatever you say will be kept in strictest confidence. It won't be used against you in any way."

She paused. "Agreed, Jack?"

He nodded. Curious if she could nudge the man and wife toward a reconciliation, he waited for her to continue.

At her prompting, the husband and wife somewhat hesitantly wrote down what each considered to be the best outcome in their situation on the top sheet of their scratch pads.

"Now, tear off what you've written and hand it to me," Liz instructed.

It was clear the husband had reservations. She was his wife's attorney, after all. Despite her promise, she might incorporate something he betrayed in subsequent arguments. Yet, for some reason—because Jack posed no objection, perhaps, or because David secretly yearned to revive his marriage, even at that late juncture—he cooperated.

Accepting the slips of paper, Liz read them silently and looked up. "Will you be shocked to learn you've written the same thing...for your children to be happy?" she asked.

The pair glanced at each other.

"What would make your children happy?" she asked.

This time, they didn't write. "For us not to be divorcing at all," her client said honestly.

"But you filed!" her husband exclaimed.

Mary-Cate Conyer's formidable defenses had obviously been breached. Her perfectly made-up face took on a vulnerable, emotionally bruised look. "Only because you started seeing Lynn Kearney," she said with a distinct quaver in her voice.

The man she'd married and subsequently decided to boot out of her life shook his head sadly. "Lynn's just a friend," he reiterated. "I needed to talk to someone. All our real problems revolve around the need to spend more time together with our family."

The words *we* and *our* weren't lost on Liz. She considered them hallmarks of ongoing attachment. Revising her first equation slightly, she aimed it at the husband. "Okay. What would make you happy *besides* what your wife said?"

His response was immediate. "Having Mary-Cate be more of a wife and mother, the way she used to be."

Not too surprisingly, Mary-Cate took umbrage. "Just because you're not as interested in your career as I am..." she began.

Liz held up one hand, like a traffic cop. "Sounds to me like those children are the top priority for you both, considering what you wrote down a minute ago and the custody battle we've been fighting," she observed. "I'm starting to get the feeling this divorce was filed as the result of a misunderstanding. What do you say Jack and I get out of the room and let you talk on your own for a few minutes?"

Hesitantly, both parties nodded.

Watching her operate with pride and something approaching amazement, Jack gave her the thumb's-up sign.

"Remember," she instructed as they headed for the door, "focus on mutual interests and common concerns for the future, not the *positions* you've adopted and what has happened in the past. I'm counting on you to keep each other honest."

In the hall outside the conference room, the man Liz loved complimented her on her negotiating skills. "If our battling principals follow your instructions, they just may reconcile and save themselves some money," he laughed. "Before long, you'll be in demand at the State Department. Now, for my most important question...how's our baby girl this morning?

Liz gave him a beatific smile. "Bright and sunny, like the weather. She's beginning to smile and coo. Last night you caught her in a sleepy mood."

He wanted to kiss her. Run his fingers through her gorgeous mop of hair. Take her in his arms. She's the mother of my child, he thought with a sense of wonder that only seemed to intensify as it sank into his consciousness.

"What do you say we go get a cup of coffee?" he proposed. "Our clients are going to be a while. And we need to talk."

What Liz wanted was to be petted and held and told that Jack loved her with all his heart. Since that wasn't likely to happen in the courthouse coffee shop, she preferred to "talk" when their responsibility to the Haynes-Conyers had been discharged.

"We will, Jack," she promised. "Soon. If you'll excuse me, I want to run upstairs and look in on Katie Howard, Judge Barnes's former secretary."

She was gone a long time, and Jack had plenty of opportunity to cool his heels and think about how to approach her. He relaxed against a window ledge without regard for the dust that might come into contact with his expensive suit. She'd been right, he thought, when she'd told their clients to focus on their interests and the happiness of their children, rather than the positions they'd taken and what happened in the past. His only question was whether she'd be willing to apply that philosophy to their situation.

She returned as their clients were just emerging from the conference room. "We want to put the divorce on hold indefinitely... talk some more," Mary-Cate announced.

"That's right," David chimed in. "Right now, we're going out to supper. We'll let you know what happens."

As they exited the courthouse, it looked as if they might patch things up.

"Guess they don't need us anymore," Jack remarked, picking up his briefcase. "I wouldn't have believed this, if I hadn't seen it with my own two eyes."

Her smile faintly pensive, despite the excellent news she had to report to Mac, Liz didn't answer him. The spotlight had shifted to them. Would she and Jack be able to work things out as easily?

"So," said Jack, filling up the silence. "What would you like to do? Walk a little in the late afternoon sunshine? Or go back to your house and play with Arden Rose?"

If she kept to her usual schedule, their daughter would be ready to nurse in about an hour. Though Liz had placed some pump-expressed breast milk in the refrigerator for Maria to warm, she preferred to do the honors herself. Still, they had a little time to waste. She liked the idea of strolling the streets of Washington with Jack as if responsibility were no object. Maybe a gentle solution to their problems would settle around them like a blessing.

"Let's walk a little and then go back to the house," she suggested.

Something in the way she said it caused his anticipation to soar. She was willing to give them a chance as husband and wife! He just knew it! Don't blow your chance, Kelleher, he ordered himself as he held the door for her. Listen to what she has to say. Try to figure out what she wants. For once, he wouldn't attempt to work things out by means of sex, or smothering her with kisses.

Leaving the courthouse behind, they started down the street, an island of two in the stream of hurrying pedestrians. Three blocks later, they came upon a small café with a row of outdoor tables. "How about something cold to drink?" Jack asked.

"Sounds good to me," Liz agreed.

After placing their order of a glass of wine for him and a sparkling mineral water for her, Jack reached for her hands across the table.

"Liz," he said earnestly, "the way you cut through the smokescreen our clients had thrown up to keep from realizing how much they still loved each other totally impressed me. I wonder if we couldn't apply those techniques to us."

Her manner grew very still, as if she'd been waiting all her life to hear those words and could scarcely believe he was finally speaking them. "I don't see why not," she answered carefully.

He dared to advance a giant step. "Speaking only of my *interests* and our children's happiness, not of any stupid or thoughtless *positions* I've taken in the past, I'd like to stay married to you," he told her. "Hell, babe... it's the thing I want most in all the world!"

Their drinks came, creating a distraction and giving her a moment to think. At last, after asking whether they wanted to order any food, the waiter flitted to another table.

"So," said Jack, ignoring his wine as his blue eyes bored into her hazel ones, "what do you think?"

Was he proposing an extension of their business-deal marriage, with the inevitable component of sex thrown in, for their children's sake? Or hinting at richer, more complex motives that had somehow grown up in the rocky seedbed of their separation?

So eloquent in court, he seemed unable to express a basic sentiment like "I love you." Well, Rosemary had warned her. For all his exterior toughness, Jack wasn't the kind of guy who liked the idea of getting hurt. To find out if that was how he felt about her, she'd have to risk asking him. Or better still, confess her own feelings, though it might lay her open to disappointment and rejection.

"The fact is, Jack, I'd like nothing better myself," she admitted. "But on one condition . . . that it be a marriage of love and not just convenience. I've been crazy about you for years, and now that you've had a chance to get over Sharon's death—"

"You little ninny!" Wine spilled, though it didn't get on their clothing, as Jack lunged across the table. "Sharon tricked me into marriage," he said. "It was always *you* I loved. You I wanted . . . the gorgeous redheaded woman I asked out first."

Coming home in his arms, Liz thought there wasn't a luckier person in all the world. When finally his kisses abated and she could speak, she suggested, "Let's go back to Georgetown so I can nurse our baby, and then home to Virginia so I can say hello to our other little girl."

"Your wish is my command, darlin';" Jack answered, brushing what looked suspiciously like a tear from his cheek.

When they reached her Georgetown row house, Maria was giving Arden a bottle, which she seemed to be rejecting. Before Liz could take charge, Jack held out his hands. "Let me give it to her," he begged.

Maria promptly threw Liz a questioning look.

"It's okay," Liz reassured. "Jack's my husband. And Arden's daddy. We've decided to get back together. Jack, meet Maria Velásquez, Arden's nanny... a truly wonderful helper I couldn't live without."

"Happy to meet you, *señor*," the nanny said, pleased comprehension dawning on her face as she allowed Jack to take Arden from her arms.

Settled on the couch with the baby in his lap, while Liz and Maria ran upstairs to pack a few things, Jack shut his eyes for a moment to bond with his infant daughter—so instinctively, powerfully and deeply that the link between them seemed forged in his very soul. "I love you, Arden," he whispered. "As much as I love Kassie. And as much as your mommy, though in a different way."

Though she didn't fuss as she gazed up at her father with curious, light blue eyes, Arden still didn't want her bottle. What she wanted was Liz's breast.

"I'll have to nurse her when we get to Virginia," Liz remarked, checking out the baby's lack of progress as she returned to the living room laden with a diaper bag and several hastily packed suitcases.

She was followed by Maria, who was carrying Arden's bassinet. Handing their baby back to the source of her next meal, Jack transferred the suitcases and the bassinet to his sedan. They're coming home with me, he thought incredulously, as he helped his wife, baby and the baby's nanny inside. Maybe I ought to pinch myself. I'm not sure I actually believe it yet.

Kassie was playing outdoors with Eloise nearby when they drove up the shade-dappled lane that led to Jack's eighteenth-century farmhouse. Recognizing her father's car, she came running. "Daddy...Daddy...Daddy!" she exclaimed.

Hungry for the sight of her, Liz noticed that she'd grown at least three inches. A portion of her baby fat had melted away. Meanwhile, her silky dark bangs had grown until they almost reached her eyebrows.

Hugging Jack around the knees as he emerged to open the front passenger door for Liz, Kassie paused to assess the tall, redheaded woman she'd once known so well. Though her face grew sober as it inevitably did whenever she was confronted with strangers, it was possible that some form of memory stirred, because she allowed Liz to pick her up and hold her close.

"I bring the baby, yes?" Maria asked.

Settling with Arden on the sun porch sofa, Liz offered her breast. Predictably, Kassie hovered close. Clearly enthralled over the advent of someone smaller than herself, she offered Arden a finger to grasp as she repeated the word *baby* over and over with wonder in her soft little voice.

"Baby *sister*," Liz instructed with a heart full of happiness. "You and Arden are going to grow up to be the very best of friends and playmates." She'd see to it that no rivalry, however subtle, developed.

As he watched the three of them together, Jack felt his happiness spill over. Everything and everyone he needed in the world was right there, in that sunny little room. Yet there was something he sorely wanted. He wondered if Liz was able to make love yet. He didn't want to push her if it was too soon after giving birth.

She settled the question without him having to ask. "I don't want any supper, do you?" she asked in a low voice when she'd finished nursing Arden and handed her over to Maria to be put down for a nap in the guest room, which she planned to redecorate as a nursery. "However, I do admit to a particular kind of hunger."

Jack laced a proprietary, infinitely loving arm about her shoulders. "You read my mind, babe," he whispered.

After the long, dry spell that had separated them, they would hole up in Jack's bed together. "Eloise," she said, "please tell Mrs. Rivers that we don't want to be disturbed unless there's an emergency."

The phone rang before they could start up the stairs. When he heard that David Haynes was on the line, Jack agreed to take the call. His former client's message was jubilant but brief.

"Mary-Cate and I have agreed to deep-six the divorce...give our marriage another try," he said. "She's agreed to cut back on her working hours and spend more time with the family. I want to thank you and particularly Mrs. Kelleher for realizing we were down but not out, and helping us start again."

Alone with Jack a short time later in the room where, henceforth, they would sleep, Liz was jubilant. "Mac's going to be so pleased," she said, flopping down on the bed fully dressed. "He's the one who insisted I come east to turn their divorce proceedings into a chance for reconciliation."

"It wouldn't surprise me if getting us back together was on his agenda as well," Jack mused, taking off his tie and unbuttoning his shirt. "What d'you say, sweetheart...let's not start a tradition of making love with our clothes on."

Liz slid obediently from the bed, as he removed his shoes, socks, trousers and shorts and assumed protection, to remove her elegant suit, nursing bra and lacy bikini panties. Still slim as a reed but shapelier and more full breasted than he remembered, she nestled in his arms.

With a groan of pleasure, he picked her up and carried her back to the bed. His first thrust, passionate but oh, so gentle, hurt a little, as if she were a novice losing her virginity. But the pain, such as it was, didn't last. She was too wet and ready for that to happen as she wrapped her legs around his waist.

Aching with need for each other after their long separation, they spiraled higher and higher. But they couldn't keep it up for long. With an incendiary lurch and inarticulate little cries that they smothered against each other, she and Jack stretched all the way to paradise.

Afterward, as they drifted down together, he told her his version of the story about him and Sharon. "I lusted after you, and you weren't available," he said. "From my perspective, you didn't even like me. Our 'outlooks' were too different, you said. Sharon showed up and came on to me. She was cute and sexy and I was feeling horny and put-upon. I thought I'd show you by dating your sister. That night..."

Hesitating, Jack wasn't sure he should continue. Talking about what had transpired between himself and her twin the night Liz had turned him down might drive her away from him again. He decided if they were to go on being married they couldn't have any secrets.

"I went to bed with her at her apartment," he admitted. "It wasn't great. In the morning I wished I hadn't. I wanted to break it off with her. But she kept calling me, so I dated her a couple of more times. After that I got busy. I felt like my world had crashed around my ears when, without any warning, she called and told me the birth control she'd volunteered to take responsibility for had failed. She was a good Catholic girl, and there'd be no abortion. She insisted I marry her. Since I'm basically a nice guy, I did the decent thing.''

Liz stared, dumbfounded at the fresh perspective he was offering her. Instinct told her every word was gospel. "You mean...that was the miscarriage she told us about?" she asked.

Jack nodded. "I can't prove it, but I'm convinced she made it happen. Afterward, without my knowledge, she went on the pill. There'd be no more children to destroy her figure and inhibit her illicit affairs.''

To Liz's amazement, Jack knew all about Sharon's faithlessness. If only they'd talked about it earlier!

"If you knew about Shar's adultery, and yet it continued, why didn't you divorce her?" she asked.

Jack's left shoulder lifted in the faintest of shrugs. "What would have been the point? The way I saw it, if I'd done that, I'd have forever spoiled my chances with you...the only woman in the world I wanted.''

His description of her sounded awfully good to Liz. Nestled there, with her head on his shoulder, she thought she knew what heaven must be like.

"Tell me the truth," he added, his voice resonating close to her ear. "You wouldn't have agreed to let me romance you following an acrimonious divorce in which Sharon fought me tooth and nail...*would* you?"

Knowing herself as she did, Liz had to admit she was a stickler for principle. "Maybe not," she agreed, "though I'd have sorely wanted to."

Jack nodded. "That's what I thought. With you lost to me whatever I did, I decided I might as well hang on to the farm, which means a lot to me, and keep what I could of the money I'd earned, instead of handing it over to Shar in the form of a divorce settlement. So I continued to put up with her.''

The picture he'd painted of his emotional life for the five years of his marriage to Liz's twin was incredibly bleak. Had he insisted they adopt Kassie in order to have someone he could love?

It was as if he'd heard her unspoken question.

''When Shar failed to get pregnant again after her miscarriage,'' he added, hoping Liz would forgive the ongoing sex he'd had with the only woman available to him, she told me her doctor said the problem was fibroids from too much stress. That's when I insisted on adopting. I wanted a child to love. Kassie was the result.''

''Thank God for our precious Kassie,'' Liz said, absolving him of past mistakes. ''Without her...''

Jack tugged her closer. ''Without her we wouldn't be cuddling here tonight.''

Liz kissed the little indentations beside his mouth. ''Of course, I love her even more for the magical child she is, independent of her role as go-between,'' she said.

''Mmm, so do I.'' He was planting little kisses on her breasts and stomach.

''What about Arden?'' she prodded.

He grinned. ''Crazy about her, too. If your career can stand it, maybe we'll end up with a houseful of kids.''

With Jack to love her, it sounded good to Liz. But she couldn't let his remark go completely unchallenged. ''Don't you mean *our* careers?'' she asked him. ''At the moment, you owe me two months of one a.m. feedings.''

''A month, actually,'' he quibbled. ''My *half* of the feedings I missed. I'm more than willing to make restitution.''

Being married to him—really married—was going to be so much fun. Home safe in his love, Liz knew she could count on their good-natured sparring to keep her on her toes, even as it resolved itself in kisses.

A moment later, she realized they already had a houseful of kids from her parents' perspective—one more than either of the Heflins knew about.

"At least you weren't the last to know about Arden's birth," she confessed. "To date, my mom and dad are completely in the dark."

Jack gave her a speculative, blue-eyed look. "Yet you told Rosemary," he commented.

Incredibly, he understood. There wasn't the slightest hint of censure in his voice.

"I've, uh, always been second-best where my parents were concerned," she added, baring a little more of her soul to him. "With them, Shar always came first. Especially Mom. When you and I married after her death, I couldn't help thinking she'd see it as a move on my part to take something that belonged to my sister. Later, when I found out I was pregnant with Arden, I knew she'd greet the news with accusations...about the way I'd lured you into the sack..."

"Technically, you didn't lure me into the sack," Jack corrected her. "I lured you. Your only transgression was to hang around, so beautiful and smart and desirable, under my roof. Despite giving you my word that nothing would happen between us, I couldn't resist."

They were past those days of yearning now, secure in each other's affection.

"We'll have to tell Frank and Patsy pretty soon," Jack went on. "They're bound to find out, now that you're back to stay, if only by accident."

Liz nodded. "I know. I'm not looking forward to it."

He'd be at her side. "Listen, darlin'," he said. "About your being second-best with Patsy... I think you should consider the source. I know she's your mom, and you love her and all that, but I've always thought she was a complete fool for not realizing what a sterling daughter she had in you."

Deep in her heart, Liz dared to agree with him. To hear him put it into words brought tears of happiness and vindication to her eyes.

"You know that, don't you, babe?" he prodded.

She nestled closer. "I'm beginning to. Heck...with you to love me, and everything I've learned through loving you and Kassie and Arden, I do know it. I can feel it in my bones."

"That's good." Having defused some of her angst over telling her parents what had transpired, Jack let his hand slide up her thigh as he renewed his quest for her womanhood.

Glowing with anticipation of another round of lovemaking, Liz couldn't resist asking one last question. "What would you have done at the restaurant if I hadn't reciprocated your feelings?" she asked.

Jack grinned, aware as a result of the teasing that her confidence had returned. She was a fine attorney and he hoped someday they could be partners as well as lovers, marriage partners and parents. "Make love to you on the sidewalk," he answered with his own aplomb in full flower, "until I managed to change your mind."

*   *   *   *   *

COMING NEXT MONTH

**The wedding celebration was so nice...
too bad the bride wasn't there!**

Find out what happens when three brides have a
change of heart.

Three complete stories by some of your favorite
authors—all in one special collection!

YESTERDAY ONCE MORE
by Debbie Macomber

FULL CIRCLE
by Paula Detmer Riggs

THAT'S WHAT FRIENDS ARE FOR
by Annette Broadrick

Available this June wherever books are sold.

Look us up on-line at:http://www.romance.net

SREQ696

This July, watch for the delivery of...

An exciting new miniseries that appears in a different Silhouette series each month. It's about love, marriage—and Daddy's unexpected need for a baby carriage!

Daddy Knows Last unites five of your favorite authors as they weave five connected stories about baby fever in New Hope, Texas.

- **THE BABY NOTION** by Dixie Browning
  (SD#1011, 7/96)

- **BABY IN A BASKET** by Helen R. Myers
  (SR#1169, 8/96)

- **MARRIED...WITH TWINS!**
  by Jennifer Mikels
  (SSE#1054, 9/96)

- **HOW TO HOOK A HUSBAND (AND A BABY)**
  by Carolyn Zane
  (YT#29, 10/96)

- **DISCOVERED: DADDY** by Marilyn Pappano
  (IM#746, 11/96)

Daddy Knows Last arrives in July...only from

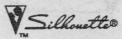

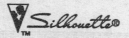